MAPLES

REJUVENATING COCKTAIL

Bhavna Khemlani

First published in India 2011 by **Frog Books**
an imprint of **Leadstart Publishing Pvt Ltd**
1 Level, Trade Centre
Bandra Kurla Complex
Bandra (East) Mumbai 400 051 India
Telephone: +91-22-40700804
Fax: +91-22-40700800
Email: info@leadstartcorp.com
www.leadstartcorp.com / www.frogbooks.net

Editorial Office:
Unit: 25-26 / Building A/1
Ground Floor, Near Wadala RTO
Wadala (East) Mumbai 400 037 India
Phone: +91-22-24036548 / 24036930

Sales & Marketing Office:
Unit: 122 / Building B/2
First Floor, Near Wadala RTO
Wadala (East) Mumbai 400 037 India
Phone: +91-22-24046887

US Office:
Axis Corp, 7845 E Oakbrook Circle
Madison, WI 53717 USA

Copyright (c) Bhavna Khemlani

ISBN 978-93-81115-10-7

Publisher and Managing Editor: Sunil K Poolani
Books Editor: Rhonda Lee Carver
Design Editor: Mishta Roy

Typeset in Book Antiqua
Printed at Repro India Ltd, Mumbai

Price — India: Rs 195; Elsewhere: US $14

Life is full of surprises and has loads to offer. There are many goodie bags for everyone. Why not take a break and give yourself some time to explore the moments you can cherish?

Don't forget, while you take a break, have your favourite cocktail or any drink that makes you feel like heaven. Celebrate life with family, friends and colleagues.

This book is dedicated to all the people who supported me always. Positivity has always been right beside me.

I hope you enjoy the journey of the four charismatic characters.

Cheers to everyone!

Dear Readers,

Welcome to a new journey. References to actual places or people are fictional.

The protagonists of this story, Ryan, Ria, Genelia and Miguel will indisputably bring a smile on your face. It is their assurance that life goes on and it can also bring loads of surprises. When we see maple leaves, the vibrant colors denote unexpressed happiness and the inner joy that fulfill those loops of despondency.

Life has so much to offer and so much to be thankful for. When we hold a glass of cocktail, each flavor represents an emotion and the triumphs we face in life. The lives and sentiments of the protagonists are being portrayed like having a cocktail.

Everyone has different tastes and like different types of cocktail that develops into a blissful ordain. Sometimes, the characters require a re-fill to quench their thirst and cheer to their victory. The refill indubitably promises a comforting taste and merriment.

Which is your favourite cocktail? Cheer to the glory of dignified manifestations and sip a rejuvenating cocktail.

— **Bhavna Khemlani**

1
CHAPTER

Life is Delicious

Taking a break from the daily routine makes it awful to cope with the unspoken grief that feels connected from youth. What happens when one hopes that someday he or she will certainly discover all the answers to the questions that were disconcerting the mind? One liberal, intelligent, kind-hearted, yet an absent-minded person would like to invite his readers to his journey of life where he takes pleasure of all emotions and thinks life could be delicious. Ryan Sahay, born and raised in London has his life curled up in a rollercoaster between his career and reality. He has the opportunity to practice photography in Thailand, which slowly escorts him to new connections that lead him to an array of problems.

"I have been waiting for the past five hours to see how life could be delicious. In fact it could be, but now it is an obligation. Oh Gosh, I hope it does not disappear!"exclaimed Ryan Sahay. He continued, "Who said photography was easy? All of this for a freaking research report and we were chosen to travel the entire way to Bangkok."

"Stop muttering Ryan," whispered Mark. He was - Ryan's roommate and a close buddy.

"I could have travelled to other places, but the course

coordinator convinced us to come here," said Ryan with annoyance.

"Well, this is a good place. With wonderful beaches to see in Thailand, we can chill and have a beer before the big day, Ryan," Mark remarked with his carefree attitude.

"What big day?"Ryan frowned.

"Silly, this is our research presentation, remember. This presentation will be our Chocó-chip," Mark said sarcastically.

"Hey, I'm starving. Let's go grab a bite, man.

"I was not talking about food. With this presentation we can enjoy the entire cake. This is our final semester and the final extra percentage we get is our target," Mark said scrubbing his jaw line.

"Yup Mark, I guess that is why we are here," said Ryan. He wondered if he wanted to attain his undergraduate degree from The University of Westminster, he had to complete it on time.

Twisting and turning, he finally fixed and positioned the tripod at the right angle, and turning the lens, he clicked.

Ryan was thinking out loud, "Oh, now I see this spectacular Smiling Moon in Bangkok city. In fact, it's an extraordinary astronomical phenomenon known as "Conjunction of Moon, Venus and Jupiter."

Ryan turned back and told Mark, "Look at the three lustrous objects in the sky over Bangkok. I am sure it can be seen from many parts of Thailand forming a 'Smiling Face' in this amazing year 2008. When Jupiter and Venus meet the Moon, there is a smile in the sky. How cool? What a beauty!"

Mark listened patiently.

Ryan realizes there was so much to know about this phenomenon.

This was his first time shooting something so unique for his photography project on astrophotography.

He noticed that with the right lighting, complicity between the technical device and seeing the world as an establishment could be illustrated as a beautiful photograph.

Ryan questioned himself all the time. This time he conjectured, "Perhaps this is the reason why I am here...to see the moon and stars assure me that everything will be fine. After I am done, I shall be evaluating and analyzing the photographs to provide justice to this magic."

Somewhere in his mind he was wondering again, whether this was a way for someone or God to alert everyone that a supreme power was always watching over us.

"Ryan...we have to leave now. I hope you got what you were looking for. Everyone has and I hope you have too and of course talking to yourself. Hmmm," his coordinator shouted out loud nodding his head.

Ryan started packing all his stuff. He looked forward to a new day with a new act.

Mark patted him on the back saying, "Yo Mate! We got to go. Don't get carried away in your thoughts or is it about your youth again?"

He looked up at the sky grinning, and considered that things will certainly work out. With excitement, Mark told Ryan, "Hey, we are going to the beach tomorrow, I guess. We need chilled beers and that Thai aroma oil massage the coordinator mentioned about. What do you say?"

Walking slowly, Ryan gets into the van back to his hotel. On the way he thinks about the exotic beaches which Thailand was famous for. A few moments later, after getting into his comfort zone, he began to hum. "Ryan, what are you humming? I haven't heard of it before," commented Mark.

"Yup, Mark, it's nothing. It is some random tune. It's a good way for me to let off stress. You can hum anything you want to," stated Ryan.

"Mark what time are we scheduled for the beach?" asked Ryan.

"Hmm, at 8am. We are taking the flight, so we have enough time tour around. We shall be staying at a resort for the night, remember," said Mark with exasperation.

"What's up with you?" asked Mark.

"Oh nothing, just making sure," said Ryan.

"Okay, Ryan for your wonderful memory, we are

going to Krabi which is located in the South of Thailand," Mark said boldly.

Ryan had heard about Krabi as a wonderful land of the sea where anyone could have his or her own privacy in one of the most exotic places in the world. He marveled with a positive notion and was quite lethargic with traveling around Bangkok for his astrophotography project. He simply threw away his stuff, bounced on the bed and dozed off to sleep.

He slept soundly that not even the sound of the dogs barking outside his hotel disturbed him. The next day, he was standing in the queue at the airport for some time.

Ryan became agitated, and when he learned that the flight was delayed, it tested his patience.

He wanted caffeine to get focused. He still felt drowsy, so he told Mark, "I am off for a caffeine shot. Do you want to join me?"

As they sipped coffee, the aroma of the freshly blended beans, woke both of them up. They felt soulful again. As they heard the announcement, they rushed and boarded on the flight. They couldn't wait to chill at the salient destination. After some time, the Captain, with his loud and unclear accent, thanked the passengers for flying with the airline. Ryan was wondering how he would survive at the place because of the accent or even the language.

As the plane landed, they got into the resort's van and headed to their destination. Along their drive, they saw the beach and were content in the beauty of the place.

They had never seen anything like that, not even in London. The driver then led them to the entrance of the resort and thanked them in Thai for the tip he was given, 'Kob Khun Khrub.'

Mark smiled and said, "Thank you," without even understanding anything.

He added, "I don't get it Ryan, but I guess walk ahead, so we don't get tied up and waste time."

Ryan smiled back, firmly nodding his head as a sign of appreciation, and proceeded to the reception desk.

The two were greeted with orchids and a glass of Long

Island Ice Tea as their welcome drink. Ryan felt revitalized and walked toward the reception desk. He had asked for his room key and made enquiries from the staff about Krabi.

Very politely, she explained, "Krabi has very secluded white beaches sheltered by astounding limestone formations. The interior of the island is filled by jungle, forest waterfalls and mysterious caves." After a pause, she added, "Sir, if you have any questions we are happy to help. When do you want to go to the beach?"

"Oh, soon I guess. Thanks," he answered. He had heard from his coordinator that Thai people were very generous with their hospitality. Ryan was relieved and finally felt he understood someone very well. Because of the accent, he was finding it difficult to catch up.

He then left to survey room. He paced toward the balcony and could see the beach. He felt so good and let out a sigh. Feeling relaxed for that day enabled him to plan out what he would do next.

"Hey dude, let's go to the beach," said Ryan persuasively.

"Oh, before that, we need to find out places we can visit today. I am also famished and would love to have some good food," Mark said enthusiastically.

"Yup, we should get going Mark." Off they went to the information desk for enquiries.

"Mark, why don't you do the honor?" asked Ryan.

"Hi, we would like to know some places to visit at Krabi and where should we start?" asked Mark. To his notice, the woman at the information desk gave a wide smile and looked dazed. She seemed new at her job and he thought perhaps she was a trainee, so he waited patiently.

"Wait moment please, um, hmm, you try to see beaches, which one?"

Mark was confused and stated, "Yup, I want to know-which one?"

Ryan raised his right eyebrow and thought it was best to wait until Mark sorted it out.

The woman was not fluent with English. She handed

him some pamphlets. It was obvious that Mark did not understand anything, so he asked another receptionist how he could get to the beach. She said, "It is a 15 minute' walk, and you can take a red colored scooter that can accommodate four people. Tell the driver where you want to go or you can use our shuttle bus and they can drop you off at our nearest beach. From there you can decide whether you want to go any other beach."

"Thank you," said Mark and asked, "Which is the nearest beach?"

"Sir," she replied, "It is called, 'Ao Nang.' It is name of beach and also has limestone."Mark was simply disappointed with the verb tense used, but had to ignore and focus on important details. She continued, "The beach is beautiful and has many food to eat. You can relax - have a massage, up to you, Sir."

With curiosity Mark asked, "Is there sightseeing and some activities?"The lady answered, "Yes, have, Sir," she grinned and added, "Hope you have a pleasant trip."

Mark walked up to Ryan and said, "We better check it out and explore. Otherwise, we can choose the location from the pamphlets."

They waited in line to get into the shuttle bus, and heard a group of people saying, "We must see the caves. It is stunning."Ryan interrupted and asked, "Excuse me, do you know how we get there because we plan to see the caves, too."

Mark patted him on his back and asked, "Are we?"

"We have company, let's check it out," Ryan replied.

"Okay," agreed Mark. They get onto the shuttle bus to see the caves.

When they got off the bus, they had rented a red scooter- to go to the cave called 'Tham Petch.' It was not too far. As they got there, they saw a local tour guide mentioning to other tourists that the caves shine. After having heard the caves shine, Ryan became excited to capture it in photo.

The laughter of the children on the beach brought a beam to his face reflecting the children's chirpiness.

It took about thirty minutes, and once they reached,

the strong aroma of grilled chicken evoked Mark's hunger. They were hungry and went to sit in a hut, ordered chilled Heineken beer, and grilled chicken with white rice. The taste of the grilled chicken served with spicy mixed herbs gave an interesting flavor. They were not so fond of spicy victuals, but were quite keen with trying out new food. They simply wanted to eat, even though they did not enjoy their first meal of the trip.

Later, meandering away, they went to get tickets to explore the beauty of the caves. Having walked for about two kilometers, they saw the cave walls that replicated diamonds. That was something they had never seen. Ryan wished he could take out his camera for a cherished memory, but couldn't. Taking pictures were not allowed. They noticed that there were natural and spectacular formations on the caves.

Feeling blissful, Ryan said, "Life can be so great when we can see what nature provides us with such exquisiteness without even asking anything in return."He turned around and added, "People should take care of it, Mark."

"Ryan, we all should," said Mark.

"You can be so lame, Mark.

"Yup, we have to take care of it. Heard of Global Warming?" Ryan added. They smiled at each other and continued to pace closer toward the caves. Both of them were lost in their own world. Ryan wondered what would happen or what would he do when he got back to reality?

Living with his Uncle's family felt like a burden to him. He could not take it any longer. Ryan's reality was a clandestine. He wanted to discover the truth about his parents for years.

At the age of twenty-two, he wanted to have a more meaningful life.

He was tired of maintaining relationships that he felt have drifted away, and started to feel detached.

Creating a special bonding with nature, Ryan found himself fully satiated with the historic sites and scenic wonders of the place. After taking pictures, he and Mark left the place and were on their way to the beach.

Admiring the surroundings developed a new sensation

for Ryan. They reached the beach and walked on the sandy shoreline.

Having basked in the warmth of the sun, the two felt indulged with a good tan. It was already four in the evening. They decided to have chilled beer and enjoy the breeze at the beach. This time, the weather was not too hot but quite cool. Ryan went for a casual walk on the beach.   As he dawdled, he held the can of beer in his hand, felt the warmth of every grain of sand under his feet, and- he was- yet again, drowned in his life patterns. He felt lost.

Observing the details of the landscape, all of the living things, Ryan sat down and watched the way the sun reflected off the water in brilliant colors of gold, blue and red. The panorama was laid out like an exotic scenery depiction in an art gallery. Everything around Krabi beach had its own distinctive feel making him feel calm and relaxed. Ryan could see a patch of sea weed and took a deep breath of fresh air. He looked at the adjoining view, saw people, and little kids building sandcastles and having sand fights.

A few meters away, he saw young teenagers playing volleyball. He felt he was at the right place at the right time. He realized he hadn't seen the beach for months and needed a break for the longest time.

Having lay down on the sand for a while, a few hours had passed by. He took out his camera to shoot the wonders of natural beauty at sunset. The clear blue water of the sea and the red-orange sky overhead was truly amazing. It was almost time to get back, and he wondered where the hell Mark was. Brushing sand out from his shorts, he walked toward where Mark was last seen.

Mark had gone to sleep. Ryan called out loudly, "Mark, Yo, it's time to catch flies."

He was squinting rapidly and they both started laughing. They cleared up and planned to try out some extraordinary cuisines at the open beach restaurant. It had a great sight of the sea, where they could watch the ships sailing by from a distance, and anyone would enjoy his or her dinner without much noise.

As they opened the menu, they noticed the list of variety of seafood, chicken, grilled meat, raw meat, and different salads. They did not know where to start as they felt their eyes were bigger than their stomach.

They ordered lemon iced tea, chicken satays, spaghetti and meatballs, and grilled prawns with spicy sour seafood dip. The restaurant wasn't lavish. It was an open air café. They enjoyed the fine meat and seafood preparations. The restaurant was sectioned into two parts where one section played lounge music and the other jazz. It all went well and what a fine meal it was, they thought.

Suddenly, Ryan's cell phone had bleeped again. He picked up his phone to check who it could be. He noticed that he had five missed calls.

"Bugger," he said in a very British accent, and added, "Who could it be? No number, perhaps someone I know."

He got up from the dinner and ambled to a quiet place when it rang again.

"Hello. Yes. Oh! Hi, Uncle Barun!"

"Ryan, when are you getting back? We got a notice about the delay in your payment for the semester. This is the third time and the deadline is tomorrow," said Uncle Barun.

"Uncle, I will be getting back in three days, and I shall visit the student counsel for late payments," replied Ryan.

"Ryan, we don't want to clear your mess. Anyway, everything else is alright here, and take care," said Uncle Barun with apprehension.

The phone line was disconnected. Ryan felt like he had gotten a call from a total stranger. Using British slang, he blurted, "Bollocks."

He had stridden toward Mark and briefed him. Mark was so carried away in a different world, and told Ryan, "Don't worry. Find a way when you get there."

"Yes, I guess so..."

Life could be delicious. What a cliché? When one was taking the pleasure of an enticing meal; unexpected calls do create disturbances as if someone added extra salt to the food making it unappetizing, thought Ryan.

Urrrgggh... Ryan wanted to scream.

CHAPTER

2

Sorting Out

There are times when a person undergoes a Eureka moment. Events from his or her past would unexpectedly rise to the surface of his or her mind and crystallizes it in a surprising way. This is how Ryan was feeling and he had a clear understanding of how these past events had affected his present behavior.

Mark stayed back for two days in Krabi and was quite happy for an extra dosage of relaxation. Ryan felt his stay at Krabi was great with a new experience being learnt. He left the airport and took a taxi back home. As he sat in the taxi, he felt awkward and this was nothing new for him.

He recalled a series of events he endured throughout his childhood.

He also understood the fact that everyone would go through many incidents making them emerge stronger and riding harmoniously on their journey. Those who cried over spilled milk would continue to moan and groan until deathbed. He knew that now was the time to make way for opportunities and think for alternatives to cash up.

"Returning back to London would be great," he thought. He finally reached home. He walked toward the door and turned around. Scanning his surroundings and his neighborhood, he saw houses, apartments and flats where uniqueness assembled with the joy of residential charm and superior location in the heart of London. He rang the bell.

Ryan's home was spacious, well-decorated with five bedrooms, an indoor swimming pool situated on the seventh floor, which revealed the beautiful landscape of London. It was a home that anyone would dream of. Uncle Barun named it the "Seventh Heaven."It was a home for everyone and a shelter for Ryan. He got his room, but felt he had no respect.

Waiting for a few seconds at the door, his fifteen year old cousin brother Aadil opened the door. "Hi! You are back, Ryan. We have alot happening here man!" said Aadil cheerfully.

Ryan smiled and gave him a 'high five,' asking him, "What happened?" He wondered that he was away for a few days and now a calamity had already risen.

He entered Uncle's paradise. Being the owner of three famous Indian diners was not easy. He surely worked very hard to build a home, considered Ryan. "Where is Uncle Barun?"asked Ryan.

"Oh, he is at the diners. If there is anything you want to eat, why don't you ask Butler Zarann? He shall prepare it for you," replied Aadil.

"Nah, I am fine Aadil. Do you have any idea where the letters kept by Uncle Barun, which was sent by The University of Westminster?" Ryan asked curiously.

There came a whine of regret, "He did mention it and was quite irritated. You know he does not want to pay for expenses he feels he is not responsible for. He told me, all this money, diners are his hard earned money and it is not for charity. He said I should start working when I complete high school. It shall make me a 'Man.' I think he seemed pretty upset."

"Okay. Anything else!"remarked Ryan.

"Yes, we have been invited for a luxurious dinner to a film festival which is in a few months. I mean next year, but don't know which film festival it is. Dad mentioned that Indian cuisine would be catered by our diner. We are all going to go. Mum said we can also take Isha this time, as she won't be too noisy. She is eight years old. What do you think, Ryan?"updated Aadil with eagerness.

"It sounds good. Finally your sister can join us. I shall see if I can make it. I have to sort out some things," said Ryan.

"What things? Finance—huh!" said Aadil wittily.

"Yup, - I will update you about it and only when it is sorted out. I shall freshen up and go to the Uni for some work. Adios for now," said Ryan.

He went to his room, locked the door and sat on his bed. Sleep ran in his mind. The last time he slept for a straight seven hours was months ago.

He was looking at his two comfortable, puffy pillows by his side. It was bizarre, but ideas came to him while he lay on his cozy bed with his Japanese buckwheat pillow supporting the contour of his head. He felt that sleep was death without responsibility. He slowly dosed off to sleep. After forty minutes, he woke up suddenly. He rushed to take a shower and headed to Uni.

Ryan enjoyed going to Uni. It was a great and peaceful place. Ryan used to tutor one of the counselor's sisters a few years ago, so he went to meet the counselor for advice on his late payment. Unfortunately, the person he wanted to meet was not available.

After waiting for a few moments, an aged man asked him, "What are you doing here? What problem do you have?"

Ryan hesitated to answer, wondering whether this man was the right person to ask for advice. After clearing his throat, Ryan decided he couldn't choose. "Sir, I have passed my payment date and I am a few days late."

The man answered, "No problem. You can go to the counter and pay now."

"Oh, uhmm, I have another problem. I don't have enough money. This is my first time and I need to pay it in installments. Do you have any suggestions?"asked Ryan with unease.

"Oh boy, we have various ways students can pay their

fees. The Uni provides an essential support service for students in many aspects. However, the installment payment system is quite a strict process and if you delay, there will be a fine of two hundred pounds for a late payment plus your tuition fees. He handed him a brochure detailing the process of payment in installments. Ryan opened the brochure and began reading...

Educating the future professionals
Payment system for students' year 2008: The rate of increase in fees will normally be limited to the rate of inflation. For late payments, additional £200 added...

Ryan closed the brochure and blurted out, "Thank you very much. I have understood this and will try to pay as soon as I can. For now I shall sign a 'Tuition Fee Installment Form', and hand it to the Campus Finance Office."Off he went to hand in the form and paid a deposit of £300. He did not know it would be that easy and now the main problem was the remaining money, he considered.

He practically came to a point where he felt like a loser and almost spent his entire savings. He was left with only £120. He contemplated with disappointment. He wondered what he should do to earn another £800 in one and a half month. This meant that by the end of February 2009, he had to clear everything, or else he wouldn't be able to complete the course on time.

"Hmm", he thought to himself, "I better head home and think what to do next." He decided to leave the dorm as he could not afford it anymore. So his last option was to shift back to his Uncle's home.

On his way out, he bumped into some of his friends and spoke to them for a while. The feeling of being updated and updating on life events was quite a fun thing. He felt he missed a lot, even though it had only been two weeks.

"All right, then. I shall catch up, soon. I have some things to settle down with," said Ryan.

"That's fine Ryan, Adios," said his friends.

He started walking away from them and was glad he didn't have to drop out a semester. He murmured, rubbing his left ear, "I am so eager to complete, so I can live with my own terms." He looked retarded. Luckily, this time no one saw him murmuring to himself. He took the tube and headed to his lavish shelter, knowing there was no escape from Uncle Barun.

Ryan wanted to talk to Uncle Barun and assure him that everything had been taken care of. After twenty minutes, he reached home and Butler Zarann asked him, "Ryan, where did you go? Uncle Barun has been waiting for you."

He greeted Uncle Barun. The mixed feeling from his side, - was surely a useless worry, despite knowing that he was an arrogant man with a big heart. Uncle Barun was quite glad to meet him and told him, "It has been months since we have spoken to each other."

"Yes Uncle, it has been a while. Aadil told me you have been invited for some kind of dinner," said Ryan.

"No Ryan, we all have," Uncle said politely.

"Uhum, yes," was all Ryan could say.

Uncle continued, "I was thinking...keep yourself free and it is important."Ryan updated him hastily, "Uncle, I went to Uni and everything has been settled. I will pay my tuition fee in installments and move back."

"Good, good, better to clear off debt, I would say. Ryan there is no free lunches in this world, that is, no free education. There is a cost for everything," said Uncle with buoyancy.

Ryan felt the heat and at the same time he avoided to get into any sort of argument. He gave a pretentious smile and asked, "Anything else?"

"No Ryan, you can freshen up and I will see you at the pool. We can talk there," persisted Uncle amicably. He wore his swim trunks and joined Uncle for a swim and, of course - the talk he had to have with him.

"There you are! Aadil, go and finish your homework," stifling a yawn even as he spoke.

"Dad I will, just one more lap to go," said Aadil anxiously. He knew that he wanted to talk to Ryan and could sense some kind of displeasure from his side.

"Ryan, you went to Thailand. How was it? Was it worth?"asked Uncle inquiringly.

He smiled in fond amusement and said with coolness, "Yes, it was for a project and it was a remarkable experience.

Uncle started with his golden preaching, "You know Ryan, self-confidence and sensibility is the first requisite to great undertakings. In the beginning I used to conceal myself that I was a strong and fast learner, but today I have overtaken my justification. I hope you know what you are doing with your life."

Ryan nodded and took a dip into the pool. He noticed that the tiles were dirty. Taking a swim, he looked up from the bottom. He could see the swirls of waves mixed with afternoon rays. The pool only seemed to look good when one was in it, he wondered.

At that moment, he could not take the pleasure of swimming because he felt he had been tied up with a series of questions from his Uncle. He took a dip, twisted and came up feeling better.

Uncle saw that Ryan did not continue to swim but stood diagonally getting fresh air, so he continued speaking, "I have a proposal for you. For the film festival we have to showcase exquisite Indian cuisine. I need some help with the design and photography to present the menu for the film festival during the closing night. It would be the gala dinner and desserts for two days. We will know the dates again. In that way it will be easier to create a blueprint of the menu for the two days of the gala dinner. Oh! It is for *"The London Film Festival 2009."* There are other bigger events, but this is also a good prospect for us to bag better deals. I shall be paid £350 for this work."

Uncle added with jauntiness, "The lunch and dinner for other days are being prepared from other five star diners and hotels."We are preparing meals for any two days during the film festival. The sponsors trust *my* choice of food, and if it hits the target, we can get the contract for eminent film festivals next time for a longer time, so it better be good!"

He thought this over for a few seconds. The moment of pause got him to evaluate his emotions and put aside his consternation. He knew that if Uncle hired someone else, he had to pay a higher price for it, and the only economical way was to ask someone he knew who would not say no. Ryan felt this was not what he wanted to do, and never wanted to work for his Uncle. It was not the case of ego, but it was the only way to stay away from dilemmas. He had appreciated everything his Uncle did for him.

The mystery behind his parents' death was still unknown to him. Ryan still never knew what exactly happened to them. With all this confusion, he realized he was being paid, which was good as he had to find money to pay his fees.

Displaying a positive attitude, Ryan said, "Yes, I shall give it my best shot, and we can discuss it later, maybe tomorrow. I will come to the diner and let me know how you want it to be done."

Uncle was pleased and said, "Eventhough the event will be held sometime in October and November, we still need to plan what we are going to do. Ryan, I will only give suggestions and see the fluidity of the work. You can talk with the chefs and decide two designs and course menus for the dinner."

Ryan began to feel disoriented, like - a nail was being hammered straight into his forehead. Keeping still, and taking a deep breath he paced slowly toward the right side of the pool.

Uncle continued talking and talking, "It will be good to see your creativity and determination. Ryan, I know you stopped swimming. Our talk is over. You can continue to swim, if you want to. See you tomorrow at the diner at 10 am."

"Sure!"He thought that one day he would definitely ask his Uncle about his parents. Maybe, - after all the gala celebrations and payments were made. He swam a few laps after Uncle left.

*****

Ryan started to feel famished. He got out, took a shower and asked Butler Zarann to prepare the spicy falafel wraps. After a few minutes, Aadil came up to Butler Zarann and said, "Yeah! We are eating the spicy falafel. Good it has been a while."

The butler said, "Aadil, wait! When it is ready, I will inform you and Ryan about it."

Ryan went for a hot shower. While scrubbing, he wondered what he would do. He had no clue about food and designs for a menu.

While being drawn to the ideas of the menu, he had this flash of this inquisitive pest. Ryan was back to his lonely thoughts, - that sometimes each person would have and shadows they ran away from. Everyone had things that are missed and remembered in the night bringing back unhappiness and seclusion. Love is missing from my life and it has been a while since I even had a girl friend he contemplated.

"Ryan! Ryan! Aadil bellowed out standing outside the bathroom.

This surely pulled Ryan away from those thoughts. He quickly twirled the shower faucet to slow down the pressure of the water to hear what Aadil was saying.

"The spicy falafel is ready!"

"Alright, go ahead," said Ryan.

After deluging, he wanted to know who was attending *The London Film Festival 2009*. He knew it was a big event. Celebrities from many countries and the members of the elite society would attend the festival showcasing extravagant new films, and critically acclaimed films from around the world.

He had seen the poster which had a separate note showing that on average 280 films from 60 countries would be made known with an Opening and Closing Night Galas, industry and public forums, celebrity interviews and there were other activities.

After viewing the note, he paced out of the room.

Uncle Barun told him, "We shall receive the festival program and the schedule tomorrow evening. We will also receive the list of all confirmed guests within a month. In that way, it will be easy for us to prepare the dinner for the two days."

Ryan asked curiously, "Isn't the closing ceremony dinner usually one night?"

"Yes, at first I assumed it too, but this time they will have it for two days. They might have a theme and many other films are going to be promoted, so it shall be a big thing. We are all invited for the two days and have our own table. It is not confirmed which two days we are catering dinner but I hope everything flows with grace and elegance. Oh, I heard they only have a thousand tickets for sale for outsiders," updated Uncle with promptness.

Uncle added excitingly, "They have a show where celebrities will showcase their movies and I heard there will be some entertainment. The tickets are quite pricy, but worth. As in £100 for adults and £60 for children under 16; however, no children below 8 years are allowed. We shall listen to music and celebrate films at international levels. The good thing is, with each ticket each person could watch two films. We have received tickets to watch any eight films. Let's discuss about the menu design now."

Ryan could see the expectations his Uncle had toward this big job and he had to accomplish it. His brow creased with fretfulness. "Uncle Barun, - we can discuss this tomorrow and I shall need to do some research on new contemporary designs and themes. Knowing it is an international crowd; we would need a fusion, and perhaps invite some sponsors for food tasting before the gala dinner."

Uncle seemed impressed with his initiative and told him, "It looks like you're thinking now," and left.

Huh, I am always thinking, what is his problem? considered Ryan. He walked toward the dining table, picked up another spicy falafel and took his biggest bite. "Yummy," he said out loud and added, "Butler, you're always good."

He took it into his room and switched on the TV. His favorite series, 'Weeds' was airing. It was a new series with a plateful of genres including comedy, crime, and drama. The last time I smoked weed was when I started Uni. Good I stopped, he thought.

While Ryan watched the fourth episode of the fourth season, Isha barged into the room saying, "Ryaaan, can I watch TV with you? Nobody wants me to watch TV."

Disapprovingly, he said, "Isha sweets, it is time to sleep. You have school."

"Yeah," Isha said and added with assertiveness, "Even Aadil has school and he is watching *Gossip Girls*."Isha began to whine and started nagging, "I want to watch TV, too."

Looking at her innocent and playful eyes, Ryan changed the channel for her. He changed to various channels, and nothing interested him. Isha then screamed, "Cartoon...I want to watch -Nemo."

Ryan had no choice. He slumped down on the bed. "Isha, sit down here and watch this. What is this about?"

With her soft voice, she explained, "You don't know the cartoon *Finding Nemo*. It's my favorite and Nemo is so smart. He finds his way back home."

That was a great description. How helpful? He thought. He did hear about animated movies, but never watched them. Anyway, as he watched, he missed his show 'Weeds,' but could not do anything about it. He considered, watching TV with an eight -year- old wasn't bad at all.

Eventually Isha fell asleep and Ryan carried her to her bedroom. He could not watch his series, but afterward, when he flipped back to the same channel, the TV show - Greys Anatomy- was aired. He began thinking how ridiculous it all was. He flipped to the other channel, Actor Hugh Grant's movie -Bridget Jones: The Edge of Reason- was aired. He continued watching Hugh Grant's movie from the middle and dosed off to sleep.

"Aah this sound; I need a new alarm clock. Looks like I am going to be deaf," Ryan said, and his hand just pushed the button off. He remembered his appointment and woke up from a very agitating sleep. He stretched himself and got off the bed. He gets this tensed smile and realized he did not change his clothes and slept with his jeans. He quickly turned the shower head, took a quick rinse and got ready.

He knew he had to meet the expectations of his Uncle and make sure that everything would be pleasant. He took his laptop, which was absolutely good for design and graphics, and within a few seconds he strode out of his room. He slurped down his coffee and stormed out of the door.

He paced briskly as he had only twenty minutes to reach to the diner. He hopped onto the tube hoping his skills were stronger than they had ever been before.

When he reached the station, he got out of the stuffy train. He had to wait to get going as there was a long queue. Fortunately, the main diner was not too far away. It was located at Mayfair, situated between Oxford Street, Piccadilly and Park Lane in the very centre of the city.

Uncle Barun had started his first diner there years ago because it was close to many beautiful parks and historical squares. It was an area where elite residents had the world's supreme shops and the most exclusive businesses.

After walking for ten minutes; he was in front of one of the finest diner serving Indian cuisine in London. For a few seconds, he admired the name of the diner, 'Seventh Heaven Indian Cuisine.' Many people addressed it as 'SHIC.' The name was hip and it brought goodluck. There were many restaurants' that had Indian food but a few served with a fusion concept. The restaurant had always been Uncle's baby and it was time for it to move up to a next level.

It was already 10:15am, so he rushed into the diner.

Uncle Barun had come out from the kitchen. When he saw Ryan, he just smiled at him, and greeted, "Morning! Show me your ideas, I am waiting."Ryan was hesitant. He took his seat and started discussing his ideas. Uncle Barun appeared in a rather good mood and was a good listener. He did not pass any judgments as yet.

He told Ryan, "If this works, it will be good for all of us, or else, I would not be able to trust your ideas in our business again."

Ryan had no words to say, but just ignored those curt remarks.

He wanted to retain a modicum of dignity. He

wondered if he should ask about the payment. Uncle later suggested, "The focus should be fusion with an ethnic touch. The food should be blended and flavoured with the taste that would suit all people. Once we have decided what kind of food we have, it would be easier to derive a notion and design for the menu. You can go on and have a word with the chefs, as we don't have any customers now. When you are done, we can finalize and discuss with the sponsors."

He went to the kitchen to call the head chef.

Ryan turned on his laptop as the head chef came out to converse about the meals and designs with him. After two hours of discussion, he finalized the ideas and continued to develop it into a presentation.

"Ryan, we have received the fax of the film festival dates. Oh, the film festival will be around mid - March till the beginning of April. Hmm…this means we have three full months for preparation," said Uncle with ardor. He kept away the fax and sips coffee back in his cabin.

After a while, one of the chefs called Uncle, and Ryan was getting edgy to inform him about the two kinds of menus he created. It was time for Uncle to decide and permit the green sign.

"I hope we can count on this culinary forefront," said one of the chefs.

He had prepared two versions of the menu and was awaiting the feedback. "Ryan, show me. You know I am not so good with computers, and yours seem to be quite complicated," said Uncle Barun.

"No problem, here," said Ryan respectfully. He showed what he had discussed with the chefs. His eyes flicking and added, "Uncle, I have not designed it yet, and this is what I have come up with."

"Hmm, this seems interesting. Some cuisines appear creative and we have agreed for sponsors to taste the flavors and check whether the blend of the spices would suit the mass. We might need alternatives for the main course. How about three types? In this way the guests can choose from the menu list. The guests shall choose his or her main course and dessert. One more thing we should not make it cluttered, or else it shall look disorganized. We can have three to four choices for main course," said Uncle with poise.

"Why not three? It will be overwhelming," suggested Ryan.

Uncle was confident with his ideas.

"I am impressed, Ryan. After about two hours of conversation with the chef and researching online, you have seemed to have done well. So for each day, we should have something different. There might be a last minute change. This is all good for now," praised Uncle.

"Thanks, Uncle," said Ryan.

"What a relief?" Ryan thought. "Have a look at this, and we can finalize it," said Ryan. Uncle Barun went through the entire food choices. While he was going through it, he pointed out the reasons with the Chef for their selection.

Looking at Ryan he continued, "You have two sets of menus. I must say very well presented."

With a smirk, Ryan got up and went to the washroom, giving Uncle his space. He also grabbed a bite from the kitchen because he could hear his stomach gnarled. He ate fried fish with herbs and saffron rice with mixed nuts which was quite relishing. He liked the blended flavors of mixed herbs, saffron, and the fragrance of cinnamon was soothing.

Finishing his meal, he noticed that it was already nearing dusk, and he wished he could have a chilled beer. On the other hand, Uncle made a print out of the menus and sent an email. He wanted to make sure that he had a copy of the selected cuisines.

Ryan sat there and could see that many customers were coming to the diner. He heard some of them ordering desserts and various types of coffees.' He was aware that it was nearing rush hour and did not want to discuss or create any disturbances for the customers.

"Ryan, I am done with this. You can pack up and have tea or anything you want to drink," said Uncle hastily. He took a final look at the menu and was already thinking about his presentation.

It has been a while since I hung out with my friends and I need a break. Friends were the only people in this world who made every stress, a stress free relief, bringing a bag filled with elation and positivity, Ryan thought. He had made many good friends and was grateful for it. Since childhood he did not believe in sharing his emotions, unless it was important. His cousin Aadil was friendly and trustworthy, but he was hesitant to be close to him.

Ryan wanted to have a drink; however, contriving the menu was an important task. As a result, he could not leave the diner as yet.

One event he looked forward to was the New Year celebrations for a new get away to 2009. He was waiting to speak to Mark and plan his night out.

Diving into other thoughts, Ryan came back to where he was. He looked at the menu over and over again. He hoped for everything to go well in the coming months.

Then with a positive notion, he considered how New Years would be fun, and glanced back at the menu. It was succinct and the selection of cuisines made him feel ravenous.

<u>Menu Style 1 (Day 1)</u>
Drinks
Pick your choice with your meal:
- **Sweet or Salty Lasi with a radiance of mango flavor**
- **Coke, Diet Coke, Pepsi, Sprite**
- **Ice Tea**
- **White wine- Gruner Veltliner, Greek Santorini Assyrtiko or Mantinia Moschofilero, Wines from Spain, Australia, Austria- Gruner Veltliner,, Chile**
- **Red Wine -Southern Italian wine, Wines from Spain, Australia, Chile**
- **Chardonnay or a crisp Sauvignon Blanc, and Champagne**
Appetizers
Each platter contains:
- **Indian fusion Sushi- Vegetarian**
- **Grilled Eggplant with Salsa sauce served with**

sautéd mushrooms blended with herbs and blue berry
sauce
- Stir-fried Shrimp in aromatic garlic pepper sauce
Main Course
Pick your choice:
- Crab cakes in tangy mango sauce, served with
spinach and mashed potato, Naan bread with
rosemary and basil.
- Fettuccini Alfredo with olive oil, tomatoes, sweet
chutney, oregano and medium spicy lime pesto sauce,
served with Caesar salad in Tandoori dressing-
Vegetarian
- Chicken Tikka Biryani (basmati rice, almonds,
pistachios and sultanas garnished with onions and
other spices) served with Saffron Creamy Shrimp and
special fusion gravy for rice, and cucumber salad
Desserts
Pick your choice:
- Dark Chocolate Tart blended with White Chocolate
and Cardamom served with Mango Creme Brule
- Gulab Jamun- Sweet dumplings, sprinkled with
coconut. Served in a warm sugar syrup and rose water
- Caramel Panna Cotta with served with cherries and
raspberry sauce

Menu Style 2 (Day 2)
Drinks
Pick your choice with your meal:
- Sweet or Salty Lasi with a radiance of mango flavor
- Coke, Diet Coke, Pepsi, Sprite
- Ice Tea
- White wine- Gruner Veltliner, Greek Santorini
Assyrtiko or Mantinia Moschofilero, Wines from
Spain, Australia, Austria- Gruner Veltliner,, Chile
- Red Wine -Southern Italian wine, Wines from
Spain, Australia, Chile
- Chardonnay or a crisp Sauvignon Blanc, and
Champagne
Appetizers
Each platter contains:

- Bruschetta with assorted vegetables and cheese topped with tangy Tamarind and strawberry sauce- Vegetarian
- Butter Chicken pizza
- Connoisseur's Mix- royal assortment of delicious chicken lamb and seafood appetizers

Main Course

Pick your choice:

- Fresh seabass spiced with chillies served with mushrooms and garnished with fresh bamboo shoots, fresh green and red peppers, showered with fresh coriander and creamy spinach
- Whole crab seasoned with fresh exotic herbs, barbecued in a rich medium spicy sauce, laced with almond, coconut garnishing served with fusion style fries
- Soft silky ravioli with creamy cottage cheese and spinach dressing, served with Indo-Chinese stir-fried noodles with vegetables and melting mushroom soups

Desserts

Pick your choice:

- Panna Cotta with rose and mint sauce with a tint of herbs
- Gulab Jamun- Sweet dumplings, sprinkled with coconut. Served in a warm sugar syrup and rose water
- Mango Mousse with fresh peaches and cream

Fortunately, for his own peace of mind Uncle said, "It seems good. Now you have three weeks to design the menu.

After you're done, I can fix an appointment with the sponsors. By the way, one of the sponsors just called and said the guests will be choosing their main course two days before the event. This means we must have no errors. Everything has to be spic and span. We must be prepared for last minute requests, so extra help might be required."

The energetic brainstorming session proved to be a success. Impressing Uncle Barun was no joke, marveled Ryan. He took it as a challenge.

"Bullocks!"Ryan mumbled. He bit his lips and waited

for the chefs to leave. Ryan whispered to Uncle, "When would be the best time you could pay?"

"Um," Uncle said and added, "After New Years! Wait for two weeks when the sponsors finalize the contract in January. You will get paid. Now focus on the design."Lowering his eyes Ryan sat back, sighed and finally felt good because he could get the money before the deadline. He wondered what would be another way to acquire the remaining money.

He started packing all his belongings and during the process, one of the waiters asked him if he wanted anything to drink. He had asked for a cappuccino and requested a special topping with caramel and cinnamon.

Ryan finished his cappuccino and left SHIC. He anticipated there will be no looking back. He knew he had to come back with an improved and adequate design for the menu.

For now, he was keen to know where his extra income was going to come from. He was long lost in his random contemplations.

Assembling his fluttering thoughts, he decided to call up some of his friends to hang out with. He decided not to go home and coveted a break from his mental stress of responsibilities.

The money issue was driving him bonkers.

CHAPTER

3

The Fortune-Teller

Trying to escape the daily routine has caused mental stress and driven Ryan deranged. Sometimes people would struggle through similar situations but in a different scenario. Another person who shares the same feeling is, 'Melina.' Her expectations have driven her fanatical.

Melina was doing her manicure and a pedicure spa treatment. After some time, one of the hairdressers told her, "A Tarot card reader is here, today. She is pretty good."

Without thinking straight and with no hesitation, Melina said, "Yes."

The session with the Tarot card reader was not convivial. Melina found it too difficult to digest all this at first. Later she realized everyone had choices and a great mind with a beautiful heart to follow. It gave birth to unwanted questions. What would a woman do if she was told that she was better off single for the rest of her life? She was a man trapped in a woman's body. She does not have to worry. She would always have everlasting wealth. She is independent and marriage is a missing ingredient of her life. Melina was thinking about what the Tarot card reader had told her.

She was infuriated when the Tarot lady told her a series

of predictions. Melina felt shallow and a wave of disappointment toward destiny.

Her mind was trying to console her heart. She would generally deny her thoughts, but this time it elicited unwanted sentiments. Would that be true? Is it a divine decree? Wait a minute. Maybe this is all rubbish. I don't mind getting married. Why shouldn't I? It would be nice to have someone to share things with, to throw pillows at, and sometimes even throw the frying pan, for fun though...it is all out of love, she conceived.

She continued to be lost in her imaginations. What would happen if I never experience sex that is prolific and is not with adulation? What if I simply left the world without having experience the intimacy that a husband and a wife spent? Well, she considered that she should have faith in the Angels that looked after her well-being and not dive into a pool of negative predictions that were made on random basis.

After struggling with her mind for half an hour she told her beautician, "Getting married is every woman's right. It is fine to be single for life but that depends on individuals thinking. In the Asian culture we might face a pressure if we are single. Being single is victory and a celebration to life.

Whether it is 21st, 22nd or even the 25th century, women are content with what they have, whether it's their career, being a single mother, being a police woman or even an astronaut. Women have reached the preeminent and perhaps that could be the reason why many prefer to be single. In fact, a woman and a man complete one other. Imagine a one-sided see-saw. It would always be pulled downwards and with the two-sided support length, it can be balanced. In the end, it is the choice of the woman."

The beautician winked at her and gave her thumbs up. Then she realized she began preaching which felt stupendous because she let loose of her frustration and distress. Melina had let out a sigh and smiled zealously.

Melina reckoned that probably expecting to hear loads of positive things coming in a goodie bag or even hearing that her life would be a bed of rose petals was a baseless assumption. It made it look superficial.

However, the short time spent at the salon gave her time to read between the lines from the indirect clues that life could just be the way one wants it to be. She knew that it could be some sort of warning but not an ultimatum.

"How about being disconnected from everyone for a while," she considered. After some time she felt a development of an overflow of electrifying current of enthusiasm and spontaneity. She was determined to take a break from having to think what should be done and how it should be done. Some things could be left to fate and miraculous events. At the end of the day with a great visionary and fortitude anyone could attain his or her aspiration, she thought.

Melina knew what she wanted to some extent. She was only twenty three years old. She had a lot more to do and learn from her existence, she believed. Her positive attitude blanketed her fear and sorrows. The only thing positive was her perseverance.

She was shattering her reverie and grasping the better tomorrow.

The next day, when she went to work, she was greeted and teased, "Hello Molly. How are you doing?"

Melina being a Chinese American conversed with her colleagues truly the American way. She answered, "My name is Melina."Few days ago, her supervisor at her part-time work place called her in his husky voice, "Hey molly, you want a lolly, the day is very jolly." She wanted to strangle his neck, but couldn't because he was her supervisor.

Her supervisor was a cheerful person. Even though Melina disliked it, she could still see the joy from his face. Her supervisor added, "So, how have you been? Been a while and heard you graduated. By the way, did not see you at the ceremony. You know my younger brother graduated, too."

Melina answered, "Yes, I had gone overseas. The head told me last minute. It is a new job and had gone for an on-the-job training to Scotland."

The Supervisor inquisitively inquired, "Nice. How was it?"

"Great. I felt akin to steam like sensation in my blood. More like going berserk. Working part-time for sales and trying my ass off to convince people to buy membership for the fitness club is not easy. I have to look for something else too. I want to continue my further studies. I need to save up. I left the US years back. I feel it's time to head to a new place and later I can get back to the US. Nevertheless, it's all good. I do love London. Anyway, I am thinking of going somewhere in Asia. I have three choices, Singapore, India or Malaysia for my further studies," Melina said wholeheartedly.

The supervisor spoke with concern, "Oh, have you spoken to your parents?"

"Yes, I did a week ago. We do speak using Skype. It is pretty great. It has been four years since I visited the U.S. I met my parents here a year ago, was a great reunion I would say. Anyway, I got to go now. We shall catch up soon. Have a good day."

Melina did have a job but not an occupation where she could earn extra cash for her further studies. The day had passed by with serious work patterns and after work, Melina walked a-long and got into the tube. She took out her IPod Touch. She clicked on her all time favourite song from *Kelly Clarkson-Since you've been gone*. After a few seconds she changed it to *Celine Dion's- I'm Alive*. Whenever she heard those songs, she felt pepped up.

The next day's routine made Melina too exhausted to talk and convince people for something she considered was bull-shit. I know, it is just an exaggeration and it is not that bad, she thought.

In contrast, the forty-minute ride to the 'Central YMCA Club'- could be sluggish but at the same time Melina could take a glimpse of the infrastructure and busy lifestyle of London. She had worked there for a year and was offered a senior sales position for membership services.

The Central YMCA was quite a club with tempting facilities and special service help for employees. They could use the gym facilities during their days off, have a free drink daily at the juice bar with a ten percent discount to the lifestyle courses. Melina loved that part of it. Many charming and attractive men were members. So it was a good stimulant for her to be alert and the beam brightened her day. She missed flirting with a man at times, but she ignored that part of it because she wanted to focus on her career.

That day, Melina passed through the fitness center to check if everything was all right and glanced at the swimming pool. Seeing people involved and happy during their workout was quite a watch. "Good afternoon, Molly. I know you don't like me calling you that, but I won't stop. It is a nice nickname for you. So what you looking at?" said the supervisor intentionally.

"Hello, supervisor," she replied and disregarded the question.

He informed, "There are two females interested in Pilates. Show them the new schemes."

"I will check to them. Have a good day."Melina spoke professionally.

As she walked toward them, she remembered the time she started work during her probation period. The supervisor was unsociable, offensive and sometimes crude. Today when she could make sales, he had turned over a new leaf.

Melina recalled a situation about one morning a couple of months ago. She had stepped out to get the mail in front of the sales department and noticed that someone had left an empty soda can in front of the mailbox area. She thought a decent person who loved keeping the environment clean would pick it up and throw it away.

However, Melina had a feeling that it would be the supervisor as he had the habit to leave his waste sometimes at the wrong places, so she picked it up and threw it in the bin.

The snooping and the suspense to find out who it may be would be entertaining, she wondered. Melina began to act like a spy. She noticed as days went by, there was no can in front of the mailbox area. She also peeped toward the supervisor's cabin and overheard him call for a meeting to revise hygiene and sanitation rules of the club. He actually changed his habit, she reflected. She was glad to see a transformed person.

She went to meet the two new eligible members. She showed them the documents, and spoke in her best possible manner. The two females bought the trial membership package for three months.

Finished, I am nearing the edge and bored of my job. Explaining customers' about the club and finding people who were interested even for a short time to join any form of exercises, whether it was cardio, kick-boxing or even Pilates is exhausting, considered Melina.

Everything changed with time. She knew she was not a dynamic saleswoman and luck was on her side. After a few months, she was promoted as one of the senior sales executive. Looking at her watch, she realized she had another three hours before she could head home.

*****

At the other end of the city, Ryan got a headache figuring out his design and how to get extra money. Time was ticking and his heart was beating even faster. He wondered where Mark was. He needed a friend.

Sitting in his room on the bean bag, - Ryan opened his lap top and went through the menu to figure out the design whether it should be simple or – contemporary - and flashy. He thought it was better to design and print the menu to be environmentally friendly, perhaps from recycled paper. This would be a new concept, he presumed.

Everything within his heart and soul revolted his ideas giving him satisfaction to his final notion. He considered of proposing the idea to Uncle. His first design for the menu was based on animation. He visualized of having famous cartoon characters around the menu holding different types of curry pots and the hookah.

He was then convinced of a menu being depicted like a celebration or contributing respect to international cinema as well.

Now he was thinking of his next theme. He liked the concept of a key shaped newfangled design. It could represent so many things like, key to success, key to new ideas or even key to celebration. His last theme was bright, sandy, with maples, signifying the friendship between cinema and the pleasure of people watching it. Ryan liked the design. It was bright and looked better.

Ryan hoped that the themes he designed would be good enough for Uncle to choose from. He had to complete it that night and did not want to have any delays. While getting so engrossed into his new project, his cell phone rang.

"Guess what? It was Mark's call - he was back.

"Hey man, where have you been?"

"I was busy after I got back and just got my act together," said Mark.

"Hey Mark, I have to deal with my tuition fees. I need another £450 for the late payment. I need a job. I only have a month, orelse I am doomed," said Ryan with disappointment.

Mark eased out with concern, "Geesh, how did that happen? Anyway, let's meet up and I need updates. So are there any plans for New Years? It's in three days, mate."

"No plans for now, Mark. I can't even celebrate Christmas because of my financial dilemma."

"Chill and everything will be alright, man. I will see you at Oxford Street, in Polka Restaurant. We have not been there for a while. We need to plan something exciting. Don't be boring, and shut up! See you in an hour, Ryan."

*****

Meanwhile, at the office, Melina was getting ready to head home. She was also giving a thought to do something different for New Year's. She wanted to spend some time with her Uni friends. As she got out of the club, she tripped and slid on her buttocks. Some teenagers looked at her and started giggling.

"How ugly! Why me?"she muttered.

Melina got up and took baby steps toward the exit and swiped her card.

When she was out of the train, she stopped by at the groceries. She wanted to relax for a few days. Only one more day to work and she would be off for three days. It was like everyone was on a holiday mood. She bought a few stuff and went home. She satiated herself with a hot bath as London was cold and foggy.

She prepared herself a light meal and switched on the TV to watch 'Oprah's Big Give.' It was a great fund raising show, attempting to make dreams come true. The show was inspiring and intense. Melina loved watching it whenever she had the time. She was almost done with dinner when her cell phone rang. One of her friends, Kathy called up to make plans for New Years.

Melina spoke cheerfully, "Hieee, I was just having dinner, and watching TV. What's up!"

"Oh well, we were planning to go for the Cruise dinner for New Years. What do you think? It will be fun. Every time you go to the church and later you're at some bar, you need a change too," said Kathy persuasively.

Melina laughed and wanted more details about the cruise. She knew it would be exhilarating.

Kathy articulated convincingly, "Oh, it is about £80 per head, with buffet, disco, fireworks, unlimited alcohol you know, it should be fun. We all can catch up. Later, if you are up for it, we can go to a pub. The cruise leaves at 8:30pm. We shall be cruising around river Thames at night. It will be fun, Melina."

Melina was twirling a few strands of her hair and said, "Fine, I will join you and I know it will really be fun. So how many are joining us?"

"We will be six of us."

"Kathy, I shall go to the church and meet you at 7:45pm near Big Ben."Melina hung up the phone and was already thinking what to wear. She realized that she had a few days and continued watching TV.

*****

Time was ticking. Mark had been staring at his watch occasionally. He was waiting for Ryan at Polka Restaurant for some time. He ordered a drink and after a few minutes Ryan walked in. They were so happy to meet. They gave each other a long time no see tight hug, and sat down for a healthy chat.

Mark asked, "So tell me how you are doing? You seemed grinded with your money issue. It happens, you will find a way. By the way, I will be meeting my girlfriend after dinner."

"Hey man, I need a chilled beer," said Ryan and waved at the waiter to order two glasses of beer.

"What you doing for New Years, Mark?" Ryan asked.

"Hey, I am planning to go to either a theme party, a cruise or may be to Planet Hollywood. Whatever it is, you are coming with us. We are all going! Our group and my girlfriend, so it is time you get one, too. You have had your break already."

With his dazzling white smile Ryan expressed, "Shut up Mark. Let's order some food. I am hungry."

Both of them had a long catching up and decided on Planet Hollywood. Out of worry, Ryan voiced, "I need to get a job, as I am tight even during New Year's."

With a quick response, Mark pointed out, "Fine. You sound irritating and I have not seen you like this before. Why don't you ask the manager if they have a part-time job offer for you? This place is constantly busy and I guess it's good and it is celebration time. So many people do come here so why don't you check it out."

When they were done, Ryan asked for the bill and Mark had to leave quickly as his girlfriend was waiting. He had a word with the manager. The manager knew Ryan and Mark as their loyal customers. Lucky him, he was offered a part-time job, and had to start the next day. He was relieved that he would earn about £120. Ryan also agreed to a night-time shift for ten days after the New Year's celebration.

What a fluke! He thought. The manager offered Ryan a position as the temporary head of all waiters. In this way, Ryan could earn up to £300, and after that he had to figure out, his next new job. He headed back home and was looking forward to a new day. That night, he slept soundly.

*****

The sound sleep sustained the troubling mind and the next day it was a feeling of a new gag for Melina, Ryan, and the rest of the world. Later that evening, Melina was looking through new job vacancies and Ryan was getting prepared for his new job sessions. All was going well. She emailed her resumes to a couple of companies so that she could get a response soon after New Years. She preferred not to apply for a sales job as she was already doing enough in the club. She sent her resumes to some hotels and supermarket chains as a part-time customer relationship officer.

Getting an undergraduate degree in Advertising and Marketing Communications was fun, and required night time shifts. However, she was never interested in night shifts. She couldn't handle the pressure and the feeling of being fatigue.

She did what she had to, and was thinking about what the fortune teller had told her. She was lost in those thoughts at her cozy corner at home and began flipping through the TV channels. She felt restless and to calm herself down she started to light some candles.

After a while she started to feel better, and realized an individual was his or her own best friend and it is in the person's hand to get hold of his or her emotion. She was looking forward to a new beginning in 2009, a new job and her new destined location for further studies.

Finally, the big day was here. Celebrating New Year's was one of the most awaiting festivities that people looked forward to.

When she got back home from the church, Melina was going through her wardrobe and checking out what to wear that night. She pampered herself and got dressed up. She was looking stunning in her lilac halter dress, and her soft curls made her look like a diva. She wore her gloves and took her stylish coat and left.

Melina reached Big Ben and was waiting for Kathy. There were so many people as it was a jovial and celebratory season. She was looking at all the people and the children jumping out of joy and excitement.

Kathy called out, "Melina, Hieee, have you been waiting long?"

"No, just waited for about ten-minutes," replied Melina.

"Sorry, you know the traffic. We can walk to the cruise. We still have thirty-five minutes," said Kathy.

Melina began to yak, "Sure, I don't mind, it is a good weather for a walk. Oh, the cold..." Catching up was like emptying a bag full of candies by sharing it with friends, presumed Melina.

It was a conversation full of spice and elation. They were striding toward River Thames - for their extravagant New Year cruise dinner.

*****

Too many people had gathered the streets. Ryan left the restaurant and was glad he made some money. He noticed that he could not live life like this, with just having enough to survive and needed money for a balance.

When he reached home, he told Aadil he had plans and would meet everyone after New Year's. He gave a brotherly hug to him and Isha.

Aadil informed him, "Dad has plans with his friends, too."

Ryan was glad he did not have to join him and left home to meet Mark. He wanted to party and was waiting for a surprise victory. He was looking forward to meet someone special, so he would feel the victory and savory from the break he had.

After some time Ryan met up with Mark at Planet Hollywood. Mark handed him the raffle tickets.

The New Year's night was thrilling. Melina stood out of the dining area in the cruise. She could feel the cool breeze surpassing her body. She felt the buzz and was having a great time. The lightings, the scenic view and the buffet were majestic. Music lovers dressed in their best and had flock to the cruise to celebrate a new beginning. She peeped outside looking at the sky, and was thinking of a fresh start with her life. She needed a change.

It had been a long time since she was away from home, and knew she could not stay away from her parents for a longer time.

She wanted to make her life filled with qualitative experiences. Eventhough, it may not be easy, she wanted to be the master of her own decisions, and sometimes thought she could conquer the world. All these beliefs were running in her mind, inspite of all the loud sound of music and DJ announcing the raffle prizes.

"Molly, let's go and dance. Here is your chilled Apple Martini," teased Kathy. Melina took a sip and danced along. She felt she was hiding something and at the spur of that moment she thought of exactly what she wanted.

Grooving to the music was all people could contemplate to celebrate on a grandiose day. So did Ryan. Doing the boogie at Planet Hollywood, Ryan toasted with his friends to a better year ahead. The dance floor was open and many kinds of dances were demonstrated. There were waltz, tango, salsa, and a live band singing to famous songs of the 80's and the 90's. Ryan could dance. Unlike some men, he did not have two left feet. He was looking around if he could spot some woman of his type or even be introduced to someone. He needed a friend and this time he wanted to meet a special woman, he thought. He was having a good time and was enjoying his chilled champagne. After four glasses, he was surely feeling different.

His bright smile and sparkling eyes, hid his feelings that night.

He took everything with a flow. There were only thirty minutes left to New Year 2009. People around were ready with their party poppers, spraying colorful springs at each other, toasting and cheering.

*****

At the cruise, Melina and her friends hugged each other and toasted to their friendship and everlasting bond. There were only fifteen minutes left to the countdown.

The flamboyant evening was escalating with happiness and exuberance. They went back to their table and took pictures. They glanced around the beautiful and colorful River Thames.

The place looked so different and magical that night. From a distance, they could hear the DJ announcing louder and louder, 10, 9, 8, 7...3, 2, and 1...Happy New Year 2009!

Fireworks engulfed the sky and everyone gave each other a hug and kissed their loved one. Melina saw many people of different age groups and the joy of extol reflected on everyone's face.

The moment was worth capturing on celluloid, she wondered. Melina embraced her friends and sent a text message to greet her parents, too.

*****

The pleasure of drinking had absorbed in Ryan's happiness. He was already feeling tipsy and did not regret not staying back with his cousins. He knew he had to make it different this time, for himself.

After the countdown, the host of the evening said a few words to make the evening more memorable. "Spread the message of unity and have high inspirations to head for all the goals you have set in the New Year. Everyone has learnt from every aspect of the passing year and look toward some more excitement in the coming year. Don't forget to stir your soul and grab new opportunities. May the new hopes arise and be seen with flawless ground. Happy New Year! Enjoy and Cheers!"

It was past 1:30am and Melina was already tired. She was walking by the River Thames looking at all the 'Happy People.' She still did not mind heading home, even knowing that her friends would not permit her to do so.

"Melina, we are going to Oxford Street. We shall probably go to a pub for a while. You are coming with us. Your house is not too far from there."

Melina replied disappointingly, "It is okay. You guys can carry on."

"No, it is just for a while Melina. Like an hour and then you get back. It is New Years and we don't even meet often," said Kathy assertively.

"Fine guys, no problem. Let's go and have some fun," replied Melina.

While Melina wanted to head home. Some people simply adored life and wanted to enjoy every bit of it.

Unlike Melina, some people were ready for some excitement. Ryan tapped to the steps of music and flirtatious moves of strangers. He wanted to have a time of his life.

After the countdown, Ryan was with some of his friends getting off the tube. He noticed the luxurious setting and glamorous lightings as he neared Piccadilly, and got through the crowd.

He managed to walk through and after a while entered the night club, Crystal. It was packed. It could be seen that the crowd at the club were hip and from affluent families. Looking at the jittery, stylish, and sexy fashion show, Ryan ordered a glass of red wine and stood there for a while. He watched the hot and stunning models walking with style on the ramp.

Ryan enjoyed glaring at the poise of models for a change. He had the patience to be lured by their beauty.

Where endurance was very well sunk in Ryan's behavior, Melina had no tolerance. Outside the 'Viwo Latina bar, Melina and her friends discussed whether they should even get inside. Then, Melina and her friends walked in to the bar which was not big and packed. They stayed there not more than forty minutes and left to the next place.

Melina was looking attractive that night and her charm could possibly attract someone, but who would that be? She giggled and enjoyed flirting with the English men as they wooed at her. She admired the attention.

All of them were woozy but were still in their senses. Melina hated to get drunk and disliked the feeling of a hangover, and never wanted to go through that again.

"Oh, Melina, let's go to NO.3. It should be okay," said Kathy.

"But look, way too many people," complained Melina.

"That's fine. We can get a cocktail and leave soon, I promise," convinced Kathy.

Melina wanted to get home as she needed her beauty sleep.

"Hey guys, I ain't having breakfast and I feel like going back home," whined Melina.

Kathy replied sarcastically, "Yup you won't. Probably it might only be lunch."

Everyone started to laugh. "Ladies, don't be Bi-a-tches!" swore Melina.

Melina joined everyone and entered NO.3. One of her friends ordered Mojitos' and a Bikini Martini Cocktail.

After some time, Melina suggested, "Guys, let's get out of here and go somewhere better. Then we can go home..."

Everyone was staring at her and pulled her leg, "What happened to your beauty sleep?"

In her hyper tone, "Well...well... screw it for a while. One more place and we leave okay."

One of Melina's friend recommended, "Let's go to Crystal. We have not been there for a while now, and it's a good place."

As Melina entered the night club she accidentally stepped on someone's foot. With a drunken voice the stranger stated, "Hey Love...my foot."

"Oops, sorry, sorry, Happy New Year's," said Melina jovially.

"Same to you, too," The stranger said with a tease.

Melina went where the fashion show was going on. She walked passed through Ryan and found a place to sit. The fashion show was good and was about to end soon.

The show stopper was a famous British model. Everyone cheered and applauded for her. After some time the dance floor opened and everyone began swaying to the music. Melina shook her head as she liked the music.

Ryan walked away from the dance floor and suddenly turned back to call Mark.

He accidentally hit Melina's head.

"Oh, I am sorry," apologized Ryan.

Melina just stared at him. With her half smiling face, she nodded her head saying, "It's okay, Happy New Year."

She marveled inexorably, this is absolutely Karma. She just stepped on someone's foot and her head was hit by someone's elbow. She was dancing her way to the crowds and went to the dance floor.

Ryan and Mark had planned to leave. Within that moment Mark's girlfriend said, "I like this song. Leave after this song."Mark looked at Ryan and told him, "You too, let's go to the dance floor."

Melina was shaking away and with every turn vouched a festive dawn, and embracing the delight of a new opportunity to a fête.

To a sudden surprise she turned back immediately. One of Ryan's friends was drunk and smacked Melina on her buttocks. Melina raised her left eyebrow, frowning, and thought that this was not being funny. She turned around and could not see anyone who she thought did it.

Ryan's friend was bouncing away and tripped. He pushed Melina and she fell on Mark. The scene was hilarious as Melina hadn't a clue what was happening. Mark balanced himself pretty well that he fell alone and not with his girlfriend.

Melina's friend got her up and she was already steaming up. When Ryan and Mark acted contrite in behalf of their friend, she marched away. She had no interest to listen. There was a bridge of silence. She was in no mood to have a debate.

Melina and her friends left the night club and planned to grab coffee. They teased her about the incident. They told her that one of the fellows was good looking.

She was upset and said with infuriation, "I am not looking at men when I fall. So please stop it now. My haunches hurt now." They all broke into a laughter.

Melina tried to forget what happened, and enjoyed her coffee in the cool weather. When they were done, Melina said her goodbyes' and paced toward the tube.

As she got on, someone from the back patted her and said, "Hey!"

What now? She wondered. She looked at him vaguely and asked, "Do we know each other?"

Ryan spoke gently, "Not yet but kind off. We just met at the night club. My friend fell over you." After a pause he added, "I am sorry about that."

Melina was annoyed and taunted, "Well, I guess it was something that I wouldn't forget. Maybe…next year you guys should be more careful."

"Sorry, I am Ryan," he introduced himself.

Melina gave a slight thought, there was no harm being kind and replied, "I am Melina," and turned her face away.

Ryan saw from the glass reflection that she was yawning away and was not so bothered. Melina felt lethargic and heaved a sigh and Ryan just told her from her back, "Wishing you a good year. Cheers."

She looked diagonally and replied, "Same to you, hoping you and your friend's don't attempt to get people fall on the dance floor," and winked with a slight smirk. She added, "Happy New Year again."

She saw Ryan get off his stop. After a while, she remembered what the fortune teller had told her, "She would meet someone by accident but not marry him."

She got off at the platform thinking all along about her night, and was quite glad she had a great and strange time.

She hated the fall and was having a bad ache. She began thinking about the whole scenario on meeting a stranger and marveled on the thoughts about what would happen next in her life? Whether she would get a new job or find new Love? Or may be both?

Everything seemed strange this time, considered Melina.

4

Why Settle for Less?

Ryan woke up late in the afternoon on his first day of the New Year. He was in a rather good mood and wished everyone a Happy New Year at home. Isha was excited to meet Ryan and sat beside him during lunch.

Uncle Barun did not say much to him. He ate lunch and proceeded back to his room.

A few days had passed and Ryan was already working at the restaurant. He could sense a new encounter feeling the stability of life. Whereas, Uncle was glad that he was not wasting his time. Ryan used to get home late and during the day time he used to work with his designs for the menu. A few days later, he showed the designs to Uncle. He did not say much and told him, "I will show them to the sponsors and let you know about it later. It seems fine for now."

On the same day, the ambience brought a necessary exertion to browse through important emails. It had been two weeks and Melina had developed a gush of negative attitude. She switched on her computer and began squeezing her sponge ball.

Leaning down, she skimmed through her emails. The feeling of being appeased was derived after having seen a reply to her job application. She was called for an interview. She prepared herself for the interview for a part-time position as a customer relationship officer. She felt lucky that she was free during the weekends.

She surmised this as a good start and began humming on the nursery rhyme 'Twinkle Twinkle little star...'

The working intensity was rising elsewhere too. The keenness to produce great work was a challenge for Uncle Barun. He wanted the best and made sure he prepared it with zeal.

The three days had passed in a jiffy. The moment for some creative tasks to accomplish was to be instigated.

Uncle Barun had told Ryan that the sponsors finalized their decision with the design and liked the one which was bright and sandy with maple leaves.

"We are going to use menu two for the first day and menu one for the second day. You're saved and I will pay you next week," said Uncle with ease.

Ryan was already looking for a new job as his due date for the tuition fees was nearing. He needed another £800, and had collected only £300. He was getting restless. He did not want to settle for anything less.

He was eager to earn more money to balance his financial dilemma. He looked through the newspapers for a suitable job.

The feeling of being in hot soup gave him no choice to be finicky. He emailed his resumes to many companies. Some of which were for sales consultants at the sports club, media and arts consultant at PR firms, and a position of a market research executive. He apprehended the fact that he did not have to compromise his choice of profession.

Keeping his fingers crossed, he hoped to receive a prompt response. After some time, Ryan got back to completing some of his reports and went to pay off the £300 at the university.

Finding a job was not an easy task. Being lucky was simply miraculous. Melina had her interview and everything worked out for her. She had to work Tuesdays through Saturdays at the hotel in the evenings from 6 pm-11pm. She knew it was going to be miserably tiring as she would not have time to socialize, nor take care of herself, but she needed the job. Managing two jobs was an art of bravery. Melina had things sorted out and also did not want to settle for anything less. She wanted the job and was getting paid well. Her next step was going through brochures' of different Universities in Asia for a graduate degree.

Sorting out a stable employment could be a pain in the neck, thought Ryan. He was checking his e-mails and eventually after a few days, he was called for an interview at a magazine company as a part-time photographer and an assistant editor for a famous teenage magazine called *Street-icon*.

Ryan was getting more serious about his career. He developed high hopes thinking of an advance payment from his new job.

*****

Alternatively, Melina had started her first day at work, and was quite nervous. She wished for nothing to go wrong. She started her New Years with a fall and that feeling of embarrassment need not to be occurred again, she wondered.

The head of the human resource, introduced her to the rest of the staff. He briefed her up with her responsibilities. She was to handle the two cafes and sports amenities at the hotel daily. She loved her work this time. Although, she didn't even start it, she apperceived positive vibes that it would be pleasurable.

With the economy and technology progressing in various directions, customer service was a challenge of the day. She had gone to the cafe, gym, and swimming pool to see if there were any problems with customers. Days passed and she was getting used to her work routine. She did undergo many incidents with customers - where she had to offer discount services unnecessarily. Some customers created problems, and asked an incentive for it.

Having heard that one aced the interview is a sweet

delight. Melina had her sprightliness and so did Ryan pass his interview. At *Street-icon*, Ryan had to carry out his first photo shoot for a group of teenagers' who were modeling for healthy lifestyle. He was supposed to go to the hotel where Melina worked. It was obvious that Ryan had no clue about it.

Ryan thought, who said teenage models did not have attitude? If they knew they were getting famous. Their attitude was full of baloney and artificial pride.

He was at the swimming pool and saw a slider and the customary made waterfall. It seemed exotic and was a good place to shoot. The photographs had to create the appeal but not create any controversy for unhealthy lifestyle for teenagers. After it was done, Ryan and his crew shifted to the gym and took pictures of teenagers exercising, showcasing how music could boost their motivation to exercise.

Melina took a round at the swimming pool area and walked past the gym. She noticed the photo shoot and smiled at some of the teenage models. Realizing she did not have time to loiter, she went toward the café and ordered a cup of coffee. She prepared a report completing the requirement of the hotel. As she was done with her work, she wrapped up and was ready to leave.

Ryan was done with the shoot and wanted to grab a bite before he headed to the company. So he walked into the café and ordered a cappuccino and a tuna - cheese sandwich.

Melina stepped out toward the exit of the café professionally and passed through Ryan.

When the waitress served Ryan's cappuccino and sandwich, he had bent over to keep his camera back into the bag. He saw her, but could not recall who she was. He was looking at her for a few seconds and then started eating his sandwich.

Melina was speaking to the waiter and asked about some details about the dessert menu. She yawned, and that very moment, Ryan looked at her again. He remembered who she was but not her name.

He got up quickly, and called out, "Excuse me, lady."

Melina replied, "Yes. May I help you, any problem?"

Ryan wanted to laugh but stopped and simply said, "No, but we have met before."

Melina did not recognize him, until he had reminded her about the drama on New Year's. Her lips quivered and she said, "Oh, Hi! What you doing here? You have a good memory."

Ryan spoke in a friendly manner, "Yes I do. I had a photo shoot, here."

Out of curiosity Melina inquired, "Are you one of the teenage models?" She winked.

"I am glad you think I am quite young. Nah, I am the photographer," exclaimed Ryan.

"Well nowadays many teenagers are over grown. So I thought...I am joking. Anyways, how are you doing?" teased Melina.

Ryan whispered, "I am good and you."

"Great! Why did you whisper?"replied Melina.

Ryan asked inquisitively, "You work here?"

"Yes...anyways I got to go now. Have a good photo shoot. See you around," said Melina with reluctance.

She jaunted out of the café and went into her cabin. She had wished she did not see him again. Melina was fascinated with the fact that it was a small world after all and how friendly he was to re-introduce himself. She completed her work and left to the station.

As she entered the tube, Ryan did not realize they entered the train at the same time. Melina took out her iPod touch and as she was putting on her earphones. She saw Ryan, feeling puzzled and looked away. She reckoned him coming toward her.

Melina carried on listening to her music and when she tilted to give space to another person. They looked at each other.

There was a slight leer on her face. Ryan came closer and said benevolently, "We meet again."

She removed her earphones and that is when they started their first ever mystifying talk.   Everything appeared so natural to Melina. She could not stop from speaking continuously. They didn't bear in mind nor grasp how they started talking without feeling conscious. Melina could feel their connection was stunning.

Ryan was not aware when he passed his subway stop. Neither did she observe when she passed hers. They spoke about work and food, that's when they passed their stop and laughed at their oblivion.

"Oh gosh, I will have to walk back," complained Melina.

"Oh well, me too," uttered Ryan.

"Are you heading home?" questioned Melina.

"No, I am going to deliver the pictures," Ryan replied and adjoined with concern, "What about you?"

Melina rendered, "Home. I want to sleep, and need a hot bathe...It is so cold."

They got off the stop and sauntered different directions. They knew they felt some kind of a pleasant sensation - a spark to a new camaraderie and traipsed their own ways. Ryan knew that he'd experienced an exceptional and a special connection with her, but wasn't ready to acknowledge the moment because of his financial dilemma. Melina felt something she could not specify and when she was lying on her bed, she thought of the conversation she had with Ryan. She denied any interest of any sort. Nevertheless, it happened naturally, marveled Melina wholeheartedly and dosed off to sleep.

A few days later, Melina was at the station, buying magazines and a hotdog. She sat down for a while and wanted to read and relax. She noticed someone coming toward her, and ignored it.

A husky soft voice said, "Melina, how you doin?" It was Ryan. What a pure twist of fate! They both glanced at each other abruptly and felt the heat.

There was a strange sensation. Ryan wasn't sure what he was feeling. He decided that he'd rather be and do what senses right, regardless of the risk. He spoke to her, and eventually asked her for her number. Melina did not hesitate to give her mobile number. Later, both of them left to their work places.

The flicker of elation in him was snuffed out like a shooting star in the firmament.

That following night, Ryan called Melina and asked her out. Because of her busy schedule she opted to go for lunch on a Sunday. They met up at Oxford Street station and carried on from there.

After a warm welcome by the waiter, Ryan gave her a box of chocolates. She acknowledged it with delight and ordered scrumptious Chinese cuisine. They shared moments of their life and had a pleasant time sipping Chinese wine.

Melina anticipated that it had been a long time since she went out on a date, and did not regret it at all as Ryan knew how to make a woman feel comfortable. Melina shared stories about herself in America and her Chinese lifestyle. Ryan did not say much about his Uncle but did mention that his parents passed away when he was young.

They had a great time and later wanted to do something fun, as suggested by Melina.

She started to feel like she wanted to scream, breathe, and walk in the cold. She guessed it was the excitement pumping up her stomach. With the weather being so cold, they agreed to take a stroll for a while and thought of taking a ride on the London Eye.

Ryan preferred taking the date slow and remembered he sat on the Ferris wheel years ago, when it had just opened. There were not many people, and it was absolutely a fine moment in the evening.

When they got into the capsule shaped seating area, they saw the view and London never looked so beautiful. They could see the city's landmarks and admire the beauty of the well designed cathedrals and architecture. It was a breathtaking moment.

Fortunately, they were the only ones in one capsule. Ryan tried to get closer and eventually held back, as he did not want to jeopardize his date.

Melina was quiet for a while and was waiting for something to happen. She glared crossly out the glass believing that may be going slow would be fine, too. She slowly rested her head on his shoulder, indicating her feeling of comfort and watched the view.

Ryan was glad that he cultivated a comfort zone and

did not want to mess anything up. After the ride, they sipped hot coffee, and said goodbye with a tight hug.

They shared the same feeling of not wanting anything to mess up the date. Before they left, Ryan hugged her again and kissed her forehead quickly, and said, "See you soon."

Melina left and he messaged her on the cell phone:

How about dinner next week? It's an opportunity to smile more often, takecare and sleep tight.

She replied: *I am smiling already, and dinner is fine. Will let you know the day. Sweet dreams.*

Everything was going smoothly, considered Ryan and was happy to meet her again.

That night, Ryan completed his assignments and had to pay his tuition fees within a few days. He built courage thinking of what he would do. The next morning, he spoke to his boss about the advance payment.

The boss was not in favor to do any advance payments; however, after Ryan had requested for £400 to pay his tuition fees and not entire salary, the boss signed the petition for £400 to the accounts department.

Ryan appreciated the generosity and assured that would never occur again. He got back to his work and had long hours of shooting, but did not whine about anything, as he did not covet for any complications regarding his payment.

Four days later, he got it out of his chest. He paid his fees and wanted to meet Melina again.   It had been a week since he had seen her, so he called her but she did not pick up the phone. Then he tried again. He was struck by the silence and began to get querulous.

A couple of hours later she called back and they spoke for a bit and confirmed for dinner and movie that night which subsided the petulant notions.

Melina met him and gave him a fortune cookie. She told him to open it after the movie. Ryan found that an interesting way to start their evening. Melina was contented and began to like him more for his unique intelligence.

After the movie, when they reached the restaurant,

he remembered about the fortune cookie. Ryan took out the cookie and removed the wrapper. He cracked open the cookie and slid out the paper. The fortune on the paper corresponded to gossiping and traveling. Ryan mentioned to Melina that they were at the right place where they could have their yakkety-yak session.

They enjoyed champagne, like they were celebrating. During dinner, Melina offered to pay the bill. She told Ryan, he could pay the next time. He did not like the idea, but agreed on it. At that moment, he forgot about his financial problem and focused on her.

He thought she was amazing person. When they finished the luscious Italian meal, they went gallivanting. As she was walking, Ryan kicked the coke can on the ground. Melina did not know the reason but began to smile then giggle. He saw her giggling, he laughed. The situation was so pure and he held her hand. They stopped by a lake, and sat down on the bench. She could feel the butterflies and hear his heart beat, as he was so close.

Melina glanced at Ryan and he said, "I am happy to see you."

He slowly brought her head toward his lips. They were so close and she turned away. She was feeling uneasy. After a few seconds, she looked back at him and he could tell she was nervous. He said nothing and tried again, this time she allowed herself to break-free. Ryan could feel his heart was roaring through his head. He did not expect himself to be this nervous, but he guessed, after a gap everything felt like the first time. He tilted down and kissed her soft lips.

The kiss lasted a few seconds, and a satisfied smile parted her lips. She saw a pair of brown eyes looking back at her intimately. They both looked and started to chuckle.

The weather signaled an affair of love. How long would this last? No one knew. Was it even love? She assumed.

They got up from the bench and left to the subway station. Ryan had told Melina about Isha's 9th birthday the next day. So he rushed to be part of the preparation. He did not want to miss it, and create any chaos. They hugged and kissed each other goodbye.

Days passed. They would meet up, sometimes for coffee, sometimes for movies, bowling or even fishing. Ryan had introduced her to Mark and other friends. Mark was quite surprised on how they met and were already dating. He could see their intimacy was growing and they were falling for each other.

A month and half later, Melina invited him home. She wanted that night to be special. Melina made some peppermint tea and headed near the sink.

Ryan sat on the sofa and asked, "Do you mind if I make myself more comfortable? I need to take off my shoes?"

"No, why are you being formal today?" She smiled and added, "Feel free." They laughed and there was a comfortable silence for a couple of minutes as the kettle came to a boil.

After having peppermint tea, they listened to soft music and talked about photography and movies. Melina smoothened out her hair and combed through the tangles with her fingers.

Ryan observed every move, and suddenly got up to switch on the TV and turned off the music. She wondered why he had stopped the music. Did he not want to do anything? She thought. Melina began to get engrossed into the TV programme. Ryan touched her back and tickled her waist teasing her. Melina felt a tingle that made her quiver through her body.

After New Year's, the peacefulness of their almost two month journey was getting more exciting.

Ryan cuddled her and whispered, "I am here." He grinned, giving her a few seconds and she said, "I know and the thunder storm is freaky. Looks like it will rain heavily."

"Yes, it looks more like it," said Ryan affectionately.

He pulled her closer toward him. He pecked her soft lips and slowly started caressing her breast. She started to giggle, and felt a shiver. Melina was feeling bashful with the intimate closeness.

Ryan said, "Sorry! But I thought it was time...um," and smiled. Melina didn't say anything. But her reticent smile was giving him an indication to go on. He kissed her again. Their lips and slowly their tongue were exploring their way. There was a soothing feeling that sent a vibe of pleasure. Slowly slouching down on the couch, he started to caress her breast again.

Melina stretched her hand and took the remote from the table. She turned off the TV, and the lamp. She switched on the music. In the darkness, Ryan could hardly make out her shape, but was quite close enough to smell the fragrance of her hair and faint perfumed body lotion. She took his hand in hers and that simple act sent waves of excitement through his body.

He could feel the heat of her body through the thin lacy bra. He slowly undressed her, and as she tried to undress him, she slipped her hands inside the shirt. Then she slowly took off his pants. She could feel that he was growing more excited, and their hearts had beat faster and faster-in sync. Melina was aroused and the frenzy pleasure slowly took hold of her- as Ryan tickled her. They got closer and he gradually kissed her breast again and back to her lips. His lips skillfully explored her body.

Then leisurely moving upward, they both glid toward each other and enjoyed every moment of imminence. Her rhythm stopped and pushed downwards. Her arm was across his throat, as she tilted her head back and moaned.

Consumed in the moment, Ryan's leg hit the lamp. It fell down - that made a loud noise. They both laughed at the disturbance.

Ryan and Melina endeavored to new excitements. They felt they were on a ride on a fantasized rendezvous.

With affection Ryan complimented, "You are so beautiful." Melina kissed his chest and said, "You too...handsome." Her eyes were twinkling. They kissed each other goodnight.

The next morning, Ryan got dressed and headed back home. Their love and avid sex went on for weeks. Sometimes, he couldn't think of anything to say. He began getting naughty and the only thing he could think of were along the lines of, "Let's go back to your place and have passionate sex."

Melina began to assume after meeting Ryan, that some guys tend to only enjoy sex or they just didn't know what to talk about? Melina hoped this was not the case with her and Ryan. She knew they became close, and something was happening. They both did not want to settle for anything less in their life.

They took every opportunity to get to know each other. Both of them became feisty.

When they met up, they often discussed about people in general? Or about taking risks, or even allowing their feelings to be taken to a new voyage. It didn't matter if it was even short, as some experiences were worthwhile, Melina had mentioned to Ryan.

Sometimes Ryan had a doubt, thinking whether they were meant for each other or not. Their silence hinted the impression that something was not right.

He thought people needed patience to be erupting at all times, or else they would end up making the wrong decision.

Who knows what rewards were cooked and ready to be presented, contemplated Ryan. All one should do is be – patient - that would be the key word. But for how long would patience retain its comfort zone. Someday it might lose its way, believed Ryan.

CHAPTER

5

The Bumpy Ride

Melina confides in Ryan about her goals. Overloaded with
work and emotionally tensed regarding Uncle Barun makes
Ryan figure out what he really wants. Melina meets her new
friend 'Ria Thakkar.' She is this new buzzing bee, which is
exemplified to happy bubbles that could pop in anyone's life.

Finally the big day was here. The London Film Festival
2009 had already begun, and Ryan wanted to invite
Melina. He wanted to give her a surprise, so he had to
have a word with Uncle Barun to check if he was okay
about it. That morning, at breakfast, Ryan had asked him
if he could bring a friend - but Uncle did not like the idea.

He mentioned, "I am given only five passes for the
two days that we are catering the food." After breakfast,
Uncle gave it a thought and suggested, "One day we can
take Isha and the other day you could bring your friend."
He had asked too many questions and Ryan answered
what he could.

Uncle confirmed about the invitation the next day.
"Your friend can join us. Tell her she could meet us at
home and we can all go together." Ryan never mentioned
to anyone about Melina. Only Aadil got an insinuation
that she was more than a friend.

The first day at the Film Festival was astounding. The night was great with a variety of films and music. Ryan and the rest enjoyed the food served by the diner. For a change, even Uncle Barun and his wife felt the dinner was not from their diner but from somewhere else. The meal was absolutely relishing.

Many types of films from many countries were screened and discussed about. The ambiance and gestures from people were hospitable.

A documentary was shown. Speeches were given by some known celebrities like Daniel Miller, Mira Knightley, Sameena Khayet, Ashley Hayek, Hugh Junkin and Chris Patel. There was also a fashion show by known models and teenage stars.

Ryan had already told Melina about the Film Festival, and she was excited as well as anxious to join his family. The next day, as Ryan was waiting for her, he saw her walking toward him wearing an off shoulder pink dress. She was spectacular, he thought. They accompanied each other and joined Uncle and the rest. She greeted them well and everything seemed alright.

The problem was that no one spoke about anything. Uncle did not say anything, but smiled to her whenever their eyes met. While Melina surveyed around she began to feel awkward. She thought, maybe he did not want her there. Having ignored the dingy thoughts, she saw what an extravagant night it was.

The night started when Ethan Law gave an opening speech. Melina was thrilled and took pictures from her iPhone, and continued speaking to Aadil.

Cocktails were served and a sustained applause greeted the name of each director presenting his or her new film. Melina felt she hit the jackpot as she got to see many well known people. Famous Indian Bollywood celebrities, like Freya Devi, Shawn Ibrahim, Karolina and Rashid Kapoor were also part of the festival. The night was worth attending after all, she wondered.

Uncle Barun was so ecstatic to see Freya Devi. One of the sponsors had mentioned to her about his diner which made him feel on top of the world. Aadil liked Shawn

Ibrahim and Karolina. Melina did not know any of them, but found Rashid Kapoor charming.

The night was like a colorful painting, with different strokes meeting and blending with one another. It was a film fraternity celebration in touch with their audience and fans.

The night went on smoothly, but the silence between Uncle and Melina continued. Ryan did not say much. He smiled at the celebrities and took pictures with all them. He knew this occasion would not occur frequently and he got a chance to meet elite people. Life does not give people opportunities like that often, he thought.

Hours later, it was time to leave. Ryan dropped Melina off and she thanked him feeling a sense of awkwardness that night. Ryan felt the same. He could tell that something was not fine. They spoke less and could not say much to each other. With eyes flashing in anticipation, they hugged each other casually and parted.

How come after a while, the feelings just didn't feel the same way, excogitated Melina. Usually in a relationship, either a couple gets closer or starts realizing that they were not meant to be with each other. In their case, they felt they loved each other, and became great friends.

After a couple of weeks, their intimacy was masked by bleak visions and the true meaning of life started to appear. Melina knew that Ryan was not the one, and he felt the same. Their mutual connection was drifting away.

She was not sure what was happening. Although the time spent with Ryan was no regret at all, she considered. She recalled the moments where they could make each other smile and uplift each other's feelings during their downfall.

Occasionally they chatted for a while, and shared about their day at work. Melina had asked about Ryan's parents and he closed his eyes. He made an attempt to remember his parents as his memory of them had diminished over the years. She tried to console Ryan, but it did not work. So she changed the subject and said with apprehension, "Forget about it. So tell me what are your future plans?"

Ryan got agitated and blurted, "What about the future?"

"Will you be working or will you study further?" asked Melina with eagerness.

The silence between them tested their intentions and fortitude. She had to say it. So she took a deep breath and expressed, "Well, I am going to continue my graduate program. I am saving up and - planned something exciting for myself. I will be doing my graduate studies, but not in London."

To his surprise and a sudden outbreak, Ryan asked, "Oh, Why? How come this sudden decision was made? So where are you planning to go?"

Melina spoke about Singapore and the educational standards there. Ryan was stunned that she chose to go to Singapore which was quite far.

He was flushed with disappointment and said, "Melina, you never mentioned of going overseas."

"Well, I have now. Ryan, honestly, we love each other's company and have grown to be so close, but not so close, like soul mates or married couples. We are good buddies and have grown emotional."

"Yeah, whatever," whined Ryan with anguish. Melina could see that he was mad and over dramatic.

Ryan stood up. He was ominous and moved around briskly. He needed some fresh air so went out to the balcony for a while.

Melina came out. She wore a pink cardigan with a matching cotton top and a long flowing skirt with flip-flops on her feet. Her curly black hair and skirt were blowing in the breeze and she smiled as she saw him.

"Ryan, please talk to me. I have been trying to speak to you for the past week," claimed Melina.

He let out a sigh and uttered, "In practicality, you may be right, but I really like you."

Without a pause, "There you go. I presumed it was love. You really like me, but we don't "*Love each other.*" It can't be all about sex, mad sex, passionate sex...it is just *sex.* Perhaps we don't regret any moment, but I will regret being with you because I can't fake this whole thing and lie and conceal my goals. You know I should be leaving London, soon. I am not staying here forever."

Her eyes began to become teary and Ryan's unacceptable and gloomy mood- did make them feel that something they cared for was leaving for good.

"Let's go for a walk, Melina. I need some air," insisted Ryan.

Quietly, they left Melina's home. She started talking and sharing about her interest in going to Singapore. Ryan just wanted to hear her speak. He didn't care what she spoke about.

"You really want to go? What about studying here for a while and checking for more options?" requested Ryan.

Melina had explained how important it was to develop a security for her life. A career path was imperative for her well-fare. She needed to bring the change and quality in her life. She was not leaving anytime soon, but confirmed she was to stay for another few months. She did not want to throw an unwanted revelation which would devastate friendship but was mitigated she brought it up earlier before it worsened their relationship.

Every time Ryan talked to her about how he felt, he became more confused. Whenever he got closer to her, he ended up feeling pulled further away from her. He took two steps back for every step he took forward.

With a comforting voice, "Ryan, we will still meet and catch up. Please don't take this as being dumped or as a rejection. We both are putting an end to something that can be dirty and create commotion, and irrational arguments in the future."

Ryan assured Melina he understood her. He was cognizant of their bonding and had no guilt of having her in his life. He embraced her tightly wishing her everlasting affluence and love.

She was depressed and stressed about breaking up in such a way. Ryan thought, it was better to go home and catch up for coffee after a few weeks. He wished this never happened and didn't like what was happening but knew Melina was right.

Ryan respected her decision and kissed her for the last time. He could see her teary eyes. She sniffed and wiped her tear that was trickling down her face.

A few weeks later, after dealing with the space and having been given liberation to her tears, she began feeling better. She felt more like her chirpy nature was back on track.

Ryan had called Melina to meet her for coffee and catch up with her. He never meant anything wrong for her and atleast their friendship could be maintained. She answered the phone and spoke very calmly.

She was happy that during the past weeks, she was able to cope with her life emotionally and wanted to get out of that estranged culpability. They eventually met and the date was finalized when she would leave.

"I am leaving to Singapore in two months," Melina updated Ryan and his facial expression was flushed, but he learnt to accept it. He wished her good luck and they continued their conversation.

Melina crossed out days from her calendar and two months had passed by with ease. She had arrived to Singapore and went through the phase a new person in a new city would.

She joined her graduate program and met *Ria Thakkar*.

She was a senior taking another graduate program. They met during a seminar and started hanging out for a while. Melina was happy she met a charming, decent and trustworthy friend.

Ria was petite, lovable, and charismatic. At twenty four years of age, she was assertive about what she wanted to do.

She contemplated about how many people would get to do what they want, and how many chose what they wanted to be? Some people lived for making other people happy, and some believed in keeping themselves blissful and contented. She always made people cheerful willingly and was complacent to see people that way. However, there were times where she cogitated that she needed someone, and eventually became her best friend by following her instincts.

When she was young, she began to realize that no one would clean up one's mess except oneself. She remembered being adopted by a famous TV personality in India at the age of two. Her step mother, Ms. Rashida Thakkar was a divorcee and a famous jewelry designer in Mumbai. She had an eighteen year old stepsister named Simmy. They did get along, but had tolerated a friction of behavioral eccentricity time to time. She considered herself a stranger in one of the most happening, energetic, enterprising and busy city around the world.

With Rashida, every step of her life ended up in a magazine or newspaper. Ria was thankful to Rashida's kind love and care in the form of materialism. She reformed her and gave her a life which she was thankful for. Rashida practically planned her life making her grow detached and believed in becoming a self-made woman. Sometimes, Ria surmised that all was fair with the upbringing and a chance in enhancing a qualitative life for a child, only if the child felt the same way later.

She attended class, had lots of assignments, but took it in good spirits.

There was a fun loving, boisterous energy to the day that gave her a great deal of power and self-confidence. She did not know what was in the air. Taking a graduate program in Dentistry was fun, but malodorous. She concluded that dentistry could also work during recession, as how could people avoid bad breath, braces, or even cleaning their teeth? She had to be able to withstand odors, and bad breathe of all kinds of people. Something different, she thought, atleast it was away from the media glare.

That day Ria and Melina were having lunch, she mentioned to Melina that she was dating.

She was curious how they met and told her about her break up with Ryan. Ria commiserated with her story. She found it strange about herself, but it was hilarious, she thought.

She updated her by saying, "I like this guy, but sometimes I feel something is wrong with this relationship. Oh well. I shall think positive. I had gone for dinner with some friends. I walked pass this table of hot guys, and went to the restroom to freshen up. As I came out, I saw a dog. The restroom was located behind the restaurant. I guess the dog came from somewhere. I hate dogs, lizards, practically all creepy crawlies..."

Melina laughed hysterically. She rested her elbow on the coffee table.

"I was petrified, Melina! I threw tissue paper and even babbled 'Shoo' several times but nothing happened. Then I saw this guy walking toward the toilet. I waved at him saying, 'Hi!' Melina, I hope you are not bored. That was the first time I saw him. He ignored me and went to the toilet. Anyways, I followed him."

Melina listened carefully.

Ria continued dramatically, "I followed him and knocked on the door. I was so scared of the dog. He asked me what would be the reason to disturb someone while they were peeing. With fear of the dog, I shouted out telling him to accompany me out because I was terrified of the dog..."

Melina was overjoyed with the spicy and juicy details of the story.

Ria felt she sounded like she had switched on a radio. She spoke continuously. She mentioned how she pushed him and held his hand tightly. He was cold and escorted toward the exit. When they were out, he teased her and called her one crazy girl.

"Ria, he was being disrespectful," said Melina considerably.

Melina was confused and asked, "Oh Ria, so that is how he became your boyfriend, so strange?"

"No there is more to it. Ehhheee, well three weeks later, I had gone for a seminar on dentistry, about latest innovations and medical treatment. After the seminar I decided to go for a spa. Apparently, I accidentally bumped into him there. After waiting for thirty minutes, I entered the room filled with sweet fragrant of candles. I felt the wait was worth it. I was in the Jacuzzi filled with rose petals and lemon peels. It was amazing - the combined fragrance of the two. I shut my eyes and dived into my thoughts, practically in another world. Guess what Melina? I heard a strange sound. I ignored it for a few seconds and then it became huskier. I opened my eyes

slowly and saw that idiot. He was topless, and thank God
he never saw me. Slowly, he turned on the shower in the
room and turned around. We both saw each other and I
screamed. I felt so creepy and embarrassed. Seeing my
reaction and condition, he laughed, took his stuff and
left. I was so pissed. Luckily, I was covered. Why did it
have to be him? Our eyes met. We saw each other very
clearly even under the dim light. I assumed I got into the
wrong room. The masseuse apologized several times. That
is how we met again, though not in a very nice way,"
said Ria enthusiastically.

"Goodness gracious! Then what?" stated Melina
curiously.

"A few days later, there was a dance party at the
university. I ordered a Martini and noticed he was already
there. As soon as I got my drink I took a few steps ahead
and he said, 'Hey, longtime no see!' I saw him vaguely
because I did not know if he was talking to me or someone
else. He waved and said, 'I am talking to you.' I responded
saying, 'has it been a long time since we met?' We smiled
cheekily. I did not know where to start and just told him,
'See you soon. I got to go.' I avoided the conversation,
Melina."

"Ria, he already sounds interesting and different."

Ria grinned and added, "It was one of my friend's
birthday. It was fun and later that evening, we met again
on the dance floor. - He introduced himself and said, 'I
am *Shawn Silveira*. Nice to meet you and I introduced
myself. He was kind of close and I felt odd. I must say he
was looking so good that day. Some things just slip off,
and feels like you can't catch the rope any longer.
Something was certainly going on. I went to sit on the
sofa and I noticed that he was looking at me. Then, he
came forward and sat beside me."

"Oh my God Ria," remarked Melina.

"Melina, my heart was beating so fast. It felt loud that
I was positive that everyone else could hear it, too. Why
did he have to look so attractive? He sat on the futon
right beside me. Hmm…his perfume was good too. I felt
my lips curve into a big broad smile. When I realized

people were seeing, it made me look silly. Shawn had brought up the incident at the spa. I did not want to talk about it, so he paused. There was nothing to clarify about, and we both laughed at the situation. We spoke for a while and he mentioned that he was working at the hotel, completed his post graduate and giving his best interest only to his career in hotel management and aviation."

"Ria, you did have a weird set of encounters. This is what we call life and its bolt from the blues. That is nice. Your series of meetings resulted in you both dating."

"Yes."

Moments later, Melina said with restlessness, "Ria, I got to go and will catch up with you sometime soon. I have loads of errands to complete and still new here. You takecare and we will keep in touch."

"Sure, see you later. It was a great chat we had," said Ria.

Ria continued sipping her coffee and her memories of meeting Shawn made her chuckle. She did not know whether her relationship with him was going to blossom to fascinating level. At the same time she thought, there was something about him that made him appealing.

She was happy and began thinking about Shawn. She found him mysterious and thought, could anyone tell whether a relationship can blossom to an interesting level? It is always mutual to make something flourish. If everyone could make things work and get the love they desired, no one would be heartbroken. Perhaps it was all about the mixture of variety of emotions, creating a cocktail which could not be sipped entirely by everyone because everyone had a different taste.

She imagined the spice of her life like a blender coalescing distinctive flavors.

CHAPTER 6

The Sizzling Battlefield

Ria was at the dorm and could feel that Shawn had come to her room. She had forgotten to lock the door. "Ria, Ria," Shawn called out.

She said, "Go away."

Shawn came closer and his lips felt good as they moved really softly against hers. She was surprised by his visit.

She still pretended to be asleep and Shawn whispered, "I'll kiss you again if you don't wake up." He said it in a very sexy way. "No, go away," teased Ria.

Shawn tickled her and said, "I mean it, I will." She did not want to be tickled so she woke up suddenly, and exclaimed, "Oh, goodness, I was having a dream."

She had this entire pattern of conversation and a strange feeling without even Shawn actually being there! Letting out a sigh, Ria woke up and sat up cuddling her pillow.

After a few minutes she received a message from Shawn:

HI SWEETY, I GTG 4 THE AVIATION TRAINING,
WILL BE BACK AFTER SIX WEEKS,
LOTS OF LOVE; WILL CALL YOU, SHAWN.

When Ria read the message, she was stunned. He never even mentioned about it. She was sure it was not a last minute plan. He was going away for more than a month. It was not like typing it as six weeks seemed any better. She did not know how to feel. She was annoyed with the whole thing. Her temperament began to blanket all the good times she had with him. She tried to ignore the whole matter for a couple of hours and then messaged back sarcastically:

HI, YES, SHORT NOTICE, ANYWAYS
GOODLUCK AND SEE U AFTER A MONTH, RIA

Knowing she had so much to do, she went for a shower and went to university. She met up with one of her classmates. She jabbered about work and updates on the lectures and at one point she felt she was making no sense.

She felt she was saying one thing at one minute and the opposite thing the next. Most of the time, she continued to jump from one issue to the next, but today Ria was most likely going to fall in a mess if she did not stop. After having learned that Shawn suddenly left, she could not cope.

Ria took a deep breath. So what? I would have more time to myself and friends. It did not even look like Shawn was serious about anything, so why was I getting paranoid? She thought.

Meanwhile, Shawn was feeling great and up in the air. He was flying so high and was quite confident about himself. With his opportunistic, manipulative and sometimes caring behavior, it was certain he would escalate in life. However, was there room for Ria? He wondered.

At this point of time, all he thought was about his dream to be a pilot and owning chains of Moroccan cafes. His ambition to achieve something was his only motive. He affirmed the fact that one had to work for it and it would not manifest by itself.

Many pilots flew through different time zones. The fact that pilots dealt with weather and operational delays could extend their workday by many hours. Shawn thought, what a magic?

Four days passed, and there was no message from Shawn. Ria's patience level was fluctuating. She was in her dental practical room, and hoped she did not pull out the wrong tooth.

Ria did not want to think of the worst. She conjectured thank God this was a dead body. I would have been fired. Who said a five years course would be easy? The past two and a half years has been hectic. She had been experimenting and continued with her extractions.

Everyone had their own drama. Shawn begun to procrastinate important things he had to do. He went for the training late. He overslept. In agitation he squeaked, "I am late."He threw his alarm clock and rushed to get ready for his training. For a change, this pilot-to-be did not shower. He brushed his teeth, wet his hair, applied some gel, wore his clothes, and dashed off to his training session.

He imagined - Do pilots actually do that some times? What happened to time management? This was unprofessional and not accepted during his graduate diploma programme. Imagine if all the passengers were waiting for the pilot, and the *zombie* arrived because he couldn't wake up on time! What chaos! At twenty five years of age, he needed to work on that.

As he reached the school of aviation, he hurried to the workshop, and found a seat on the last row. Aviation chiefs were to share ideas and exchange views concerning a wide range of aviation concepts. He was saved and no one taunted him.

The lecture started and Shawn took out his laptop to take notes. The workshop was about attitudes, skills and knowledge in pilot training. The lecture went on for an hour, and then continued with a video clip.

There was a thirty-minute break and all the students were analyzing the aircraft parts. Shawn enjoyed every moment and was waiting to pilot his baby.

Toward the end of the class, Shawn's classmate was cracking up jokes and made fun about aviation. He laughed after hearing a joke with a sound of a chipmunk on Singapore Airlines: *Thank you for flying Singapore Airlines. We hope you enjoyed giving us the business as much as we enjoyed taking you for a ride. Happy flying! Your magic pilot!*

Shawn warned his friend to shut up before they would get kicked out. They were laughing away, and finally after a while the workshop for the day was over. He packed up and felt he needed to shower.

Later, he noticed something at the doorstep. It was a letter that was not for him. A company error, he assumed. He did not want to deal with it and forgot about it for a few days.

He also never called or sent a text message to Ria. Shawn was so involved with his intense training and chilled with his classmates. Stop being a jerk, he called himself.

Beep Beep, Beep!! Ria quickly got her phone out of her bag, wondering who it could be. She had already given up on Shawn, after sending him an email and two sms' - and received no reply. She wondered if whether he was alive or dead.

Ultimately, after two weeks, Shawn messaged Ria. He told her how busy he had been genuinely and did not want to create any excuses.

She saw his name and had this mixed feeling of being happy and hurt at the same time. After reading the sms, she did feel missed for a short time and later found it did no good to her. The message from Shawn did not cover up for the two weeks of silence.

His excuses seemed fake, but Ria tried to forgive him after reading another sms from him:

HI BABY, HOW R U DOING? R u waiting 4 my message?

. -*- .

('. ')

=(,,)=(,,)=

So sweet honey

THANKS FOR UNDERSTANDING

Ria was pissed and thought, they were dating for goodness sake, and he asked me whether I was waiting for his sms. I am busy too. I have a life, and it takes only a minute to sms, five minutes to send an email and two minutes to call. It was so easy for guys. When the woman had put forth an effort, guys would ignore and take it for granted. However, when the girlfriend had eased out and did not do much, the boyfriend would become anxious. It was like a see-saw affect. "Whatever," she said out loud and did not sms back. She took five days of controlling her emotions. She eventually felt guilty, and sent him a message:

HELLO SHAWN, GOOD 2 HEAR FROM U AFTER TWO WEEKS,
BEEN HECTIC HERE, TOO, HAPPY JOURNEY INTO THE WORLD OF UR
DREAMz, GOODNITE, ☺

She looked forward to a lovey dovey sms. She did miss him, but could not do anything about it. She made the effort to call, but it went on voicemail. Her effort seemed futile.

Weeks later Shawn arrived and went to the university to meet Ria. He waited there for a while, then went to the library, and loitered around the café. He was getting apprehensive, but still did not see her.

Shawn was looking forward to read a message from Ria. It had been two days, but still no update from her. Now Shawn's patience level oscillated. He called her, sent a message and finally thought of leaving a message at the apartment. He started postulating that maybe she was upset with him. He was too late with his assumptions. She was disconcerted.

Possibly there was another reason why she could not be reached, he wondered. He went to the apartment again, and waited in front of the room for a few hours. He conceived that he would have to camp here tonight. Shortly that night, he sat in front of her apartment on a sleek chair and dozed off to sleep.

A few hours later, Ria saw him. She patted him, and he woke up. "Shawn, what are you doing here? How are you? How was training?" The words rushed out of excitement.

Shawn did not say anything. She continued, "I was away for two days in Malaysia for a seminar. Since you were busy, I thought I would tell you about it, when you get back. Sorry about that."

He just looked at her and was being a good listener.

"Well, I was waiting for you for hours." He got up and gave her a tight hug.

She invited him to the apartment. They drank a cup of coffee. He updated her about the six weeks of training. They chatted like long lost friends and eventually lightened up.

She had mentioned to Shawn, how much she had missed him. Shawn was so endearing. He teased her, "I missed you more."

Ria rested her head on his shoulder and fell asleep.

The next morning, Ria awoke with the sun's rays on her skin. She felt the tingle of a blush on her cheeks. She looked at Shawn and his faint perfume fragrance was still uplifting. She freshened up, made coffee, and breakfast. Experimenting for the first time, she managed to make pancakes with blueberries, cheese omelets, rolled bacon with sausage stuffing.

Twisting and turning, Shawn woke up. He stretched and felt refreshed. He said in his husky voice, "Oh, wow what a long night."

He kissed her forehead and they ate. "Thanks, Ria! That was kind of you. This is like a feast," complemented Shawn.

With sarcasm Ria uttered, "Looks like you're still on pilot mode." She winked at him. Ria continued, "Hey, it has been about four months. Time really flies."

Shawn was confused with the dates. He did not want to create drama. He agreed with her and said, "Huh! Yeah...it does."

Ria ideated, don't think, don't think, don't think, and continued with her breakfast.

Shawn hurried up. Before leaving he told Ria, "I will call you. It was a good night." He kissed her cheeks.

Ria thought, during the four months they dated, they had kissed twice. They had snuggled, kissed, but she hadn't felt any intimacy. She washed the dishes, and went back to sleep. At that point, she did not want to develop any kind of emotional trauma for herself by analyzing her relationship with Shawn.

He was too busy with his projects and practical

training. He did send Ria messages and did write her an email for the first time. She respected his effort.

On the other hand, the year was heading to the end of the journey of 2009. Two months to go and it was another new year, reckoned Ria.

*****

Shawn was waiting for his acceptance letter. The suspense was getting intense and a few weeks elapsed. He had received an acceptance letter for an exchange program in training for a pilot license in Australia. He felt on top of the world. Then he thought about Ria. He had to talk to her about it.

The exams had gotten over and Ria was excited to catch up with Shawn. It was their fifth month anniversary. She wanted to do something fun and cool, but was running out of ideas.

Brrrrzzzzbrrrrzzzzz... "Oops, the phone was set on the silent mode!" murmured Ria. She picked it up and felt sad that it wasn't Shawn's. She inferred, perhaps he had forgotten about it. After the second month anniversary he had changed. She no longer received surprise gifts.

She finally called Shawn, hoping he would remember with a little beguile.

Ria greeted with love, "Hi Shawn, how are you doing?"

Shawn replied with pleasure, "Oh, hi babes - How are you?

"I'm fine. Exams are over and have been thinking about you. It's been a few days. I've missed you," said Ria devotedly.

Ryan was preoccupied with other thoughts. He was not hearing Ria vigilantly. Inattentively, Shawn said, "Missed you, too. So, tell me, what have you been up to?

She got annoyed and spoke obdurately, "Shawn, I just told you about my exams and stuff. By the way, what are you doing? Isn't it a great day today?" She continued using tricks to get him to remember, but it wasn't helping. She waited anxiously to hear something from him.

Shawn apologized and changed the subject about

taking a holiday. He remembered and out of excitement he said, "I have something to share with you. Let's meet up around 7pm."

"Hmm, okay. Sounds good!"

Ria wondered, damn! He did not remember I guess. I will meet him later and see what happens. Maybe he would come up with a surprise. She could not let go of the fact he forgot those special things that brought them together.

When they met, Ria was moody but tried hard not to show it. She had expectations after the first two surprises. She doubted if he really remembered. It would have been great.

Ria and Shawn gave each other a tight hug and he kissed her cheeks and slowly her forehead. With just that, Ria's frame of mind was already stabilizing. She was not a woman with usually high expectations and respected the people who remembered cherished occasions.

At that moment, she tried not to spoil the evening with her doldrums. She understood the fact that he was a human too and sometimes boyfriends could forget things.

"So where are we going today, Shawn?"

He replied politely, "Oh, I was going to ask you that. Well your pick, Ria."

She spoke affectionately, "Let's have dinner by the lake." River by the lake sounded perfect to Ria. Holding hands and just enjoying the ambience was romantic, she marveled.

After dinner, there was something bothering Shawn. He eagerly waited to tell her about his acceptance. "Well Ria, there is something I want to tell you," said Shawn with restiveness.

"Me too, you forgot something."

Without hesitation he said, "What did I forget?"

"Shawn today is our fifth month anniversary."

Feeling puzzled, he stated, "It was? Uuuhhh sorry again! I am forgetful with birthdays and anniversaries. Wishing you a happy fifth month anniversary," he stood up and hugged her.

"Well thanks, but don't you think you usually forget your own. It is upsetting, even though today we had a great time. Our special day would have felt more special," said Ria with ease.

"Stop making it a big deal. Please take it in a positive way, Ria. Anyway, we did have a great time. These things happen. Well I had to share something with you, but you don't seem to care."

"Don't change the subject, just say it. Does that mean you were acting the whole time?" Spoke Ria contemptuously.

"Stop getting agile and be quiescent," said Shawn assertively and continued, "Whatever! I don't want to spend the night arguing, and figuring out whether you're actually happy or not. We met after a few days and I wanted to genuinely meet you. When you called, it felt good."

She was bugged and considered it was better not to say anything. Shawn did not show any importance to how she felt but rather wanted to spill out what he was keen to say. She took a deep breath and was unruffled. He was getting too upset and began to show his temperament.

Before Shawn would taunt or get hyper Ria spoke in an unflustered manner, "I meant it. I was really happy to see you. Why divert it to a misunderstanding? Fine, you were going to share something. Let's talk about that."

"Where should I start? It is good news. I received an acceptance letter from an exchange program in training for pilot license in Australia," said Shawn dramatically.

Within a split second, the whole scene changed.

"Wow, Shawn! That's great news!"

"Today was good. I feel things are working out. Let's leave Ria."They went for a walk. He went on and on about his pilot training and how he would become a pilot and would live a luxurious life.

There was a point where Ria felt frustrated. She was so happy for him but was also feeling strange because he never mentioned about where she was in his life.

She was a woman full of optimism, but never knew she would be in a relationship with empty promises.

Sooner or later she would have to change to another woman with idealistic expectations in accepting life's realities. She did not want to share this with Shawn, knowing they might end up with an argument again.

Ria thought, what about a meaningful relationship? Who was going to have an aspiration to maintain that? That night Ria was very confused and was distressful. She was having a battle with her emotions, which bombarded her mind. She knew she did not feel good, and could not share it with anyone, not even her mom. She felt alone. She could not even call her friend Melina because she had gone away to the States for a holiday.

Ria had a negative feeling about this whole relationship. Two days later, Shawn wanted to meet up. He sounded uneasy and impatient. Her heart pounded as she thought all negative possible. The two days since they had met had been murky.

She felt controlled by her sentiments later. He hugged her with fervor when the met, and actually gave her a quick peck on the lips with predilection. "Hey, Ria, how you doing and feeling?" asked Shawn with concern.

Shawn showed great happiness during coffee and said, "I am going to Australia tomorrow evening, for a few days. I plan to check out the training center and full-fill formalities. I needed to meet up with you and let you know about it. Remember last time, I had to leave out of the blue."

"Uuh, yes, - I'm glad you told me." She was relieved he said nothing negative.

The whole idea of him traveling made her miss him more. She was happy to spend some time with him. She kissed him goodbye, wished him a safe flight and left back with a good note. She did not want to develop any unpleasant feeling again. However, she did not know what would happen when he got back.

Ria spent her days pampering herself, going to the gym and following up with her assignments. She emailed Shawn and loved the pleasant days.

One week passed by and Shawn had arrived. She began thinking pessimistically again. Her sanguine behavior was vanishing. Eventually, she met Shawn and he had alot to say about his travel and the training course.

They spoke for a while and he informed her, "Ria, there will be a lot of traveling going on in the next few days. The good news is that I am starting after New Year's. It's in a month's time."

"Oh, okay. What about Christmas?"

"Let's see, perhaps I might be in Australia. Will let you know about it," stated Shawn genially.

"So we won't be together for Christmas, and then who knows you will say even for New Years. You just said that - you shall be starting soon. What is happening here?"

"I just don't get you at all, Ria. Am I missing something here? Why are you over reacting? You should know during my training hours, - I will not be here. It can be for a few weeks or even for a few months."

"We should talk about this, Shawn."

"There is nothing to talk about. Ria, understand one thing we are not children or even in high-school. You and I are focusing on our careers and that is important. We must understand this significantly."

"We cannot jeopardize all this by acting like a teenager. By the way, it is not like we are getting married! We enjoy each other's company and are dating."

She froze and said nothing. She wished she could have disappeared, or whack him, kick him or even throw him into the river. How could he say that? She considered.

"So Shawn, you think all this was for fun? Killing time the past five months? How could you think that way? You made it sound so ironic," said Ria in a crisp tone.

"All this time whenever I made efforts to meet you, it was not bogus," justified Shawn.

Shawn said in a defensive manner, "Don't think the worst of everything. You are a positive person. I just don't think this will work. I valued every moment spent with you and this won't give us anything. We argue occasionally. You are also concentrating on dentistry. I do not mean we have to share the same thoughts. We are very different, but we can still be friends." Shawn continued without thinking of his choice of words, whilst she tried to block out all the information.

Ria deduced, what was he saying. Was it easy for women to date for five months and not feel anything? She was going crazy now and did not want to regret knowing Shawn. She accepted his unexpected traveling, which surely taught her how to be strong and showed her the reality that some things don't work.

"All right, looks like we cannot walk on the same road! We are different. Firstly, I thought we could join hands and be on the same road passionately. Looks like that person will never be you."

"I would want to maintain our friendship and hate to leave with a disaster note. I can't believe we are breaking up like this."

"So, how did you want to break up?"

"Shut up and stop being a loser!"

He smiled and hugged her tightly. He whispered in her ear, "I am sorry this did not work out. I felt this after I came back from the training. We have different purposes and are here for different motives. It does not come near to anything close that brings us together, and we should not comprise and create a chaos."

She was teary-eyed. She could not believe this was happening to her three weeks before New Year's. She knew it was better now than waiting for the worst to come. They parted and she felt someone she cared so much for was leaving her.

"If there is anything, stay in touch. We met by accident and it was a funny one. I will always miss you."

What a moron! She thought.

He kissed her forehead and said, "Let me drop you home. Please don't say no."

The silence was killing her. She was hurt and at the same time trying so hard to feel normal.

As they reached the apartment, she said, "Shawn, it was good to know you. We shared moments of joy during the days we met. Our first meeting was brief, but from the second you made me feel special and developed a venerated friendship, I was captivated. Although, I feel deeply hurt now, I know it is better for both of us, yet it still doesn't feel good."

When Shawn saw her teary eyes it made him feel uneasy and regretful. He thought practically and rationally.

He was staring at her and told her, "I will never forget you, and I would continue the journey of friendship. Whatever the occurrence, this is the betterment for us."

He left and Ria stood there watching the taxi pulling away. She felt terrible and started to weep. She hurried back to the apartment. She remembered telling Melina that she had felt something was not right, but did not know what it was. She did not know she would discover it after five months. She felt a wave of nausea and her blood pressure reducing.

Ria thought, sometimes with a sudden jerk, a tornado of negativity, sadness, and death to a happy relationship arises.

It may become visual, leaving no answers of hope. Why? What is this moment of misery got to teach me now? Why did this have to happen?

Chimes of Hope

When a person undergoes a period of overwhelming issues, he or she would prefer to hibernate and seek for answers. Everyone has different ways to figure out things and takes each day as it comes, including Ria and Ryan. For a change, they rest their happiness on 'Hope.'

Can recession stop people from being blissful, breathing fresh air or even living a happy life or lifestyle? That was certainly not possible! Ria had various questions and answers in her mind.

She wondered, in fact, it was during the tough times, when everyone should feel grateful. They should open new ways for beatitude to breeze in. Doing something about it or finding alternative ways are the chimes of hope during the recession of relationships.

Days passed and Ria was still not over about what had happened. She sure lost a great friend whom she thought would eventually create a special bond. She did not hate Shawn, but did not love him enough to convince him to reconsider his decision. Although, she knew something was not right she wanted to work it out like normal people would do. Shawn had pointed out the obvious and closed the chapter to their affinity.

She had a few weeks break and decided of going to India to her family and friends to celebrate Christmas and New Year's. Ria had not visited home for two years. She did miss her mother and sister. Catching up with them on Skype was not enough. She necessitated a vicissitude. She reminded herself that in another two years, she would be a qualified and a self-made woman.

She thought of messaging Shawn to wish him the best for his pilot training. She did not want to be one of those women who believed their consociation was the end of the world.

Inspite of having a feeling of some spinning negativity in her world, she decided to text Shawn. Suddenly, she realized she had to choose her words carefully.

Hi Shawn, how r u doin, X'mas is around the corner,
Thought of visiting family for new years, wish u the best for
pilot training,
Takecare

She did not expect to hear anything. She got her ticket and the next day at the airport as she was going to switch off her phone, she received a message from Shawn. She frowned and said to herself, "Wrong timing idiot!" She quickly read the message:

Enjoy Christmas n new years, Will be celebrating in Ausi,
Glad hearin from u, 4get the past,
Wishing u a happy journey to new yrs, Cheers

When Ria read the sms, she definitely knew that the decision to go to Mumbai was the right thing to do now. She switched off her phone and put on her ear phones. She felt the wetness, wiped her tears and took her power nap.

*****

Where Ria almost sobbed to get some rest, Ryan completed his undergraduate course and was on cloud number nine.

He was riding on a gesticulation of prosperity and that there was a great deal of hype causing a whirl of activities. Ryan was working for a while as a part-time photographer and editor for certain columns for *Street-icon*. He liked his job and wanted an opportunity where he could travel and do something larger than life.

He seldom remembered Melina and did not want to look back, even though he hadn't heard from her for a couple of months. He was all right about it. Uncle Barun was happy for Ryan as he looked at things differently.

Deep within, Uncle was still angry with Ryan's father's behavior that caused his death. He never spoke to Ryan about it and desired him to be a self-made man and never sought him to do the same mistake his father did.

Christmas was near and everyone was getting busier in a celebratory mood. The diner offered a variety of sweets and desserts as part of the Christmas festivity. Uncle's diner was struggling during the time of recession. He considered if he had a helping hand, he would never think of shutting it down.

Time was running out and Uncle wanted to have a word with Ryan about taking care of the diner. By then, Christmas came and left, leaving Uncle confused and more restless about the business. He knew he had to speak to Ryan before New Year's revels. That evening he asked Ryan to keep himself free to talk. Ryan wanted to avoid it as he felt he had just graduated and did not want to do anything to satisfy others. He was growing selfish inside and knew what he was thinking was ridiculous.

That night, Uncle and Ryan were sitting at the dining table and were discussing about sports and the New Year's celebrations. After a few minutes, Uncle asked, "So Ryan, have you put a thought on your career? What do you plan to do?" Ryan was silent and blank.

He turned to him briefly and gave him an exhausted smile. He said abruptly, "I am already working part time and I am thinking of going full-time. I would continue with photography and editing. Why, Uncle?"

"Well Ryan, there is a lot to say. You're a young man. Business is not too stable. I was thinking if you could give a hand with the work at the diners because I was considering of shutting one diner in January after New Year's. It is no point leaving it opened and dragging it out. We are in a loss. Anyways, are you willing to help out?" said Uncle with consternation.

He plainly replied, "Uncle, I don't think I can do it. Perhaps your decision about shutting down one diner is a good idea. Go ahead. Do what you think is suitable and the best for the family."

Uncle was quite disturbed by the way Ryan was showing his concerns toward the diner, and his frank opinion did not do anything to soothe his feelings. Instead it brought back that self-attitude in Ryan which reminded Uncle of his brother. He plunked himself down onto a chair by the bed.

He felt this rush of restlessness. "You are just like your father. Selfish and self-centered! No one told you to leave everything and work at the diner. But you could be helpful to give some of your valuable time. At the end, you and Aadil would be responsible for this. It is not like the diner would be buried with me. As time goes by, I don't want to face the option of shutting down all of the diners." He could not take Ryan's frankness and had blurted out of agitation.

The conversation triggered the moment that had been buried for years. Ryan wanted to know about his parents and did not like being called as a 'selfish and self-centered' person.

"Uncle, sooner or later you would have to accept the fact that when I travel for work, I may not be available. At that moment I can only help out occasionally," Ryan said frustratingly.

"I don't need your pity. First think and be available by being part of the family," Uncle said arrogantly.

Ryan raised his eyes and gazed out of the window absently.

He had to turn and say something. "What family? I have always been here and tried to ignore the petty things. Today, I want to know about my parents and the reason why you are fuming. Regardless, I need to know. Please tell me!" requested Ryan.

"No, Ryan. You don't deserve to know," said Uncle defensively.

"Why?" Silence spread a magic spell over the atmosphere in the room. It was incongruously eerie. They argued and Ryan pleaded Uncle.

Eventually Uncle had to say something. "It all started when you turned four years old. You were playful and your innocence united the family. Until one day, your parent's argued about money, and your future. You began going to school when you were four," Uncle said with regret.

He added, "Before that, you were home-schooled. Your mother always wanted the best for you. After three years of marriage, your dad, my brother changed. He became so ambitious, manipulative and selfish. He used most of the money in investing in stocks and bonds. He lost everything. Your mother got so stressed. She was getting pressured for having a second child and she quit her job so she could conceive. She wanted to make your dad happy and maintain the harmony, but I guess harmony died in that domicile."

"It was not about you, but it got worse when you turned five. When your mother was four months pregnant, she passed away from a heart attack. It was sad. After about six weeks, suddenly your dad quit his job. He missed her and could not deal with the thought of living without her. He was going through depression," explained Uncle.

Uncle added after a short pause, "Seven months later I found out that your dad was into drugs, drinking, and started smoking. He could not handle expenses for your school and I brought you home. The foundation to a stable mind and security was affected. It was getting difficult to takecare of you as you missed your mother. Your nanny quit the job, too. Your dad went for therapy, and spoke to various psychiatrists. There was no improvement and this whole thing was instigated by giving up. A week later, he took an overdose of drugs and died. He had just left a note. It was for you and me. He mentioned to give you the letter when you turned nineteen years old. But I decided not to give it to you as I was afraid it would upset you. He wrote how upset he was and if he could change he would, but he could not. He apologized and requested me to raise you."

He could not believe what his ears were hearing. This was something so shocking.

Uncle noticed how clearly distressed he looked. "Uncle, um, I would like to read the letter," he said reluctantly.

Uncle went to his walk-in closet and got the letter. It was time for Ryan to read the epistle. Ryan's hands were trembling. He opened the letter and read:

Dear Son (Our Hope),
Greetings to my big boy! I hope you are taking this well. I never even imagined I would have to write a letter to my son to win his heart back again. The day you were born, we welcomed you with open arms and later as you were growing up, I felt I deceived you. I was unable to sustain the love you deserved. I shall not ask for forgiveness, as I feel not worthy of it. I bless you and hope you shall allow love, laughter to reach your heart always. There is unconditional love around you and opportunities in your life.
Thank you for reading and lots of love to you my son. My brother will always be by your side and has in-depth affection for you. Bless you and wishing you prosperity. You're a grown up and a young man now. Mom always wanted the best for you, and will love always love you...
Blessings from the father who desired the world for you always.

Ryan read the letter over and over again. He could not believe his dad had written something to him. This was the only thing he had that belonged to his father. He turned and looked back at Uncle.

Ryan managed to say a few words. "Uncle, dad may have made a big mistake, but realized it too late. I am so sorry. The best I can do is work part-time for a few months and when I get a better opportunity I shall consider that. Aadil can help us, as New Year's celebration is coming up soon."

The words failed to pass his lips. For the first time in years he embraced him whole heartedly. Finally, Ryan felt his curiosity about the matter of his parents was answered. He could see the hope of doing something credible for his life and his Uncle.

Uncle was glad as he could see the slight spark rising and a new beginning to a united family.

*****

Everything appeared to be conventional. Ryan was in a spectacular frame of mind. He felt fabulous and was convinced enough to feel at home again.

However, Ria had just arrived in Mumbai and Ms. Rashida was away for a jewelry exhibition for a few days. She missed home and felt it did not welcome her by her loved ones. I may have all the luxury, but no one to talk to, wondered Ria.

Late evening, she was glad that Simmy approached her well and seemed happy to see her. They spoke for a bit and she wanted to get hold of herself. She wanted to revamp her life. What a strange fact of life, but yet so pure and true. No matter where a person lives, one can get all his or her answers while the other is still searching for them. The good thing was, there was hope for the better, no expectation, but the positive thoughts would eventually uplift spirits, imagined Ria.

It was close to Christmas. Ryan was very much engrossed with his work and helping Uncle at the diners.

She loved her privacy and wrote about her needs, her wants, and what she could do to allow opportunities into her life. Her mother arrived just in time for Christmas. She updated her during their evening tea. After tea, she accompanied her to work in order to divert her mind.

Mrs. Rashida planned a high-profile high tea for Christmas and wanted Ria to meet people. Ria was not keen for it as high tea was not her type. What fun was it to drink tea at a slow pace? She enjoyed the cafes and informal gatherings. She only liked spas and dining at five star restaurants. Maybe, this could be a good way to entertain guests, she pictured.

She was quite involved with the high tea arrangements.

She made her guest list with Simmy and discussed the kinds of flavored teas, coffees, snacks, and desserts that would be available. Ms. Rashida designed her invitation cards. Ria looked around and grasped that moment of feeling part of a real family's festivity. Seeing everyone joyful, she felt complacent.

The day for the high tea Christmas celebration had arrived. Socialites in Mumbai knew exactly how to grab the opportunity to commemorate, expose and express gratitude to life. All they needed was an excuse to rejoice.

There was so much of excitement. Glittery candles, chocolates and return gifts, shot glasses, wine glasses even various decorations like the Christmas tree, lights, mistletoe, and nativity scenes were on purchase.

That evening, within the glamorous clings, cheers and greetings, Ria felt lost. It had been a while since she had to do a lot of chit-chat with people whom she thought were phony. She realized that even if people were acting fake, the bottom line was, they were having a great time.

The high tea ended pleasantly and people got the chance to win a raffle draw. This made the evening more suspenseful and mirthful. Time flew and Ria took a deep breath as she recalled what she would do for New Year's.

She began getting irritated that she hadn't heard anything from Shawn all this while. She began to accept that it was completely over between Shawn and her. What was the point for any relationship to carry on when it was not even prevailed from the heart? It was simply disgraceful and not fair for both sides, analyzed Ria.

She decided she was not going to allow the negative thoughts ruin her good day. She hoped for the chimes of happiness to blossom her life again.

Three days later, Ria received a letter. As she began to open the seal, her mother barged in and told her, "We are going for a birthday party. Get dressed up quickly." She kept the letter on the bed and went for the birthday party.

Ryan could see that everyone had different formalities and responsibilities in life. He was working very hard to save the diner.

The New Year Fête 2010 was just a few days away and hoped for a new prospect. No one knew what was going to happen next. It could be fate, coincidence, opportunity or a result of something that had been occurred before.

Ryan faced his new challenge heartily. He wondered if it would either be a new ride of pleasure or a misery to a new mystery.

Last year was a roller coaster ride. What does the New Year 2010 have to bring now? Projected Ria.

Mid-Nite Sundae

Ria and Ryan were very much involved in stabilizing their frame of mind. Ria was coping and trying to settle in Mumbai knowing this could be her future permanent address. There was yet another person in Mumbai who loved every bit of it. Genelia Silveira had big plans making her surroundings a better place. Moreover, new relationships are being developed and a new sizzle was going to buzz. Miguel Clayton arrives creating an itch to a new relationship. He lives in Chicago and comes to India for business purposes. He befriends new people and fosters new affairs.

Doesn't anyone ever crave for mid-night snacks? Is it normal? Or is it a disease or symptoms of pregnancy? Any kind of snack, having chips, chocolates, yogurt or even ice-cream is as good as a great sundae, ruminated Genelia. She was marveled with all sorts of junkies that could be relished at night.

Genelia Silveira usually had her cravings. At night, she would want to eat a burger or even an entire Pizza. Unfortunately, not one of these was at service because of her awkward timing.

Once, she wanted to drink Diet Coke and eat dark chocolate at 2am. There was no 24hour supermarket available near her home, so Genelia called up a couple of her friends, but no one picked up the phone. Eventually one of her friends answered, thinking it was an emergency.

"Hey, it's me. Sorry, I really need diet coke and dark chocolate. I know it sounds bizarre, but I want to eat it," Genelia said intensely.

"Gina, why don't you hire a personal servant who works from mid night till early morning?" Genelia's friend spoke lightheartedly.

"Oh come on, do you have any of that?" Genelia said sarcastically.

"I do have a Diet Coke but no dark chocolate. Will choco-chip cookies do?"suggested her friend.

"Sure. You're a darling. I will be there in a bit," Genelia said with excitement.

Genelia drove to her friend's home like a maniac. She was imagining herself with her Diet Coke and cookies. As she reached, she gave her friend a tight hug and added, "Thanks a ton. See you at college next week."

Genelia drove back home, putting on loud music and sipping Diet Coke. She could feel that her temptation to snack at night was fulfilled. Life was a grand delight, she thought. Genelia felt cheerful, insightful and wasn't sure why many people couldn't appreciate life?

When it concerned her career she loved to be persistent and had the credence. At times, she would long to go for a holiday to revitalize her spirits.

The twenty three year old young woman created an admirable impression every time she met someone. She loved reading and pottery. With her expansive nature, she liked to be noticed and appreciated.

The sun rose and Genelia was still in a deep sleep. When she woke up, she had an urgency to procure a new book to read. She pondered on what book she wanted and was not concerned in the philosophy crap. She thought authors wrote them to brain-wash people. Books could revolutionize an individual's life for the better, but not that way, contemplated Genelia.

She got dressed and walked down-stairs of the town house. She had told her mother she was going out to the book store. Genelia's mother was not as easy as some mothers would be. She was very demanding, forgetful and hyperactive. Nonetheless, her mother was also kind-natured toward children and loved her own family.

There were days when she made it to the Sunday mass. At times she was pushed to go to church. She gave most of her time to refine her ambition.

Genelia tutored middle school children at home - to save up some cash for her career. She had no keen interest in doing her Masters and was waiting for the longest time to be in a good position. She wanted to open her first ever digital library in Mumbai for high-school and university students. She believed it was important to accommodate journals, articles, and video clips to aggrandize the students' level of education.

At the same time she wanted to have her own company to promote and encourage sanitation with the focus on building more toilets. She hated the pollution and inconvenience in rural areas, or even at sightseeing localities. The tourist spots lacked good bathrooms and being a hygiene freak, she wanted to gift women essential value. These two things had been in her mind since she completed high-school. Now she was working her way to it.

"Jesus Christ, always be by my side. This country desires for a makeover. Let me be the one, - Love you Jesus," Genelia wished.

All this would be a great contribution towards our society and the future generation. All the more better, it would help with keeping the country clean and would do some good with concern to global warming, considered Genelia.

As she walked into the bookstore, she took out her anti-bacterial gel and wiped her hands. She wanted to feel clean.

Looking through many books, as she skimmed down the tall aisles noticing the book, 'Who Moved My Cheese?' She found the title very catchy and read the summary at the back. She cogitated reading it to her students. She loved her students.

Her students adored her personality and her teaching approaches. They always told her, "We are going to inaugurate your digital library." How sweet and thoughtful of them? When her eyes met another book: 'Stealing Heaven,' she thought, "What on heaven would that be about?" She also went through the précis and picked up the book.

Opening the book she saw a picture of maple leaves and - she was driven into an emotional ride.

Genelia loved maple leaves. She loved the color and felt it indicated love and emotions that could be into reflected to a person's life. The brightness reflected all positivity and denoted a helping hand in disguise. Her admiration towards them was special. She reflected it being a way of looking at life showing miracles and consoling someone during difficult times.

Genelia bought the books and left to the supermarket. She purchased some mid-night junk and foodies. She knew her sudden cravings drove her insane and she could not drive to her friend's house every night. She wondered, now I was like that and what would happen if I ever got pregnant. Perhaps my craving would drive my charming chap fanatical.

Her desire to attain a double undergraduate degree in Bachelor Degree of Ayurvedic Medicine and the Fashion Communication made Genelia the brain-box of her house. She received her first degree in Ayurvedic medicine and two semesters were left to complete her fashion communication degree. She hardly had time to breathe. She spent most of her weekends teaching pottery and English.

Waiting for her next academic achievement made her face challenges most of the times. Her friends always found her at a tug of war on two extremes, 'Ayurvedic and Fashion.'

She believed that, Ayurveda was the next fashion to the health industry and would help many people who couldn't afford expensive hospital care. More and more people were becoming aware of this phenomenon and the natural ways of healing. She wanted to merge her dream establishment of a digital athenaeum with the Ayurvedic clinic for the youth.

Fashion communication would help her in designing, styling, photography and creating the artistic graphic for the digital library. She hoped she succeeded with her dream and could only save up enough for herself and her family.

"Well, another few years to go. What matters is how much authenticity we can continue doing for ourselves and people around us? So keep going Genelia you can do it, never lose it baby," she said out loud and went to sleep.

For a change, that night there was no sundae craze for Genelia. All she could think of was her big term project.

The following morning she awoke to someone calling out, "Ginaaaaaaaa..." It reminded her of a bee whizzing in her ears. It was her great Ma. "Wake up," she called out several more times. "You told me to wake you up at 8am. Aren't you late? It is almost 9am, - What time is your class today?"

"Holy wacko! Ma, I am late. The National Institute of Fashion Technology (NIFT) is a forty minute drive. Aahhh, I hate morning classes. Okay, please tell Maya to make me the kiwi smoothie and no breakfast. Not enough time. Quick! Ma, Thanks," said Genelia hurriedly.

When she reached NIFT, she realized she had forgotten her graphics design and space layout portfolio in the car. She briskly walked in class which had already commenced. The professor had ignored her. She sat down at the nearest computer and when there was a break she went to get her portfolio.

Oh lord, I got to stay here extra longer now. I need to discuss my portfolio with the professor and want to be acquainted with what he thinks of the digital library and Ayurvedic clinic for the youth under one roof, conceptualized Genelia.

She showed her portfolio to the professor. He went over it and remarked, "Good thought, but your work seems incomplete. In the business world there are no delays. Only perfectionism, innovation and punctuality will give you the green ticket. Genelia, where are the photographs?"

"I am looking for a professional Canon camera. I mean I don't have one, only a simple digital one," justified Genelia.

Genelia added, "I am sorry about it. I promise I will give it to you this week. Sir, do you know where I can get a camera?"

The professor replied, "Well Genelia, you can ask the student council for a rental. It can only be rented for four days, after that you have to pay a fine."

She was thankful and said, "Oh, okay sir, will see to that. Will finish the portfolio and get back to you soon, thank you."

"If you don't submit on time, your portfolio will not be accepted. It will simply be rejected and you just have to retake the semester with a new portfolio. You are capable of completing it, so don't take it for granted," said the professor with concern.

"Yes, I am aware of it. This means a lot to me. I appreciate your encouragement," acknowledged Genelia.

She went to the student council room, made some enquiries, and rented the camera. For the next four days she did not sleep well. She wanted to make sure everything was completed with perfection before submitting it. She had a week break and was keen to work on her valued project on sanitation. She began researching and discussing the subject with her friends.

She listed down some ideas and planned a visit to the Tourism Authority of India in Mumbai. She wanted to fix an appointment with the assistant manager of marketing and sales department. She knew she needed help from the tourism authority for her sanitation program to promote a clean, secure and a brighter India.

When will this come about, Jesus? murmured Genelia. She waited naively to receive an answer but knew she had to start and she would definitely consummate it. She began to create a business plan.

Genelia asked her friends, "Let's go watch a movie, as you know the next few days I will be tutoring and need to save up some money. I was also working on my business plan and need to buy a camera. I can't look for a rental all the time."

"Fine Genie," her friends teased her.

"What Genie? It is Gina," exclaimed Genelia.

Her friends added, "Listen, Genie. Let's watch some nice spicy - type of movie. We all need a great laugh, and bring the newspaper so we can check the timings." They all carried on with their movie plan and when they reached the cinema they realized they entered the wrong one.

"What the hell! Genelia this is the wrong one, we are supposed to go to cinema 6 and we are cinema 9. Where are the other two?" said Saachi with confusion.

Genelia whispered, "Oops, yes, we are in the wrong one." They giggled and were blabbering away. Genelia and her friend Saachi got out of the cinema and quickly paced toward cinema 6.

The movie had already started - and as they took a few steps Genelia missed a pace and tripped three steps down. For a few seconds Saachi wondered where Genelia went. When she saw her - she giggled and helped her get hold of herself.

All of the popcorn fell down and Genelia had broken her stiletto's heel. "Freak! My heel, it is difficult to amble now. What's going on? mumbled Genelia with annoyance. She stood up and went to her seat. Because she had hit her buttocks, she could not sit properly. As they sat, they saw their friends and updated them about their careless mistake.

Why is it whenever I go somewhere something has to happen? Grumbled Genelia. She ignored her aching butt and concentrated on the movie.

Saachi pinched her and asked, "How are you doing on your booty?"

Genelia raised her right eyebrow and flipped her middle finger. They both could not stop smiling about the way she slipped. It was like a penguin sliding down a snowy hillside.

When the movie ended, Genelia bought her rum and raisin ice-cream and sat down. She ate every bite with obsession, and enjoyed every bit. As she got up to say her goodbyes, she felt something sticky on her right thigh. When she put her hand behind, she fumed. It was a chewing gum. She started to act peevish in a continuous manner. "Guys, do something." Her friends began to laugh.

"What's with you and your luck today?" taunted Saachi.

"Whatever! Saachi bring water and tissue. Get this out please. I wonder which dum ass did this. I wish all the chewing gum in this world gets stuck on his or her hair," said Genelia contemptuously.

She added with frustration, "I don't want to do anything now. I am heading back. The movie was great and with this additional spice, the fall and then chewing gum wedged on my thigh...it is better I leave!"

She said her goodbyes again and went home. That night was quite funny as she could not sleep on her butt and twisted and turned all night. She just kept smiling to herself recalling the lame incident.

*****

Alternatively, away from India, twisting and turning in London, Ryan woke up in the middle of the night. He finally thought to make things right. Few weeks had passed. New Year's for 2010 came and left being a great delight to many. One of them was Ryan. He was happy that the diner was picking up just in a few weeks.

That night he could not sleep, so he cleared his drawers and found a letter. He was stunned as he always made sure he read all his letters. - He took out the letter and - read his acceptance as part of the photographers' campaign UK 2010 fighting poverty, promoting hygiene and a safe sex society. This was a UN photographers' campaign UK 2010.

Ryan was so happy. He embraced the prospect and stared at the letter reflecting his new project. He switched on all the lights at 4 am and started jumping on the bed with stimulation. He then realized he had to speak to Uncle about it and did not want to miss this opportunity.

The first thing in the morning he called the company to find out details about the campaign. During breakfast he spoke to Uncle and he was quite supportive about it. He was prearranged to meet the head coordinator two days later.

All the chosen photographers from UK were to be notified details of the location and the time period of the campaign. This was a big thing where various countries would work together and photographers would showcase their photography through the message of fighting poverty, promoting hygiene and a safe sex civilization, contemplated Ryan.

He was eager to be part of this exhilarating campaign. He had never been part of any human development project and wondered why everything was getting suspenseful and fun.

The morning had arrived where Ryan had to go for the meeting. As he arrived there, everything was professional, and inspiring. He was introduced to other five photographers. They were told, "You would be working in teams with other photographers from other countries. The countries chosen for this campaign are Africa, Vietnam, India, Cambodia, Laos, Myanmar, Bangladesh, and Eastern Europe, America, Philippines, Nepal and a few other countries."

The coordinator brought the list of who was going to which country. After naming others, he came down to Ryan and said, "You're going to India with Austin. This campaign starts in three months and all of you need to develop a theme for your subject. By the way, all of you know your subject of focus. Austin and Ryan your focus will be poverty, perhaps the slums in India."

Austin and Ryan just gazed at each other, and thought the slums.

Ryan grinned and knew they had no choice but prove their skills and capabilities. The team with right competence would be noticed and receive higher commendation.

Ryan and Austin planned their days and started brain-storming for their work. When Ryan got home, he shared

it with Uncle Barun and Aadil. They were all happy about
it.

Uncle asked, "How long would this be for?"

"Well the campaign is only for two or three months.
Uncle, I don't remember going to India at all," replied
Ryan.

"You did, when you were three. You wouldn't
remember. Your dad's friend, I mean one of our friends
live in Mumbai," said Uncle.

"Really! But I don't know whether I would be going
there. It depends on our target of cities, which are part of
the poverty and better living emphasizes. Let's see, will
update you," said Ryan.

He had plans with Mark for beer. They hadn't met up
for a few weeks and wanted to catch up. Ryan wondered
what this new journey would bring, as in three months
he would be encountering a new ride.

In contrast, Genelia's a week break passed by in a jiffy.
As her classes started, she felt too absorbed into it. One
of the weekends, while reading her book *Stealing Heaven*,
one of the students wanted to confide in her. She was
worried for him and knew he was probably facing
something not nice. She could smell trouble. After the
English class, Genelia asked Dev, "Come on tell me, what
it is?"He was stammering and did not know where to
start.

He gathered the guts and spoke up, "I have a
girlfriend."

"Okay, it is fine to have a girlfriend, so what
happened?"asked Genelia.

"Well, I have done a terrible mistake."

Genelia asked curiously, "Did something, what do you
mean? Did you beat her, Dev? Well that is not good. You
know you can't beat anyone, especially a girl. You got to
respect her."

Dev voiced out, "Wait, I did not beat her." After a
pause, he said, "She is pregnant. Don't get mad. Please,
I need help and I think she is about two months pregnant."

Genelia exclaimed, "Dev, come here!" She was so upset.
She told her mother she will be back after an hour.

When Genelia got into the car she smacked Dev's head. "What you were thinking? You're only sixteen years old. How old is your girlfriend?" She said reproachfully.

Dev informed, "We are the same age. I know you probably think we are stupid."

She took him for a drive. Dev and Genelia were both in this mind maze. Genelia could not believe what she just heard. She knew about dating and sex being common. But not pregnancy! It was something so huge to deal with. What rubbish? She thought.

Genelia complained out of the ordinary, "What you guys going to do? This is bad, and irresponsible. If you guys were above eighteen years old, probably I would smack you in any case and tell you, take responsibility. But now, you can't even takecare of yourself. How on earth are you going to solve this matter?" She lets out a sigh.

Genelia added, "I can't help you Dev. This is your problem and you should speak to your parents. Fix it. I can't afford to lay another 100 kilos' on my head. Please and I can only advice. I wish well for you..."

Dev said in a calm voice, "You are different. You are always ready to lend a hand. Please give us your guidance. I want to make this right. It happened and her parents cannot know anything. I was thinking of going to a far away clinic to see a doctor and maybe aborting."

"Dev, hear me. Abortion is bad and illegal. I don't really support this but this is your choice and decision. By the way, you told me she is two months pregnant, right. Well, I don't know any clinic of that sort. Please think about this carefully. You will have to call and ask for an appointment. Remember, I can only advice and be your moral support. Please study at the age of sixteen and don't create new problems to disgust and dishearten people. Your girlfriend should confront her mother and think about her family too," Genelia opinionated.

"For now you go home, do some research and I shall make inquiries, too. I need to meet you and your girlfriend tomorrow for coffee. All this has to be very natural and after you made the appointment she needs to see a gynecologist for a checkup. We will meet tomorrow at four," spoke Genelia disappointingly.

Genelia met Dev and his girlfriend, Sana. "We need to see the gyno tomorrow. I have made an appointment. Please drive us there Teacher Genelia. Don't refuse and I know what we have done is really is deplorable. Our parents will never forgive us as we are not responsible enough for a child. If an abortion can't be done, I will certainly confront my parents."

"Let the gynecologist suggest what you need to do? I don't really know where the clinic is. You need to find out the address. Hoping everything will be fine and you're healthy again. I can imagine if your parents knew this, they would be devastated. They send you to school to be respected and responsible citizens and you get pregnant. Please think about this. This is all no good. Anyways, I will see you both at 7 in the morning outside here," said Genelia with distress.

"One more thing, I can only advice to an extent, more than that you need help from your parents. I shall take no responsibilities for this mess..." added Genelia.

Sana hugged her tightly and said, "I have never been so petrified and you're my mom, my friend for now. I feel guilty and know this was not supposed to happen. I hope everything gets okay." Genelia was in a different frame of mind, and knew she was just being their well wisher and watching over.

The next morning, they drove to the maternity clinic and Sana was nervous. Genelia did not go inside with them to the meet the gynecologist. She waited in the car. She opted not to be involved and wanted them to take responsibility for their mistake. The gyno did an ultrasound and a checkup. After an hour the gyno briefed up to Dev, "Sana is about one and half month pregnant. If she came two weeks later she would have faced serious problems and she is also very young."

"Nowadays teenagers get carried away and never think of any consequences. When they are in a deep muddle then they think about the parents and smell the responsibilities. Anyway, we have two ways of abortion:

medical and surgical. We shall try the medical approach. You're being prescribed pills as it is the first 49 days of the trimester. So pills can be wise to take, these pills needed to be taken two times a day only after you have eaten breakfast and after dinner. You might even feel dizzy, that way you must drink a lot of water and if possible for the first day don't go to school," elucidated the gynecologist.

Genelia was feeling suffocated and prayed. She asked Jesus to forgive her and the kids. "I know they are not innocent Jesus, but they need help to create self-realization of guilt. Everyone deserves to learn from their mistake," she contemplated.

"If these pills don't work, you need a surgery and also need your parents consent with identification signatures. This is quite serious. Abortion is not advisable to anyone. You will not find many clinics for this kind of stuff. Please be careful and stay responsible. See you after five days for a checkup, and if you feel worse you need to visit immediately."

Later that day, Genelia was updated and she told Sana, "For the next visit you guys are going yourself. Sana, I hope the pills work and you don't have any adverse effect. I would still say to talk to your mom about this. You can always tell me how you feel, too. Dev see you next weekend for class." Genelia dropped them home and wanted to go to the beach. She drove to the nearest beach and sat on the sandy seashore.

Genelia dealt with her stress by going for a fast drive and listened to loud music. She felt so good watching the waves and the sunset. She felt like the whole day was in front of her and she just got it out off her chest. She got up and drove back home.

That night she had her craving and around midnight she had chocolate ice-cream with peanut-butter spread. Luckily, they were available at home and she did not have to disturb anyone. She ate, heard loud music, and also checked her messages on Facebook and Twitter.

Two days passed and she got a call from Dev. He told her, "I am getting this paranoia and wondering how I would break the news to my parents. I would be killed for it, and probably be sent to a military school."

"You should be! You have three days left. For now, let's hope for the best..."Genelia got off the phone and started with her next assignment for college. She had loads to do and felt she was exploring her skills by multi-tasking.

*****

However, in the same city, some people wanted to go for a holiday even for a few days. Ria wanted a vacation before she went back to Singapore. She wanted to rediscover India.

She spoke to Simmy persuading her, "I want to go for a trip. Let's do something! I really need a break."

Simmy refused and asked, "Why now?"

"Simmy, sometimes we don't have to see occasions, making a random trip is fun."

"No, Ria I am not interested. Let me think about it. I will update you again."

She felt this pinch and thought she simply had no one to ask for any trip. Some of her friends were already out of town and she needed a break before she went back to the world of bad breath - the world of ideal dentistry. She had this love and hate relationship with it.

After New Year's, Ria travelled back to Singapore. A few months later she visited Mumbai for another project and wanted to go for a short trip. In the mean time she started off with her assignment and had to do some minor research on dental technology, so she made an appointment with a few dentists to interview them. The best way she thought was not to sit there and hatch eggs but to forget about hatching eggs and complete the work that was being undone.

*****

Doing things the right way was vital for Genelia. Some things felt undone in the right manner and she went through her novel. She looked at the picture of maple leaves and got a call from Dev. This time, Genelia was getting more agitated and hoping she would hear good news.

Feeling tormented Genelia asked, "Is she alright?"

"Yup, she is fine. She got her menses, but she is in a bad shape."

With a relief, Genelia said, "Please be careful. There is no next time and no baby making. See you in the weekend," and disconnected the line.

Genelia was back in equilibrium. In the same busy city Mumbai, Ria got a call from her friend that she was back from Bangalore. She said, "Finally the IT seminar was over and the digital age is killing. How have you been Ria? It has been over six months since we met. - Let's catch up for coffee and go for a short trip. I need to tell you this, now. It can't wait for coffee. I lost my virginity and the seminar did bring a new sex life to me. I feel I have met my prince charming and we have been dating for two months, now."

"Glad for you, more than that we are meeting and the short trip sounds absolutely delighting. I need a vacation, too. See you at five for coffee, the same place."

Ria was glad and loved the idea of the trip. What a happenstance? She wondered. She met her friend for coffee and - they chatted away. Ria's friend, Denise had mentioned that her boyfriend Dhruv would be joining them.

Since Ria was on her two weeks break away from Singapore, there was enough time to plan for a new ride. She had dinner and continued with her assignment.

A few hours later, Simmy barged into the room and asked, "What you doing, Ria?"

"I was planning to eat frogs, Simmy. You know it is a new delicacy in town. What is it? I am doing my assignment and updating stuff on Facebook," said Ria sarcastically.

"Remember what you were saying about the trip few days ago? Well, we can go. A few of my friends are interested and one of my friend's cousin brothers is here from U.S.A. So we all planned to do something," said Simmy enthusiastically.

"Well Simmy, today my friend, Denise, mentioned on planning a trip, too. So we can all go together. I hope not many people. So where should we plan to go for three to four days?"

"Actually, we have planned something different. It is like a road trip for seven days."

Ria was surprised and added, "What? A seven day-road trip! So, this means you guys have your plans. That is fine. We can do something else."

"No, it is not like that. It's a plan that everyone is okay with. You need a holiday and this is perfect. A new kind of holiday, and for you it is a new experience. Well Tanish's cousin, *Miguel Clayton* and his friend will be joining us. Basically, it is a trip to show India."

"Who is Miguel Clayton? Have you met him?" asked Ria curiously.

"Yes, I met him a couple of times. He is here for a few months on a holiday or work, God knows. He lives in Chicago and seems different. Habitual wise he is quite inquisitive and likes to know about everyone," briefed Simmy.

"Hmm…"

Ria had decided to give an excuse and not to go for the trip. Just then Simmy persuaded her, "Chill, this is going to be fun. No excuses. You and Denise are coming. I'm glad we could all go for a trip. This is different and I think Miguel is your age. You need to pep up! Singapore doesn't make you all happy now. It shows on your face."

"A Road Trip should be fine," said Simmy and kissed her right cheek on the way out of the room.

"God you're so bossy, Simmy."

Simmy stopped at the door, - "No, I am convincing," and she wiggled her booty.

Ria started mumbling to herself, "A Road trip…how annoying."

It would be better to be traveling with people whom I knew well, thought Ria.

Now she had to make a choice either not to go for a holiday, or experience a new ride. She took a deep breath and thought out loud, "Go with the flow, lady."

À la mode Road Trip – Part 1

What happens when one does not want to meet new people and has to meet new people? He or she might endure turbulence? Ria chose the unexpected and was looking forward to bear the consequences. Miguel was a new question to many people's life and Simmy's behavior would be a colorful firecracker.

Planning a road trip is exhausting, Simmy thought. She had to give details to Ria and knew she would scream and say, "I need a holiday, not a yoga session."

Ria updated Denise about the road trip. Denise was excited as she hadn't done this for a long time. "Where are we going and what about the accommodation? I need to save up some cash lady. Well, I shall catch up with you later," said Denise with delight.

Ria disconnected the line with Denise and started surfing on the internet. She also watched her interviews with the dentists to analyze the reports. Her mind was running like a spiral network. She was thinking about the trip. Her pondering thoughts were like an on and off button. Eventually, she managed to trace out those silly thoughts.

Simmy had gone to have a discussion about the road trip with her friend, Tanish. She met Miguel who was originally born and raised in Chicago. He was good with his listening skills. After an hour of a long discussion and reaching no conclusion, Miguel suggested, "Use the internet!" With his strong American husky voice he added, "Guys, we live in the digital age."

Everyone stared at him. For a split second everyone had forgotten about it. Miguel took out his Sony laptop and Googled the tourist attractions near Mumbai. They had many choices and screened out to a few like, The Elephanta Island, Bassein Beach, Pune, Khandala hill station and Mahabaleshwar hill station.

Their choices were based on hours, activities, heritage, and night life.

Simmy found it interesting as she had neither been to Elephanta Island nor to Mahabaleshwar hill station. Miguel was new to the rest of the places except for Khandala hill station, which he had been to many years ago.

He was talking to his friend Ira who had just arrived a few days ago to meet him. She had known Miguel for a few months and had never been to Mumbai. Ira was quite friendly and talkative unlike Miguel. Ira being a Bengali was from Canada who met Miguel randomly in Hawaii during a vacation.

They were quite excited for their road trip and decided to take the lead. The others were fine with it as there was so much to prepare and plan out for a road trip in India. The roads were not too friendly and the traffic always had an angry sight. But their keen interest to see the beautiful places did not stop them.

Tanish wanted to get together a good crowd for the trip. He implied, "We would be around 10 people, so we don't need any ordinary car. Now we need a 12- seater air conditioned luxury bus. The luxury coach will have facilities we can use for seven days. All of us need enough space for our luggage, picnic box etc. I know a car rental service where we can get a good deal. We can all share the budget and take turns for driving. So what do you think, guys?"

"I think it all sounds good," Simmy said and added, "My sister, Ria would also like this."

"About the driving part, it is better we have a driver. What say Simmy?" hinted Miguel.

"Miguel, I think this is good and let's go ahead with it. The whole thought of driving for seven days would be crazy. We are looking forward for a good time," exclaimed Ira.

So they decided to have a driver. "I shall make the list of where we are going, how many days and accommodation in each place? In this way we shall know what we are doing," said Ira pleasantly.

"Ira seems quite systematic," Simmy said to Tanish. She felt this strange bossy vibe from her. Tanish just winked at Ira, indirectly telling her it was okay to carry on. Tanish was twenty two years old and got along well with Simmy.

"We have already finalized the places, and we should check the prices for accommodation to know about the promotional packages in March. We can review more about this tomorrow," informed Miguel.

He looked at Ira and said, "Should we go out and chill? I would like to show you around. Just ignore the traffic."

"No problem, baby, it sounds all good. Tonight why we don't go clubbing? I want to see the night life here, too."

"By the way, don't call me baby," said Miguel with a frown.

"No, you're my baby" nudged Ira.

"Ira, we are going to Splash. It is a popular nightclub. We shall go with Tanish's friends. Let's check it out. It should be fun," suggested Miguel. They drove around Mumbai city, saw the hawkers around, and stopped by to have some Indian Masala Tea.

During the night when Miguel went to Splash with Ira, Tanish and his friends, he was quite happy to be around her. It was great that she had come down from Canada to visit, thought Miguel.

"What would you like to drink? Or is it the usual Appletini," asked Miguel.

"Yes, I would like the same. Thanks," teased Ira.

Miguel went to the bar and ordered the drink. Later he went to sit on the stunning cubic white leather sofa with Ira. Miguel asked, "So what brought you here? I mean we have not met for months, everything fine?"

"Yes, Miguel I needed a break. I trust you, so thought of catching a flight here for a few days. Seems the few days have ended up in ten days," Ira added, "What about you? You are in India for a few months, so antithetical."

"Well, it's a long story. Put it this way I am here for a break, too. My job brings me here and I am working with this advertising firm. Handling some financial and advertising projects is no joke. I had to come here for some important meetings," Miguel added, "You needed a break Ira, here in Mumbai."

"I wanted to get away, somewhere far, far away…the road trip seems like a good idea," said Ira.

"Hello! What are you both doing on this loveseat?" said Tanish astonishingly.

"We are making love here. Can't you see?" said Ira sarcastically.

"Ooohh, Fine, cut it guys," said Miguel.

"I want you guys to meet my friends. Let's go to the dance floor."

Miguel and Ira went to another corner where the rest were seated. Ira was quite talkative and mixed well with the rest because of her charming sarcasm. However, Miguel did not say much.

Tanish's friends' found Ira friendly and outspoken. He had introduced Miguel as Migi. So they ended up calling him Migi. Miguel usually hid his true personality from everyone, like he was wearing a shield.

One of the friends was quite attracted to Miguel and flirted with him. She wanted to get to know more about him. She knew he was here around for a while. Miguel could see how overfriendly she got. He played along, danced with her, spoke to her, but did not get too close. He was not interested in any sort of commitment.

The night passed as if it never came. It was too quick to realize, as the early morning was so much of a rush because of the traffic jam. Miguel reached his office for a meeting, and was being introduced to other executives. He shared his views and brainstormed on better financial plans for the advertising company.

After a few hours, he was asked if he could work in Mumbai for six months to train the junior staff and would be given accommodation at a serviced apartment with an additional luxury health club membership service.

After giving it a thought, he said, "Yes, I would stay in Mumbai for a while. I do have necessary privileges from health insurance to travel mileages. This will be a great experience to work here."Let's see what the six months ride would be? More work and more joy, he assumed.

He was escorted to his cabin and was introduced to a group of people. He had a pleasant conversation with his new team.

"Ira this is great! You have put the entire trip quite well. So I guess the seventh day, we should be back in Mumbai. Now we have a brief overview about the trip," praised Tanish and added, "So you're the one getting the sandwiches, right."

Ira pushed Tanish away and said, "Yes, in your dreams." They both started laughing.

"Look Simmy is here, too. Ira is quite productive," pointed out Tanish.

"Miguel has found some information," updated Ira.

"Since we are leaving, this information needs to be informed to Ria. She is quite a choosy lady. Hoping she is up for this. Even if she is not, I am dragging her with us. We need to have an adventure," Simmy said cheerfully.

"So Simmy, what does Ria do and stuff?" asked Miguel inquisitively.

"She is studying for her dentistry and the rest you can ask when you meet her. That way, it shall be a mystery," replied Simmy and winked. Simmy told everyone, "See you all in a few days. We have a week to prepare and then the entire moronic behavior shall subside."

"I have started a new job in this city. Don't want to screw it," said Miguel favorably.

Road Trip Itinerary (7 days - March 2010)

Place	Accommodation	Days Spent	Places to visit
The Elephanta Island:	Eat /refresh at nearest resort	A day trip	The Elephanta Island and two temples
Bassein Beach:	Bassein Extravagant Hotel	Stay for the night	Bassein main beach
Pune:	Eat /refresh at nearest hotel	Look around	See city and drive pass to Khandala
Khandala hill station:	Hotel Ballerina	3rd day-stay one night	Rock Climbing/hiking/lush green hills
Mahabaleshwar hill station:	Dreamland Hotel	5th day	Waterfalls/Venna Lake/Wilson Point
Back to Mumbai-Train to Rishikesh Rafting Camp- 6th –8th day---------------Back to Mumbai			

P.S-: All hotels are budget hotels/bring: card games /picnic mats/mosquito repellents/tissue paper/sandwiches'/mineral water/first aid/meds/tents/towels/umbrella/ clothes and yourself .....

Miguel shifted to his new apartment and was getting comfortable. He liked it. This place was up-to-date and I can survive, he thought.

There were a few foreign expats in the serviced apartment and he had a beer night with them. He liked it and when it came to work, he was punctual and tried to impose it the American way. During meetings and training sessions he was a good leader for the organization. Sometimes, his strong personality was quite intimidating to the juniors.

Miguel's mother was a Guajarati (Indian) but his dad an American. They met during med- school and then there was no looking back. He was not interested in being a Doctor and liked what he was good at.

Days passed and he was already working long hours and had his beer night occasionally with his colleagues.

*****

Simmy had updated Ria about the intact trip.

"I have to tell Denise about it. Will let you know if she can make it. Perhaps she won't."

"It is fine if she cannot make it. You are coming right," said Simmy frankly.

Simmy added, "Ria, after all these years, we never got a chance to hang out. Maybe this short trip will get us to spend time with each other. By the way, I am thinking to go to London for undergrad at the end of the year. God knows how often we would get to spend time with each other. You know Ria, you're also doing dentistry and moving on."

She got emotional and said, "You call this a short trip. In any case, yes, will let you know by tomorrow. I will call Denise right now."

She called Denise, told her about the trip and Denise was up for it. She thought Denise was quick in making her decision, but she did not want to go. She whimpered with tension.

A few days later, Simmy gave Ria the itinerary. She had informed her that Tanish would leave at 7am on

Sunday to pick them up. They had four days to go and the countdown had started.

Ria was all set for packing and shopping. The next day she took her list to buy the important things and showed them to Simmy.

"Ria, you're quite prepared."

"I know I know..." said Ria.

Three days passed, Miguel took all his belongings and the cigarettes, too. They were his friends. He felt lucky enough to get a week off. Ira and Tanish took the sandwiches' and a carton of beer.

That morning they were all late and picked up Ria, Simmy and Denise at 8:30 in the morning instead. Miguel was the first one to get down. He greeted Simmy. She introduced Ria, Denise and Dhruv.

Miguel scanned Ria quickly. He surveyed the curvy petite 5ft 2inch young lady.

Ria just smiled and said, "Hello, and excuse me."She took her hand bags and kept it at the back of the luxury bus. As she stepped up, she met the rest. She did her greetings and sat on the last row. She took out her shawl, wrapped it around her and was waiting for the bus to leave to the first destination, 'Elephanta Island.'

After an hour, Ria took out the brownies to break the ice. She got up and passed it to Tanish and his friend. Tanish asked Ria, "So how is Singapore and the Dentistry?"

Ria politely responded, "Good Tanish. Glad we are going for a trip. I needed a break."

Ira over-heard that and said, "Me too, we all need a holiday." Ria got up and went to sit with Ira. She began speaking to her and they hit it off. They took pictures and Ria found Ira friendly but with a large- dose of attitude. She could be domineering unknowingly, she wondered. The whole environment symbolized true holiday fervor in the month of March. Ria got up and passed Miguel. They both looked and smiled at one another. She went to sit two seats behind him.

Miguel got up half-way, complimenting her by saying, "The brownies were nice."

Ria nodded her head with a smirk. She took out her iPod touch and played her music. That solely meant not ready for any conversation.

After an hour everyone decided to get down and freshen up at McDonalds. Everyone felt so much better, and decided to have breakfast at the restaurant. Ria did not say much. She grinned, nodded and was feeling weird, like her emotions were in a Viking movement. She ate and went back to the bus. She continued to listen to her music.

Miguel had bought a peach sundae for everyone. He offered it to Ria. She did not feel like having it, but did not want to say no. She took it with politeness, had a few spoons and left it. She was in no mood.

Miguel told Ira, "The Elephanta Island is not too far way, just a 10km ride away from the Gateway of India in Mumbai."

After some time, they reached the Island by a fifteen minute ferry ride. They were at the most congenial place, named by the Portuguese. They saw a large stone elephant on its seashore. Every part of art in the caves was related to Lord Shiva. Miguel told Ira, "Elephanta Island is quite a beauty and extraordinary." They were all energized and agreed to form two groups.

In Group one was Denise, Dhruv, Simmy, Tanish and Ira. In Group two were Miguel, Tanish's friend Addy and Ria. The idea of splitting up in groups was Ira's and everyone approved of it. That way no one would get lost, and they started to explore the Elephanta caves.

On the topmost of the island's hill, and scenic view, marshland and sea, were the Buddhist stupas. As they entered the cave, they saw the anthology of shrines, fine statuettes of Hindu Gods and Goddesses and carvings. Each of them was very much drawn towards the finest natural architecture of the caves being built more than 500 years ago.

The caves were carved from the rock face. The cave inside was slightly wet and humid. One by one everyone started to sweat.

To make it humorous, Dhruv took out his portable

fan. He had extra two of them so he lent it to Ira and Denise. "You're quite resourceful and damn nice," Ira said flatteringly.

As they walked deeper inside the caves they saw a chamber and a courtyard. When they looked upward a sculpture of a shrine was to be seen. It was a three headed Shiva, known as Trimurthy (three headed-Lord Brahma, Vishnu and Shiva) which was wonderful. It was spectacular! It surely portrayed the creativity of Indian art, marveled Miguel.

"Hey, it is full of mud," said Ria and started sneezing. "Well, it is a cave, Ria," said Miguel.

"Thanks, I thought we were inside a royal palace," said Ria with annoyance. That was when they actually said something more to each other.

Miguel was trying to be friendly to her, and did not want issues with any woman. He added, "You see, I thought so too, that is why I re-assured you. I hope you don't mind," and smiled covertly.

Ria wanted to whack him. "Walk ahead please your highness," said Miguel.

"Thanks. I appreciate it," said Ria. Miguel stopped before it got into a sizzling argument.

"This place reverberates spiritual energy," said Ria astonishingly.

"Yes it does," said Dhruv. His voice echoed. They could feel that they were in a different world. Having seen every detail of the cave and taking loads of pictures, everyone was cheering for their first location of their journey. The boys were comfortable with their soft khakis, shorts, and flashlight. They were prepared to be the bodyguards if anything happened. Men would always be Men, thought Denise.

Ria could see that every part of Elephanta Island was amazing, very scenic and had no regrets. Hours just passed so quickly. When they got out of caves they all separated from each other to get some air. There were many monkeys around, so they had to be careful.

Ira took out her sun-glasses and put it on her head. One of the monkeys knocked her head so hard and took away her glasses. She began to scream saying, "I am dying, I am going to die, my head..."Later she whined about her Chanel sun-glasses. Everyone started cracking up and Tanish took pictures of her. This was the first intense humor that lasted for a while.

Ria could not stop laughing loud. She felt bad for Ira. "Next time, sweety, get a fake pair of Chanel sun-glasses. The monkey is probably posing amongst his other monkey friends. Who knows he wanted to be in trend too," consoled Ria. They giggled at the situation.

Ria added, "Buy a new one. Let's go into the souvenir shop. Probably you get it there." There were many souvenir shops and Ira bought some random sun-glasses for the time being. They decided to chill at a food stall.

Tanish was taking a video of everyone, and each had to say something about their heart-felt apologies for Ira. Miguel was lame, he expressed, "The monkey was lucky to have escaped." Denise and Dhruv were having a good time talking to Ria.

"It is good to come out like this, Ria." "Yes Denise, been a couple of years, you know," said Ria.

Miguel was taking pictures and he overheard their tête-à-tête. He asked Ria, "Hey, when was the last time you went for a road trip?"

"Never been to one," said Ria bluntly.

He asked again, "What about trekking, Ria?"

"Not that either. It is not my kind of hobby."

"That is okay. You will have a new experience."

"I am looking forward for the rest of the trip. The caves were great. I really liked it. It takes one to a different era of time," said Ria politely and they smiled.

"Miguel," called out Ira. She added, "Let's take pictures of fishermen and the view is great. Come with me." He accompanied Ira and Ria continued her chit chat with Denise.

Late afternoon, they got back to the ferry and were off to their next destination, 'Bassein Beach.'

Ria started to feel the cramps in the bus. It came and went. She ignored it and got irritated.

Tanish rejoiced to his loud music.

Ira and Miguel started playing chess and the rest were snoring.

Ria was not feeling too good.

What was it? She thought. Then she assumed it may be food poisoning. Few seconds later, Oh no! It might be is something else, she freaked.

10

CHAPTER

À la mode Road Trip – Part 2

Miguel and Ira were having a great time playing chess. Ira was good at it and had won twice. After two hours, the coach stopped for a while for some evening snacks and coffee. Ria went to the rest room and panicked. She felt she would explode from within like a ripe zit.

The last thing she wanted was her women issues to drop by, thought Ria. She got her monthly period.

After she freshened up, she went to a small dodgy store. They sold napkins, which she never used. Ria thought, she had no choice, emergency calls. She felt Mother Nature spoke to her, "At the moment you're out of order, you need to adjust."Whenever Ria faced this, she addressed it as out of order since she became restless and lethargic.

She bought them and quickly put them in her bag. As she took a couple of steps, she turned around and walked toward the bus. It was not to be seen. What is going on today? She wondered. She waited for a few minutes and Tanish patted on her back and said, "Lady, we are not here to lose anyone. Where did you go?"

"Oh well...I did not see you guys and thanks for coming. I was going to call you anyway."

"It is okay. Everyone was wondering, and suddenly Denise saw you from a distance so I rushed to call you. Let's go."

When Ria got into the bus Miguel picked on her, "You petite, it is difficult to find you."

She furrowed her brow that meant, mind your own business.

She looked away and told Simmy about her out of order issue, she laughed and said, "Poor you. She added, "We are heading to the beach. What you going to do?"

"Well I thought of staying at the motel for a bit and catch up with you guys later."

It was 4:30 in the evening and they were not even half way near Bassein. So Ria took her shawl, got comfortable, put her feet up, and went to sleep.

Everyone was doing their thing. Ira was sending messages to her mother about the road trip. Dhruv had switched on the movie, 'The Hangover.' Miguel cracked up at the silly humor during the movie.

Denise was napping. Half way to their trip, - they stopped at a resort for dinner. Ria stayed back in the bus as her cramps were occurring as unexpected guests. "We shall get you something to eat then, Ria," stated Denise with concern.

"Thanks have fun," said Ria.

Ria and Miguel quickly glanced at each other and looked away. They sensed some kind of opposition and took each other as a challenge to face. What was it? Maybe it was a casual look! What is going to happen during this trip? This man is bogus, thought Ria.

"Miguel baby," called Ira jokingly and added, "I want a massage."

"In your dreams!" They entered the restaurant and it was crowded with many tourists.

In the restaurant, after the waiter took other people's order, Denise skimmed through the menu and ordered grilled chicken salad sandwich for Ria. Everyone ate their meals and was back in the bus.

Ria felt quite sleepy and felt her energy level dropped by 60%. She was glad that Denise brought her something to eat. She acknowledged her generosity and said, "How solicitous and how was it?"

"You know the diners, tourist spots, but good food. Ira was worried about food poisoning. You know foreigners with the foreign tummies." Ria devoured her sandwich and dosed off.

They finally reached Bassein Lodge. The driver was also accommodated in the same place and everyone took their bags and checked in.

Ria described to Ira saying, "Bassein was a quiet place where tourists could take pleasure in solitude away from the hustle and bustle of horded cities."

"That's nice. Well all the young ladies split up in two rooms," directed Ira politely.

Ria and Denise were in one room. Simmy, her friend Lena and Ira were in the other. Ria was glad she had enough space to sleep and relax.

"Denise, I will take some pain killers and sleep early. In case you guys want to look around at the night life please go ahead. Don't want to exert and will join you guys tomorrow," excused Ria.

"But, Ria, we will go for a while, not too long," persuaded Denise.

"Give me an hour to relax. Please, if you guys are in a hurry go ahead," requested Ria.

Ira had called Denise and told her, "We are leaving for a ride to look around the place and we will meet in the coffee shop in twenty minutes. See you guys!"

Ria would not be up for it, presumed Denise.

"Have fun and update me about it later," said Ria. Denise was off to meet the rest and told them that Ria would not be joining them.

"After the Elephanta Island, Ria seems to be kind of off-beat," said Tanish with concern.

Simmy told him, "You know the women issues."

"Oh okay. Got it totally," teased Tanish.

*****

In the interim, Ria started to go through some magazines. She loved her space for a while and decided to go for a hot bath. While putting her coco butter lotion on her legs, she considered to tour around the hotel. She wanted to see if there was anything interesting.

As she got out of her room, she walked toward the lift. She waited for a few seconds and chose to stride down two floors. She was loitering around the lobby and noticed the hotel was not too big. The hotel probably had about sixty rooms, including the coffee and internet café. She went outdoors, and saw the swimming pool area. It looked nice during the night time and not too bad. The hotel was small but looked like a high-end bungalow, imagined Ria.

It had two separate swimming pools with a water slide and three meters away was a unique waterfall. On the opposite side was a small playing field for children. Opposite the swimming pool was an open- aired restaurant lighted with multihued lanterns. The entrance was draped with satin and printed sequined sari type materials. Very creative, she pictured. Ria felt herself soothed there more than going with the others.

The name of the open bar restaurant was a little strange - *Cozy Pozy*. She sat down and asked for the menu. When the waiter beseeched her about the beverages she questioned him, "Why is the name of this restaurant Cozy Pozy?"

He smiled, and said, "Madam this is because it is quite homely and we have every décor adequately positioned giving it a welcoming atmosphere for all our guests and..."

She stopped him by complimenting him, "Nice." God knows what would be the next thing he would talk about...chairs or tables, she presumed. She did not want to know the whole geography and history. "I would like to have a hot chocolate and a blueberry crepe. Thanks."

She was looking around and saw that there were not much people. Then her eyes caught the sight of pamphlets and brochures. She got up and took some of them. She read through and circled some interesting information.

We only have a day and I want to see some remarkable and exciting places, considered Ria.

She noticed that there was the beach, Old Portuguese fort ruins, churches and hot springs. She wanted to go the hot springs and sit by the beach for a while. It had been ages since I could do that, she thought. She wanted to rediscover her goals and get in touch with her inner self.

She took a bite of the blueberry crepe and sipped her hot chocolate. She felt like heaven and smiled to herself. She was there for a while and gazed at the stars. When she was done with her hot choco, she took a stroll around the pool for a while. She began taking some pictures. She wondered what and where the rest would be.

She texted Simmy: *how it is going girl?*

Simmy texted back: *we are at some open bar. Ira and Miguel have gone to buy some souvenirs.*

Ria never texted back. She just wanted to know what they were doing. Her curiosity was killing her. She sat by the pool for a while and laid down there for a bit. How nice it felt. How often could a person do that? When everything was so tied up with career opportunities, one does get to go to the beach or hill stations, scrutinized Ria.

After some time, she got up and walked pass the restaurant. She entered the lobby then went to the café to check her mails.

She completed her replies and as she got up from her seat and turned around, a tall about 5ft 10inches, slightly tan, dark grey- eyed, physically a fit man was in front of her. She moved toward her left and quickly turned back. It was Miguel.

Before he could say anything, she remarked, "Sorry did not realize it was you. How was the city? What you guys bought?"

He simpered and added, "Bought some wrist bands and key chains. Ira bought some embroidered fabrics and scarves."

"Oh, scarves, - I wanted some scarves too. Perhaps tomorrow," spoke Ria zestfully.

"Well, tomorrow we decided to see the sunrise and breakfast back at the hotel. After that we can hang-out at the beach," suggested Miguel.

"That sounds good. I would like to see the hot springs and the church. Is it possible to see that before we go the beach, Miguel?"

"Yes, we can talk about it with the rest. We are meeting in a bit for drinks and cards at my room. Join us," invited Miguel.

"Thanks and see you later. Have fun!" said Ria.

Miguel saw her leave and thought, why did she say have fun, wasn't she coming?

When Ria reached her room, Denise was like, "I thought you were sleeping."

"I will soon my dear. Now you tell me what you did?" Ria and Denise were catching up. After some time, Ria told Denise, "You go and seriously I am feeling zzzzzzzzzzz in my head, mind and soul. I got to sleep, feeling so sleepy now."

"Fine, you are coming tomorrow morning. Remember, the sunrise," demanded Denise.

"Yes. Will certainly come for that, will wake up at 5am, you should too. Go drink and play cards. Good night," teased Ria.

The card games went on till 3am. They all left to their rooms to take a short energizing sleep and planned to meet at the lobby around 5:45am.

The morning was exceptional and serene as Miguel felt the early morning freshness was very enlivening. After meeting at the lobby, they went to the beach to see the sunrise. They sat by the shore on their towels and were watching every step of the sun. It was so stylish and beautiful. It had risen with charisma. Ria stretched herself, making herself feel cozy. She loved the warmth and attention. The sun's rays were benevolent, she thought.

"The impressive beach has become one of the major attractions today. The stunning fusion of natural beauty with chronological and sacred significance that Bassein town offers could never ever be complete without the splendid beach," described Ria to Dhruv.

"The white sandy shore was just perfect for all sorts of things. The palm trees encompassing the beach added to its scenic sumptuousness," praised Denise.

Everyone was so moved by the natural beauty and later it started to get hotter. "I want to see the church and hot spring, please...don't want to miss that," said Ria ardently.

"Fine, we better get going to have breakfast and see those places as we need to get back to the beach," said Ira.

"Let's go...I am hungry!"expressed Ria. After that comment, everyone was staring at Ria, wondering what the sunrise did to her. Ria felt the frenzied rush of act and was at an appease shape of mind.

Tanish teased Ria, "Now you are being normal." Ria just smiled and went away.

Everyone ate their American breakfast, felt refreshed and left for the church. As they reached the Holy Christ Church they were quite surprised by the maintenance. It was cracked and the paint was falling. There was nothing inside the church, only artistic work from the Portuguese time. Merely the façade of the church was marvelously carved and maintained.

Ria clicked pictures of the Church, Denise, Simmy, Ira, Tanish, Lena and Miguel. They were posing and making funny faces.

Their next destination was the hot springs. The driver described, "It just gets too hot and nothing is special there. He recommended, "Why don't you all see the city during the day and go to the beach for a while? That way we can leave for Pune soon in the afternoon. Going to Khandala would be a long drive, Sir."

Miguel said to Tanish, "The driver speaks Hing-lish." Ira laughed at Miguel's strange sense of humor. Everyone was getting a good laugh. Ira then asked, "Why is it that every truck has, 'Horn Please' imprinted. I have never seen many trucks like that. It is so monotonous. Why are they reminding each other to horn when they horn anyway? Everyone cracked up. She surely loosened up everyone's languid minds.

"Let's go to the city. I don't mind purchasing some shawls," insisted Ria jovially. After touring in the city and buying shawls, everyone headed back to the hotel to take stuff they needed for the beach and checked out of the hotel.

As they reached the beach, it was quite sunny. Slowly the weather was getting better. Tanish took out his two big red colored umbrellas and put in on the sand. Ira had spread the two bed-sheets, which Ria gave her.

Ria offered everyone her baked brownies and raisin cake. They enjoyed the moment by playing UNO. Ria played two rounds and won once. After some time she wanted some space from the rest, so took out her pillow and rested down on the sand. She felt the warm- brown colored sand on her back, which felt like a massage, she deemed.

She began having envisioned about what she wanted from her life in the next five to ten years. She wondered where she would travel to see the world. How about winning the lottery? She was in a dream world. This was what she wanted from a holiday. She loved to dream and rediscover moments in her life.

The boys decided to play volleyball and the girls ordered something to eat from the hawkers around. After some time, Ria got up and strolled by the beach. She was back to her past thoughts thinking about the old things like being an orphan. She then halted and turned around to see Simmy. She saw herself in her world, and was fascinated with fate. She reckoned, perhaps I was meant to be here, but for how long.

She took her camera and clicked away. She was thankful to be part of Simmy's family. She sat down about 10 meters away from the rest and suddenly thought about Shawn. It had been couple of months since they broke up, but she wanted to know how he was doing. She was happy that she hardly thought about him, felt it was something that came and left. No regrets, she considered.

The boys were playing volleyball. Ria's thoughts were running in a whirl pool. She could not even hear when Miguel called her to join them to grab a bite. She was in

dreamland again. After calling her couple of times, Miguel
went to her and called her closely, "Ria."

She turned toward her left side and looked straight
into his eyes. "What?" she asked softly.

"I called you a couple of times, but it seems you are in
another world," taunted Miguel.

"Oh, I did not hear you. I am not hungry. Why don't
you go ahead?" said Ria with irritation.

Miguel just pulled her gracefully and whispered, "No
excuses…you petite, you will disappear. We have a lot
more to do in this trip." She just went along and liked the
push for a change. It didn't usually happen, she wondered.
Everyone ate and drank beer making it a worthwhile
picnic. Denise and Dhruv were getting cuddly and
throwing potato crisps at each other.

"Well people, now we are off to the next destination.
Wow!" said Simmy.

After some time all of them got into the coach for the
next destination, 'Khandala Hill station.' Tanish
questioned, "Are we stopping in Pune city for a while? I
wonder what would the last destination be,
geographically we are going back and forth. Only the
driver knows."

"Tanish you asked a question and answered it
yourself," commented Ria.

Miguel laughed. He noticed she had a sly humor. Not
bad, he pictured. He had switched on his music and was
chatting using his new Blackberry Bold. It was interesting
with its touch screen facilities, he could edit the power
points so easily and for a while he was back on work
mode. He had been a workaholic, and all this time he
was away from it. He missed it. He was determined of
doing the training video for his team, so that there would
be no hassles.

Miguel emailed his parents updating them about his
trip and not coming back to Chicago for the next six
months. He knew his mother would be upset about it. He
could not help it and did not want to lose this opportunity
either. He messaged her: *Career call mommy! Have to accept
it, will call very soon, and miss u.*

Later, he got up and went to sit next to Ira. They talked about issues on relationship. Ira mentioned about her abortion and that there had been no other choice.

Ira revealed her fiancé being back in rehab and she couldn't handle the stress, so she broke it off. She could not deal with baby and work. Ira's voice was low with grief. "It was all such a chaos, - Miguel. I hated it completely," she said fervently and her eyes were teary.

While Ria was listening to music she tilted her chin upward and could see that Miguel was hugging Ira. He kissed her cheek. She saw how happy they seemed.

What kind of happiness was this? Was it the contentment of friendship or more than friend happiness? She felt everyone had someone, and probably whom she could consider more than a friend was yet to come, she wondered.

Ria was always figuring out other people's life, and she knew she had to work on hers. She looked away and watched the view outside. She saw the horizontal nature of crop landscapes especially the perpendicular elements, such as streamside vegetation and farmstead structures. She was quite dazzled with the traditional Indian farmers plough and saw the keen love toward agriculture. She had never seen that much enthusiasm anywhere in the world. She took some pictures again from the window and took a nap.

A few hours later they had already reached Pune, and they decided to drive pass through it to Khandala. Miguel noticed the ancient woodlands, flower-rich grassland meadows, areas of dense scrubland, and the horse tracks linking to surrounding countryside. Miguel told Ira, "It was interesting. One cannot see the country side much in Chicago."

"Yes. It is so fresh and the weather is amazing and equally blessed with natural beauty and bounty," agreed Ira.

Nearing the hill station, Ria, Miguel, and Denise could see a spectacular view of the lush green hilly surroundings and small lakes. Miguel had asked if the bus could stop on the side for a while so everyone could chill for a few minutes at a small restaurant for tea or coffee. "I need fresh air, waiting to go for trekking, hiking or even rock climbing guys," expressed Miguel.

Ria looked at him, she knew it, she would probably be the guard to protect everyone's stuff. She wasn't going rock climbing or even trekking. She would rather sleep at the hotel or go somewhere else. Eventually they stopped for a few minutes and Miguel was taking a video of the view around. Later the rest got into the coach. Ria and Miguel were among the last ones. As Ria entered, she lost balance and tripped backward into Miguel, and he slipped back on the ground.

"Hey petite! I am alive and breathing," teased Miguel.

Ria quickly moved aside and apologized, "Oops. Sorry I tripped." They both got up and Ria got a scratch on her elbow and Miguel hurt his butt. "My ass!"complained Miguel.

She turned back and said, "I said sorry." Ria sat on her seat and took out the bandage to put on the scratch.

Noticing every beauty, driving on the curvy road, they reached Hotel Ballerina. The hotel was good as it was located on the hills. It looked inviting, thought Ira. They went into their rooms and could see the green nature, "What a beauty Ria?" said Denise.

"Hey, they have Ayurvedic Massages. Cool! I will do a massage. I love massages and spas. Finally! This hotel is quite enhanced than the previous one," said Ria candidly.

Khandala is a paradise for adventure and Miguel enquired about activities that he and his friends could do - he was fast. He was told, about trekking and hiking, and how it would be an unforgettable experience.

"Sir, the Karla hills and the popular Duke's Nose peak are the ideal places to indulge in rock climbing. There are peaks and scenic views up the mountains," outlined the receptionist.

"What can we do first today? It is 6:00pm in the evening," Miguel asked.

"You can go for rock climbing today and later at night you can see the city," suggested the receptionist. He went and told Tanish about it.

Miguel updated Denise, "Tell the queen Ria to come along, too. See you in the lobby in ten minutes." Ria went along and mentioned to Denise, "Rock climbing is bearable but trekking not acceptable." Denise hugged her.

They had to saunter for half a kilometer into the hills for rock climbing. Ria looked forward to the new experience.

Would anyone do anything silly? Anything is possible in this trip, imagined Ria.

Miguel and Simmy implored the security and got their way out for an extra hour. Ira and Tanish stayed back and wanted to swim so they carried on with their plan. Miguel had given all his possessions to Ria, including his Blackberry.

Ria took out a towel, her mosquito repellent stickers and her new book, *The Classroom*, - a suspense thriller. The book was recent and written by a new author. She was excited to read it while the rest did their rock climbing. As she lay down on her square shaped cushion, and started reading the preface. She noticed that it was getting dark, so she took out a flashlight and continued reading. Her brain was reverberating around in high gear.

The book was quite interesting, very grasping and she almost finished chapter one. The key for her was not to speak, but to keep processing internally. She had already started visualizing each character and was nearing chapter two. This was her first time reading a comedy thriller in a jungle.

"Ria" Denise called out. She added, "This is not too bad. Life is short and I feel I am losing ten pounds already."She looked at her and started giggling. She wished she could record what she just said. Ria got back to her reading and ignored all the noises from the jungle.

Miguel was having a good time. Although in the back of his mind he always knew that what goes up must come down and vice versa.

While he was climbing up the rocks, he was thinking about his work, his failed relationships and was taking every moment as a challenge. He let out every bit of his anger, stress and had fun at the same time. Miguel found rock climbing a stress reliever. He could feel that his upper muscles were doing a great job. With about 7m of rope left, he gave a sharp tug and shouted out to Simmy, "You doing well?"

She did not answer him and he saw the rope kept on going. Being about 20ft high, he tugged the rope again. It kept going until he felt there was none left. He had no way of knowing what kind of position Simmy was in. If he'd been able to place any gear or slip, he could have pulled her off. That would be painful for both. So he went slow and called out to her again, "I guess we should start heading down, the rope is about to get over. May be another meter and we head down, okay."

Simmy gave him thumbs up and they continued climbing.

Miguel started to head down and stopped for a few seconds, wanting to drink water. As he opened the bottle cap, had a few sips and was putting it back in his back pocket, the bottle fell. He heard a loud shout, "Ouch." He quickly looked down from about 10ft and saw Ria pointed her middle finger.

Miguel waved and she showed her middle finger again. He laughed out loud. He figured out she was annoyed.

When Miguel got off, he told her, "Hey, sorry about earlier."

"Your bottle hurt my head. I was reading and I felt some strange wild animal or tiger just jumped on me. I felt at that moment I was going to get killed, but then it was just a water bottle."

Miguel was adamant, "Really a genuine accident."

They were waiting for the rest to come from the rock climbing. As Denise came down, she was cheery. Simmy gave Miguel a 'high five' and said, "This was so cool."

The night was still young, Tanish and Ira were by the pool for hours having booze. The rest went for a shower and headed to the pool. Ria went with the flow.

Later, Denise told Tanish, "I heard there is a bonfire party at midnight near the peak."

"Awesome, Denise," said Ria.

"Actually, it's good, the breeze and booze," remarked Tanish.

"Good Ria. You needed a break, remember," reminded Denise.

After dinner all of them headed to the bonfire up the hill. It was crowded with many people. There were two bonfires on two sides. It seemed like almost two hundred people were there. It was quite vivacious. From Indian Tea, beer, vodkas, marshmallows up to cocktails, wine and sandwiches were all available. Miguel took a look thinking it was interesting. He saw a band playing some songs of the 70's and 80's. Ria took pictures and told Miguel, "Not bad. It is something good for a change."

"Yes, Ria it is great. Let's join the group with the band," said Miguel with countenance.

"No, you can go ahead I shall go to the one without the band," persisted Ria. She paced toward the group where people were roasting marshmallows and having wine.

Miguel walked where the bonfire was lit and saw the band playing. He saw foreigners and locals toasting with their beer glasses. The midnight breeze up the hills was amazing. Bright yellow orange flames danced, flickered and people watching the bonfire were in high spirits. The fire was as hot as lava and symbolically the warmth burned the core of Miguel's soul. He went with the flow and enjoyed every moment. He thought, one more destination and back to reality.

He sat beside some German men who had offered him beer. When Miguel started, he sure did not like to stop. After some time, he bought some hotdogs from the food counter that were especially fixed for that night. Denise was in her romantic world, filled with joy and getting to know Dhruv even better. She hoped it would always be special between them.

Miguel, Ira, Tanish and his friend Addy were drinking beer and having hotdogs. The night air was at the most comfortable temperature anyone could ever fantasize. Miguel was having a great time whilst Ria was sipping her margarita.

Simmy and her friend were doing Tarot card reading and were quite excited about that. Ria spoke to people from Greece, London and Malaysia. She took pics with them and even got their emails.

Sometime later, she was looking up the sky at the stars and thanking the Almighty God for a beautiful night. She was looking away and at the same time she was talking to these girls from Malaysia, who were on a trip around Asia and India was their last destination.

Ria was glad she met new people whom she would connect with in the future. Later that night, the band played all sorts of music, such as: reggae, classic soft rock, and dance music to stir up the passion in all who would participate.

Many people began dancing with happiness and holding their booze. Ria liked the dance music that was playing and joined Ira and Tanish. Miguel was jumping and shaking his ass, as he was tipsy and acting goofy. Ria giggled at his inane attitude and wondered how silly he was.

She was wandering away and Miguel caught hold of her hair then her hand, and stopped her. He asked, "Hey petite stay, where are you going?"

She knew he was tipsy. "I am quite tired and was thinking of chilling around where the café was. Perhaps you guys can catch up there, later." She let go off Miguel's hand. She went to the other side that was slightly quieter. She could see that there was a railing around the area for safety purposes and the guards announced the party getting over at five-thirty.

She sat down and waited until everyone was ready to leave. So she bought a cup of coffee and sat down on the bean bag. A few minutes later Simmy came up to her and told her, "Why are you alone here? It does show that you are being dreary."

"Sitting down alone for a while does not indicate being dull. Everyone here has the liberty to do what they like. You too, I am having a great time and I am chilling," said Ria frankly.

"Whatever, Ria! You're missing out on the perky moment and you even refused seeing the tarot lady."

Ria was just stunned with the way she was talking, but could see that Simmy was tipsy, too.

Miguel came and sat down beside Ria. When Ira saw them from a distance, she joined them and suggested, "Why don't we all go hiking tomorrow? I mean today. We rest for a bit and meet at the lobby for breakfast at 8:00am."

"Sounds great, Ira! Hiking, I like," expressed Miguel as he started to yawn.

Ria was flabbergasted. Hiking! She thought. She did not say anything, just looked at them vaguely and thought this is the time she would want to do something she liked as well. She decided she would not go hiking.

*****

Miguel looked at Ria. His eyes were so expressive and conveyed depth. She could not make out what was it. He seemed so different, like he was hiding himself. She just smiled and gaped away. When Denise and Dhruv came, they were up for the hiking trip. Denise glanced at Ria and knew hiking was something she would never go for. The rest may find it stress relieving and relaxing, but she found it adding more stress, recalled Denise.

The next day after breakfast, Ria joined the rest to go to the peak. From there they had planned to go hiking for a few hours before checked out. She decided to stay there for a while so she could continue her novel, do her meditation and go for an Ayurvedic head oil massage.

Simmy started grumbling and did not bother. She wanted to be with Tanish and Lena, where the actual fun was, she believed.

Everyone undergoes different experiences, have opinions and why not, everyone has an individual and sensible mind, considered Ria. She was wondering what was wrong with Simmy. She did not want to upset anyone, but just for a while she wanted to think about herself. What was wrong with that? She presumed.

She told the driver that she would head back to the hotel in about two hours. The trip was getting interesting and things seem to be more bumpy but manageable. Miguel wanted Ria to come along. He looked at Ria, did not say anything, wanted to, but did not.

Denise encouraged Ria, "Go ahead, we shall see you soon and have fun with the massage," - she whispered and winked.

Ria believed that at the end of the day, a friend was a friend, the moral support was always inspiring. She wanted to meditate and be mesmerized by the beauty of the lakes. She did not want to miss the connection with the natural exquisiteness and recognized that she would not be coming to Khandala Hill Station for a while.

On the other hand, everyone else was getting ready with their hiking suits and gears. Miguel and Dhruv were the leaders. Miguel started walking behind the guide, Mr. Tony, a South Indian with a heavy, husky and curvy English accent.

Miguel had put on his light waterproof jacket. As he was zipping it, the zip broke, and in a hurry the map of the area flew away with the wind...

He did not realize it, and everyone was following him and the guide. The guide alerted, "You will see a waaterrrrfal, so get ready to be wet. We all have to pass the waaterrrrfal. Some of them began snickering to his accent. They tried to take pleasure in his natural humor.

Most of them had a backpack with all the necessities. Ira had taken some notes to add in her journal about the road trip. The boys had biscuits and sandwiches in their backpack, while the girls had cake and cup noodles.

The guide saw a large rock with a white-painted arrow. He told Miguel, "We are on the right track. Walking further along the path brings us through a narrow bush lined passage that opens out into a wide plateau. Please be careful and watch your step. It is slippery," warned Tony. As everyone walked every step, they came to an open reservoir and could see tall and massive mountains on both sides.

Everyone sat on the rocks for a while and took pictures, admiring every natural beauty. Tony informed, "Going downhill, we will take a path through which water flows and walk pass the waterfalls. Ahead of that, there is a resting place, so all of you can relax for a while until we walk further." So far everything was going smooth and it was invigorating.

After walking for about a kilometer, they saw a small pond and a resting place. They sat down and chilled there for a while. Miguel told Ira, "Would have been nice if we got our sleeping bags, but we can do this next time. It's quite a good spot!"

"Yes, very natural, there are many bugs though," pointed out Ira.

"What do you think? We are here for hiking, its outdoors," taunted Miguel.

Surrounding the pond, were palm trees that covered the sunlight making it easier to sit down under the sun's rays. Miguel took out his sandwich and opened a can of beer. He was humming a random sound of music.

"Hey guys, hiking can also go on for a week, but we are going to experience it for a few hours. Is it alright if we leave for the other hill station a little later and experience the magnificent panorama we all have in front us now?"requested Miguel.

"Sure, but not too late, even Ria is all alone," said Ira favorably.

Tanish added, "She could have come with us."

"Well, Tanish, she does not like all this. She has come with us everywhere, even she can choose where she wants to go, right. Guys, think of democracy," voiced out Denise.

"Yes Denise, democracy it is. We shall leave a little late," cheered Miguel with sarcasm.

For a while Ria was on his mind, but he wondered, why? He tried diverting his mind and it worked.

Tony told everyone, "There is an emergency rescue service here, so no one should be worried."Miguel was eating away and drinking beer. He opened a bottle of water and was having digestive biscuits, and the others decided to have cup noodles.

At that particular moment no one had notions about other things, but only hiking. Afterward, when Miguel was traversing, he did not see the branch, he slipped and skid down a meter away. It was quite comical with the way he tripped and accidentally chipped his tooth. His jaw began to hurt and he did not realize his tooth broke until Ira told him.

He was bleeding and Simmy gave him cotton and told him to take a panadol. They did not stop their hiking and went ahead. Miguel did not take the panadol and said, "He would take it in a bit."

Miguel's pre-molar tooth did look out of shape and funny. Everyone was teasing him about it, and commented, "You need a dentist."

"Hey, wait a minute. Ria is a dentist," reminded Tanish.

"She is," said Miguel and added, "I guess it has been past two hours. We need to see how long we all can walk ahead."

Ria on the other hand felt placid. Every breath taken was unsullied and soothing. The minty fresh air and the greens had a revivifying effect on her senses.

She was over with her meditation and sipped green tea at a small cafe. She continued with her new novel for a while and enjoyed the quiet time. At some point, she began wondering where everyone was. She had a feeling everyone would be late after all, everyone was on a holiday.

Miguel went ahead, and started to feel woozy. Eventually, he took a panadol and began shooting a video of the surrounding. With the sound of birds chirping, odd sounds of animals, snakes hissing and being enthralled by nature's beauty, Miguel realized that he must appreciate the dedication of the Supreme power and life to understanding the world's beauty.

Everything Miguel was shooting was spectacular. After having hiked for about four hours, they all decided to head down. Tanish talked about Ria and wondered what she would be doing.

"Somebody should tell her to request the receptionist for a two hours delay for checkout. That way we won't have to pay extra," suggested Ira.

Simmy exclaimed, "She might be sleeping or in a massage right now. We can send her a message."

"Don't tell me she is having her massage for four hours," spoke Miguel mockingly.

"She would probably be doing a massage or seeing the lakes. Something like that," briefed Simmy with aggravation.

Miguel was quite impressed with her way of putting life into a plate of enjoyment. She seemed quite contented, he thought.

While striding downward the hill, due to the steep decline, the guide slipped and sprained his ankle. It became difficult for him to walk and neither Miguel nor Dhruv could remember the way. Miguel realized he did not have the map and the cell-phones had no network. They had to walk around a kilometer for the cell-phone to work. Tension began to rise as they could not get through the emergency rescue service. Once they started hiking back down the mountain, Tanish's head was filled with thoughts of fear and concern.

He wondered why the guide didn't have a walkie-talkie. All of them walked carefully and eventually made it to the pond where they had relaxed.

Miguel had called the emergency rescue and they were there in twenty minutes. Tony was fine and everyone was out of the hiking place.

Denise had texted Ria, and she replied: *got back from the lake, at the head oil massage, will be done in an hour, the receptionist gave us extra time, n u guys should head back soon, enjoy.*

Ria was having an awesome time doing her head oil massage. The masseuse was massaging her forehead, and then her outer ears with circular movements. The herbal oils effectively restored balance, calming her mind, and helped to reinstate her natural state of happiness, and an inner sense of wellbeing.

Later, she walked out and as she entered the lift she bumped into Miguel and Ira.

Ria asked them, "Hey, where you guys going?"Miguel looked at Ria abruptly and walked pass her.

She was annoyed with his cold attitude. Ira replied, "We are going to consult for a first aid or a doctor about his chipped tooth."

"Oh, what happened?" asked Ria with concern.

"Will update you soon, at the moment we need a first aid," spoke Ira with worry.

"Sure, no problem," said Ria in a calm voice.

Denise had updated Ria and told her, "It was frolic. We had the pleasure of a good laughter but when Miguel's tooth thingy happened, then the guide's ankle; we thought what would happen next. But I guess everything was fine and now we are back here."

"We should get going soon. I shall take a shower as I feel oily and sticky," said Ria.

Everyone met at the lobby and was ready to get into the coach. Tanish had told Ria to see Miguel's tooth. He was tentative and didn't want her to see it. She saw it closely and said, "Don't worry, let me see if I have to remove it," and she smiled. Ria added with her soft voice, "It is not a major problem. You need to fix it through cosmetic dentistry. You're not going to die."

Miguel liked the way she assured him coolly. He told her politely, "Thanks," and he did not know what else to say. For some reason he was feeling strange standing between Ria and Ira.   Whenever he saw Ria he always felt heated up as if they would end up firing each other.

Ria went back to her seat and they were all ready to go to their last destination of the road trip 'Mahabaleshwar hill station.'

Simmy asked Ria, "So how was your massage? You could have done that in Mumbai, too. We had fun. You should have come and missed it again."

Ria was abraded with Simmy's sarcasm and told her, "I missed nothing. I equally had a great time."Simmy glowered. Ira and Denise noticed her and smiled at Ria. The beam indirectly indicated her, don't worry.

Miguel read on the pamphlet that Mahabaleshwar was one of the largest hill stations with its magnificent valleys, cascading waterfalls, serene lakes, and large vista of greenery. He took another panadol and went to sleep putting his legs up on the seat. He desired an energizing nap.

The driver had switched on loud Bollywood film music

and on the quiet side was the cuddly intimacy of Denise and Dhruv. After a few hours the sky began to grow dark. Dhruv held Denise's hand. She loved the warmth and secured feeling. She could feel a shudder through her body. He kissed her cheek and slowly her neck, and gradually on the lips. It was a long enduring kiss full of zeal. Then leisurely he whispered in her ears, "I guess we should get married. I love you and want to be there even when you grow old and wish for you to be the mother of my children."

Denise was stunned and said, "Yes, I mean you are serious about this."

"I would like you to announce it only after the trip, when we get back. Is that fine with you?" requested Dhruv.

"Of course, I love you. It would be nice to see you grow old." She gave him a peck on his chin. They felt they were in a world of volcanic pleasures and were in high spirits. Deep down, Denise was happy that Ria had asked her for the trip. She wanted to tell her, but had to wait for the right moment.

They all reached Mahabaleshwar hill station at night and the weather was remarkable. Everyone was feeling fresh as if they reached their first destination. They entered their three stared hotel called - Dreamland Hotel.

Ria questioned impertinently, "How many dreams are going to be fulfilled here?"and looked at Ira. Then they burst out laughing. Ria was scanning the hotel and met up with everyone at the lobby. They went for dinner by the hills and later to a Moroccan hookah lounge. The experience of hookah in a cool weather was like a moment of delirium, presumed Ria. She liked the hookah with the peach-mint flavor, and Black Cherry, French Vanilla Mint, and Pina Colada were ordered by others. All the flavors were extravagant and the night was a smooth ride as elation was sizzling in the air.

That night was a bit strange between Simmy and Ria. Simmy began growing jealous and did not quite like the closeness everyone shared with Ria just in a few days. Somehow, she always tried to accept Ria as part of her family, but sometimes the evil inside her played with her head. She cared for her, but grew envious whenever her friends got closer to Ria.

Moreover, Ria had an argument with Simmy that night on being proud and seeking attention. She was quite surprised as she behaved in that manner after a few years. Maybe Simmy was searching for more attention, but for what? Assumed Ria. She assured her that everyone still loved her the way she was.

That morning, after the tiff between the step-sisters, and a mouth-watering Continental breakfast buffet, Ria and Ira mentioned they wanted to see the lake, waterfalls and go bungee jumping, whilst the boys reminded everyone about river rafting.

"Hmm...let's see how the day goes, we have several activities to finish today and we've decided to head back tonight, or else why don't we all head back tomorrow afternoon, that way we can experience everything everyone wants. How does that sound?" said Tanish. Denise was up for it and finally after a discussion, the rest agreed to it constructively.

The day trip started with seeing the waterfalls and the lake. They went to two falls and watched them flow through the heart of the place from a fundamental part heightening the beauty of the place down a steep hill and endowed with an enthralling effect with its illuminating silver water. The water seemed milky and was so refreshing high up in the hills.

Denise surveyed the surrounding. She felt pulled toward a new world of dreams filled with lusty and passionate pleasure. She took Ria to a corner and shared her moment of bliss. Ria was thrilled and glad. She hugged Denise and told her, "Wow! This is great news. I am so happy for you." Surprise whispers arose near the lake reflecting the joy of happy souls.

When they reached the Venna Lake, the luxuriance surroundings and luminous water was admired. There was boating and fishing facilities. Simmy did not mind boating, so she went with Tanish for a thirty-minute ride. She told him, "I am upset with my sister. Sometimes we just don't get along."

"It is very natural to occur among siblings," comforted Tanish.

He also upraised her mood and added, "Ria is an adult and she knows how to take care of herself. If she doesn't want to participate in something she doesn't want to, that's not wrong. We are all on a vacation and that is the whole purpose of this trip. So don't torture yourself Simmy."She was quite stubborn and changed the topic.

When they were over with the boat ride, everyone was off for bungee jumping. Simmy told her, "You're different and it is very easy for people to like you, but for me I have to work harder on that. I have many friends, and they are all my friends first, so please never take them away from me." She tried to speak to Simmy and was worried why she was acting bizarre.

Ria was in a bad mood and hated what Simmy said. She did nothing and would never manipulate anyone to hurt Simmy, considered Ria. During the bungee jumping, Ria screamed so loud and tears were trickling down her eyes. She felt lost and contemplated, what was she even doing there? First Shawn and now Simmy, this is making me crazy.

When she got down, her face was red like a tomato and Miguel noticed it. He went ahead for his bungee jumping but could not stop thinking about Ria. He got off and found a way to speak to her, but she changed the topic.

Miguel tried and told her, "I am going to buy a can of beer. You want to join me?" She agreed. She bought a bottle of lemon soda and asked him, "How is your tooth? Feeling any better?" With a part being chipped off, he looked funny. She grinned, then he smiled and they bursted out into laughter.

Simmy was behaving like a spy. She became quite observant. She noticed and reckoned that Ria was getting too comfortable with Miguel. Ria noticed Simmy staring at her and told Miguel, "Simmy is waiting alone. Let's accompany her.

She offered Simmy a lemon soda. She was sarcastic and her tone began to become repulsive. She walked away from Ria and Miguel saw that. Then Denise asked her, "Why was Simmy speaking so loud and rudely?"

She told her everything, and Denise got pissed off with her. She added, "This young girl needs to be told off. Why are you taking shit in the first place? You don't need it."

Ria had nothing to say. She was confounded with her attitude.

They decided to have lunch and Simmy sat away from Ria making it quite obvious.

Ria did not know what she had done to begin with.

The À la mode Road Trip...was ending with an Ugly Twist, considered Ria.

11

Detox of Thoughts

Miguel began to have thoughts that he wasn't keen to give any importance to. Simmy invited more melodrama into her life, which in turn created more questions in Ria's mind. She sought ways to live life by letting go off contaminated thoughts and making new friends. Ryan and Genelia managed to sort out their busy life.

Ria reconfirmed her thoughts and dealt with the chaos her sister was trying to create for extra attention. She ignored her and after lunch, they drove back to Mumbai to catch a train to Rishikesh.

On the seventh day they reached Rishikesh and the road trip was not as sophisticated as Ria contemplated. It was a rise of suffocation for her.

That evening everyone decided to play cards and have drinks in Simmy's room. Tanish had a list of movies in his laptop. He had asked if anyone was interested in the latest flicks of 2010.

Ria was excited and she blurted out, "I haven't seen Alice in Wonderland and Takers, lets watch that."

"We are not here to watch Alice in Wonderland," said Miguel astoundingly.

Simmy pointed out, "Yes Ria, not interesting for the

night. I shall switch on the new Justin Bieber song for a while." Ira was fine with anything.

Denise said, "Takers should be interesting, I guess." Everyone voted for watching the Shutter Island. It was a horror movie and Ria disliked it. She wondered why people made them in the first place, but kept quiet for the sake of Simmy.

As the movie started, everyone was quite engrossed in the movie except for Ria because she had to watch it with abhorrence. Miguel did not care much because of his work. After about thirty minutes, Ria went for a walk quietly and told Ira she would be back soon. Simmy went behind her asking, "Are you going to sleep or a massage now? Why are you always finding ways to disappear? Just stay here!"

Before Ria could even say something, Miguel came out of the room, so he could record a video message for the conference he had on Monday morning. He saw Simmy was picking an argument with Ria. He tried to stay out of it, until he heard Ria saying, "I am coming back soon and I am not going to sleep. If I did I would go without your permission. Why don't you go watch the movie? You are gonna miss it. I will be back."

Simmy was loud and told her, "Maybe you are right. You should have not come and walked back inside." Ria was hurt and wondered what the hell was wrong with her.

She let out a sigh and noticed Miguel saying something to Simmy. She peered over Miguel's shoulder and said, "You have many people on your side and making my vacation a pain now." Miguel's tight-lipped depicted his annoyance.

Ria's lips protruded and she asked, "What is the problem? Why have you been acting strange the past few days?"

"I am not weird, you are. I am going to watch the movie and don't want to waste my time on you," said Simmy rudely.

Ria felt humiliated and turned away. As she left, Miguel came behind her and asked her what was going on, but she refused to tell him. He felt disturbed because the dainty young woman with a sweet radiant face had a sad glint in her eyes.

"I will be back, need to get some fresh air and wished if I could detox this moment. See you soon," said Ria impulsively and added, "By the way, why are you here?"

"I am going to record a video message. Could you help me?" questioned Miguel.

"Hmm…Sure, where do you want to do it? Your room or at the lobby?" agreed Ria.

"The lobby sounds good. Let's go there," proposed Miguel.

She went to the lobby and helped Miguel shoot the video. There were re-runs and she got to see Miguel on his professional mode. He was good and charismatic, she thought.

They began to talk about their work and he questioned, "What was wrong with Simmy and you."

Ria disclosed, "Just the usual squabble between siblings and also may be the fear of losing good friends. She is young and will do fine. We are leaving today anyway. Miguel, I shall see you in the room later…"

She walked toward the lift and Miguel went back to Simmy's room. Ria went to get her glasses and began to weep. The melancholic sensation aggravated thoughts she wished she could run away from. Why was it when I was actually having a good time, my sister made me feel so low, she recognized.

The movie was half way done and it was getting messy and bloodier, everyone did find it scary at only some parts.

As Ria entered the room, Miguel looked at her but did not say anything. He started to notice every move of hers and asked her if she wanted a drink. She was alright with a can of Diet Coke. She mixed vodka in it and her emotional level oscillated.

The timing of the movie was leaving everyone in the ghostly mood. "Anyone wants to play UNO and watch another movie," proffered Ria. Ira liked the idea.

Tanish suggested, "Why don't we watch Takers?"

Simmy looked at Ria again, noticing that her plan worked and when she asked earlier about watching another movie no one was up for it. She did not like that again.

They all enjoyed playing UNO. Simmy won once, Ria thrice, Miguel twice and the rest once. Everyone who lost had to bottoms up. Nevertheless, the movie was quite humorous and suspenseful. It made the night continue sinuously.

Around 3am, Ira said, "I am sleepy." Everyone decided to meet at the lobby by eight for breakfast and go for river rafting. That night, Ria could not sleep properly, so she went to the loggia.

Outside at the open balcony, she saw Miguel and Tanish. They were palavering. Tanish had grabbed a chair when he saw Ria coming toward them. He offered the chair to her and they talked about the trip.

From the first day up to the seventh day they got to know each other better and saw many exciting places. Tanish spoke about Simmy and cheered Ria, "Don't get disheartened. You have always been strong and compassionate."

She felt his quick intake of breath; then his hand stroked her hair. "Thanks Tanish," said Ria and hugged him.

Miguel asked, "Ria what about your future plans and when are you going back to Singapore?"

"In another two weeks, I am off for about a year. I don't plan to visit during short breaks. I will try to get a part-time job at the hospital."

Tanish was feeling sluggish. He said, "I will leave. See you guys in a few hours," leaving Miguel and Ria alone.

Ria rolled her eyes and looked away. She took a deep breath, expressing, "I love this kind of weather, love the night always, What about you?"

"I am not a night lover but I like the evenings. You know the sunset and stuff," replied Miguel.

"Yes, that is good too," said Ria. Then they looked away.

Miguel took a glimpse of Ria, and teased her, "Hey petite, it was nice to meet you." She began to laugh and said, "You can tell me that when we leave. You know the goodbyes, but thanks, nice to meet you, too."

He found Ria different and focused. The common thing between them that night was the stars and the moon. After some time of silence and smiling at each other, Ria got up and said, "Goodnight."

Miguel was actually waiting for her to get up, and then he would too. He embraced her and she was surprised. She did not know he could be so warm and his goodnight kiss on her forehead felt different. It actually felt good, Ria marveled.

She was frustrated earlier and the hug made her feel human again. She had a pleasant sleep.

After breakfast, Denise and Ria were talking about romance and commitment.

Ria told Denise, "You guys are in love but, he never actually proposed."

"Yes, we spoke about that. He said that when he gets back he has a surprise for me...I am so happy."

After some time, they got into the van in Rishikesh. Having reached the place for river rafting, the environment made everyone feel on the go. The weather was great. All of them were split into three groups, which made it exciting. At every raft, there was an expert as he would know the intensity of the river and there would be guidance for a better judgment.

Each of them had to show their ability as a paddler swimming through the rapid and fast flowing water.

However, for safety purposes a consideration of the swiftness grades were fixed. The expert explained, "The grade of the water was two and the rapids are of regular medium sized waves easy and gradual bends. The passage will be easy to recognize although there may be rocks in the main current, or even overhanging branches. It is more likely that after two or three hours the grade of the rapid may increase to three, this means the rapids will be of fairly high waves and the passage may be difficult to recognize. So how long are you interested to go for river rafting?"

Ira and Ria said, "Not more than two or three hours."

"Fair enough! The rapid is pretty good to handle. Hence, please decide who will go in which raft," said the expert.

Simmy opted to go with Tanish. "I am happy to go with my boyfriend and Ria," said Denise cheerfully.

"I don't think so Denise. The love-birds can reunite after some time. There are times when we must do what we do not wish to do and times when we find ourselves with obligations that must be met!" Each raft has room for four to five people. "We have to separate like this, look at this pattern display I drafted:

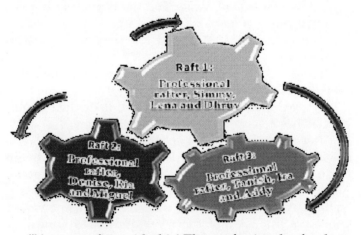

"You guys fine with this! The professional rafter has a walkie-talkie, too," opinionated Tanish.

"Sounds good," agreed Miguel with elation. Everyone started to put on their safety jackets and their helmets. Excitement was in the air!

The sounds of the river began to demand the attention of the rafters. Laughter thrived as the rafters were drenched. The boats departed into the river's swift current. Challenging sounds of the fast-moving water grew louder and louder. The rafters knew the moment had arrived. Nervous and uncertain the team cautiously listened to the commands of their river guides.

Ria was drenched and enjoyed the moment. Miguel was screaming away, Simmy glanced at Ria and looked back toward the swift current in front of her.

Each one of them paddled to their best. Some were hit badly by the swift wave. It seemed that the water had just given Tanish, Denise, Lena and Miguel a tight slap on their face. Was that a message or a warning? presumed Denise.

Rapid after rapid, eternal reminiscences of smiles and amusement, the rafters were enlightened by the exquisiteness of the river. Three hours had passed. The fast-moving water left an impression on everyone. The professional guide told each team that it would be better to head back and reminded them about the swift rapids.

So everyone paddled toward the right side to get a grip and stopped.

The vegetation and fauna was breathtaking. Floating along and enjoying the alternating trade of the shade from a cliff and the hot sun warming and tanning their skin was astounding. As each raft got to the deck, other guides had ropes to pull closely to the path where everyone could get out easily.

As Denise got out of the boat she slipped but got hold of herself. The waves began to become swifter. Then it was Ria's turn. She could easily step out of the boat but Miguel was in such a hurry that he accidently pushed her. She slipped and fell into the water. Very cleverly she caught hold of the rope that was tied around the raft.

Miguel panicked and grabbed her hand. He was so worried. Simmy got apprehensive, but when she saw the extra care Ria received from everyone, she grew envious.

He apologized and gave his towel to Ria to warm herself. The feelings of stress he had carried with him for so long was subsided. She was alive and in good shape. She had a muscle pull on her left arm making her feel achy all over. Ira comforted her.

Simmy came toward her when she was alone and asked her if she was fine. She did try not to say much and did not want to create any seen. She talked to her about how exciting the river rafting was. While they were talking Tanish came and hugged Ria. He added, "Thank God you are alive, dentist." Ria and Tanish began to giggle.

She frowned and told Ria, "Nice try, you have stolen

the show and have become the drama queen for today."
Ria could feel that her jealousy and insecurity was back.

Tanish looked at Simmy and told her, "What is up with
you? She would have drowned if she did not get hold of
the rope or if Miguel did not catch hold of her."He paused,
as if he regretted speaking anything to her.

Simmy was very upset and that was the last thing she
wanted to hear. Ria asked her, "Did something happen,
did I say something to upset you?"

"Well, since we have come for the trip your actions
have been very greedy for acceptance and attention. You
have tried your best in making things difficult for me and
whenever I wanted to do something, no one agreed, and
your ideas worked," said Simmy disrespectfully.

"That was a coincidence and based on majority," Ria
added, "How could you even think I would be doing
anything to upset you."

"You have been like this ever since you have been
adopted," said Simmy sarcastically. It was more like a
rerun on her memory, Ouch! Ria was furious but
controlled her temper.

Simmy's voice became louder. Denise came and after
a few seconds Miguel. Simmy went on and on about Ria
being adopted and told her, "You can't capture and
influence relationships."

Ria was in pain. Her eyes shifted downwards uneasily,
with a glint of gloom in them. The atmosphere turned
tensed at once.

"I am really sorry, but this is the truth I have been
seeing for a few years, and you should fix it," accused
Simmy.

Simmy was so bitchy and insensitive, thought Denise.
Before Ria could even say something, she continued,
"Even though we have been step-sisters, I have tried my
best because I care. That is why I also insisted you come
here, but it was my fault, perhaps you should have carried
on with your type of vacations."

"You are over reacting. Everyone adores you, and how
come you behaving like that," pacified Ria. Simmy left
and got into the coach.

Miguel, and Tanish, were stunned and tried to comfort Ria. Denise had told Simmy, she had always had a big misunderstanding about her sister.

Ria decided to stay back another day at Rishikesh. She regretted the fact she had agreed for river rafting. Staying back in Mumbai would have been the right choice, she thought. She wanted to be alone and felt her life just stopped for a moment to think about her choices in life. She did have a good time in the road trip but did not know it would end up repugnant and disheartening.

"In a while, everyone will meet in the lobby. Ria, - are you sure you want to do this? It is not safe," said Denise. She spoke to Denise and insisted that she would stay back one day, she had enough money. Denise could not stay back with her, due to work commitments. .

Ria went to the reception and asked to shift into a single bed room for one night and an arrangement of a train ticket back to Mumbai. She thought self-realization was so essential.   Maybe in this way, Simmy would give it a thought, and she'd realized what she said. When anyone said anything unpleasant to anyone, one should understand and know him or herself enough to realize and recognize one's choice of words and see the place before he or she just blathered, reckoned Ria.

"Why do people forget the good times? If they adopted me, they did something good, a great merit, and then why regret later for attention, or for acceptance. Some things we choose to do and some things we accept willingly to do for others," confided Ria with Denise.

She was tied up with a series of thoughts and felt she was developing a spider web. She needed fresh air. She wrote a note to Simmy: **We shall surely sort out our issues, will be great if this is just between us, for the sake of old times and some respect and love if left any. See you soon. Have a great journey back...Ria**

She took a deep breath and gave the note to Denise to pass it on to Simmy. Ria shifted her stuff to another room and did her goodbyes.

She planned to visit a clinic to sort out her muscle pull. Ultimately, everyone left but Simmy did not have any guilt whatsoever. On the way to the train station, Denise gave the note to Simmy after a few minutes. When Simmy opened the note, she read it and realized that she should have not brought up the adoption part. She then threw the chit under the seat.

Ria was settled in her new room and made enquiries about hospitals. She was told the hospitals were quite far, and there was a Homeopathic clinic which was a twenty minute ride. She did go and after waiting for an hour she finally got her turn. Her pain was increasing. The nurse had rubbed ice on the sore spot for a few minutes to reduce swelling. Then the nurse repeated the process after some time. This time she added ointment and massaged gently for about thirty minutes. She could feel the heat and the ache was quite unbearable. The nurse wrapped an elastic bandage to the muscle that reduced movement and said, "Using a bandage works best. You should come tomorrow morning for therapy as it has been swollen."

After getting the treatment she left back to the Hotel. She knew she was all alone, so she decided to go the lake before she went back to the hotel.

Nature's natural medication would be the best ointment for her muscle pull and the bruise her sister carved. On her way to the lake, Simmy's words were echoing over and over again.

When Ria reached the lake, she could see the shocking beauty with vast grassland spreads around the mere. She was blessed she felt. She sat down with a cup of tea and was thinking about various situations. Finally she got her mind into control and meditated.

After meditating, she slowly opened her eyes. She saw that with the ray of light from the sun, the lake looked mysterious, and very artistic. Under the blue sky and white clouds the lake surface was just like a beautiful large color palette. She loved it. She captured the exquisiteness feeling so much better.

She felt she had the power to detox her mind and the ability to filter her thoughts to regain her balance of mind and expanding wisdom again. But still she could not stop crying, feeling terrible and tried to think positive.

*****

Late evening before sunset, she went back to the hotel. She had some pain killers and took a nap.

When she woke up, she went to the café. She ordered a cup of coffee and as she opened her novel, someone was standing in front of her. She could sense that someone was staring at her. She began to feel uncomfortable and as she looked up, she was stunned. She could not believe who she saw.

It was Miguel! Her mind was juggling and confused, why? What? And how come! She asked him, "Oh, how come you did not leave? Who else stayed back?"

He came closer to her and asked, "May I sit?"

She did not say anything so he sat down. Miguel asked, "Where did you go? I have been waiting for a couple of hours."

"I went to the clinic for medication. Why did you stay back?" asked Ria with curiosity.

"Well I don't know, really don't know. After a pause, he said, "I thought of giving you company? I felt really bad what happened and everyone had to go back. I did not feel right. It is a matter of a day, so stayed back."

She wanted to throw up. One problem was not solved and another popped up. "Okay, hmm...I just ordered coffee and was going to read a novel," uttered Ria.

"Sure, go ahead. Now I know you are alive. I need a nap. See you at the lobby in two hours, so we can go for dinner," mentioned Miguel.

Miguel wished he could just sit there and dig out. He wanted to ask her so many things, such as, going for a walk with her, talk about how she felt. He could see that Ria desired to be left alone for a while, and did not want jump to anything.

She saw him leave and had these strange feelings. She felt a breeze of mixed feelings. She did not anticipate Miguel to stay back. She started to feel dreadful and the feeling of nausea was not subsiding. She wondered what she would do next. She read a few pages of her novel, and while sipping coffee she looked away at the evening sky fade away. She returned to her room to freshen up, and was having difficulty changing her clothes because of her muscle pull.

She got dressed and started to watch TV. She flipped channels and dosed off. Suddenly she realized that Miguel might be at the lobby. She rushed, looked around at the lobby, but he was not there. She thought she was late but he arrived after twenty-minutes. "I had overslept and woke up thinking about you," pointed out Miguel.

She wished if he was not around. Now she felt this binding and could not break free. Ria said, "I was just going to leave for an early dinner."

"Alone," teased Miguel.

"Yes, Miguel. Why not? They have two restaurants in this hotel," said Ria.

"Do you like Arabic food? They seem to have nice Kebabs and Falafel wraps here."

She wanted to blow him away and added, "That is fine. Arabic food is good and I haven't had it in a while."

The blustery weather, made the night more tempting to walk. They walked to the restaurant, and he asked, "How are you feeling about the muscle pull?"

"Well it aches, but will get better. I still don't get it. You surprised me by staying back, anyways...I like the weather here, and I am glad I stayed back."

"Yes, I agree. It could be true that you need a break, but staying back? You can speak your mind, you can say anything and I can listen," said Miguel calmly.

Ria said nothing. She was ahead of him and then turned back and said, "Thanks for asking..."

They entered the restaurant. She ordered a lemon soda and said, "Miguel, go ahead and order. Oh, by the way, I don't like lamb so much, but only kebabs are fine. How about ordering fish or prawns for a change?"

"Yes, that is fine, Ria." Now she talks, thought Miguel.

He ordered and talked about his life and friends in Chicago.

"Getting an opportunity in Mumbai was good, and in a couple of months I would be back in my cocoon," updated Miguel.

Ria talked about her liking towards dentistry and how amusing it was to be around the youth. They did not realize, but the two did click. They actually had a conversation and did not kill each other.

Later that night, Ria and Miguel decided to go to the peak. The weather was good, and they went with the flow. Miguel was chatting on his Blackberry and checking his mails. He requested the head that he would return to work after a day.

She had a bad muscle ache and requested for a cup of green tea. She relished the tea during the time the weather was at its best behavior. They sat down at the café down the hills. The ambience was soothing, fulfilling and flamboyant.

They exchanged emails and cell numbers. That was a start...of friendship.

"How did you meet Ira?" asked Ria.

He told her about it and they chatted about health, animals, and movies, career opportunities, traveling — briefly and changed to soap operas' and TV series. It seemed that both of them ignored the talk about love and commitment.

Various types of birds made noise and they could hear the animals scurry from one bush to the next as if they were running from someone. The bugs constantly buzzed past Ria's ear as if it reminded her that they were ready and waiting to unspeakably bite her. The sound of crunching leaves became rhythmic, and the difference between the peaceful woods and the chaotic campsite was amazing. Every second there was a new sound to be heard.

After some time, they decided to leave and Miguel had asked if she was keen on watching a movie at her room or his.

She was hesitant and decided that it be his room, that way she could give an excuse and leave earlier. She went over the list of movies. He looked at her and said, "Well, I remember you wanted to watch Alice in Wonderland, go ahead and watch that."

She was surprised that he was vigilant. The movie went on. They laughed and ate fries with vanilla ice-cream.

Miguel had ordered cinnamon and apple flavored tea for Ria. When the movie was over, she was falling asleep. He had already slept beside her. Sometimes a simple night, a simple gesture could bring about a feeling of happiness and a restful feeling, Ria thought. She slept soundly and the phlegmatic ambience developed a peaceful feeling.

Her heart and mind were on him. She was bereft and the air that she breathed seemed void of sustenance without his presence. A strange feeling was pricking her, so she woke up in the morning, looked at his calm face and wrote a note: *Thanks for the movie. I am in my room.*

She ordered breakfast in her room and was napping.

Miguel woke up and noticed Ria had left. He had a pleasant time seeing her wrap up her positive feelings. He called her and she had asked him to join her for brunch.

The morning brunch was a tribute to a rising friendship.

"So what time should we check out, Ria?"

The line between his deep set of grey eyes looked ingrained over the strong nose and pink lips accentuated by his tanned skin. "Well by noon. After checking out, I need to go the clinic for ointment and massage," pointed Ria.

"Sure, we will. See you at the lobby at noon?" He was thinking about her. He did not know why on earth was she in his mind? We are so different, he wondered.

So did Ria. She felt a weird sensation again but ignored it.

After the clinic, they headed to the train station. She had been able to think straight and her frame of mind was in good shape.

He was happy and felt refreshed to get back to work. After taking pain killers and antibiotics, Ria began to feel drowsy in the train. Unknowingly she dosed off and her head was slumping down. She could feel her head titling side-ways so she put her head back up, and then it happened again.

She turned and her right arm leaned toward the seat. After some time her head was slumping backward, not being aware her head caught balance, she was resting on Miguel's shoulder.

He was looking out the window pane. He looked at her strange and abrupt position. He did not want to disturb her, so he tried peeping but could only see her forehead and her eyelashes.

A few hours had passed and Ria was squinting. She had a bad headache. She hurled her body slowly and sat down in a complacent position. She was waiting to reach Mumbai.

Miguel could sense the movement of Ria's elbow. He woke up and smiled. Miguel said with a tease, "Now it is my turn. I am so sleepy. He stretched hitting her shoulders and said may I lean on you."

She gave him a strange look. He said, "I am kidding." His deep voice was mellow but his stare sharpened with suspicion.

Hours passed and they were almost near Mumbai. Ria bought digestive biscuits and a cup of coffee. She had asked about Miguel's job and his intention in staying back in India. Miguel had described about his job and his passion toward it. His terse voice ended the conversation. It was clear he had no time for chit-chat.

When they reached, two children pulled Miguel's khaki pants for some money. He doubted the money was for the right reasons. He offered to buy chilled yogurt drink with mint and sandwiches.' The kids agreed with the treat. The joy was captivated on their face.

Miguel offered to drop Ria home first. She watched him clear his throat and fiddle with his neckline. "We should keep in touch. You have my number and it was nice to meet you. We got to know each other better." He hugged her and kissed her forehead again.

"Sure. I shall keep in touch and meet you before I leave to Singapore," concurred Ria.

Ria met her mother and spoke to her for a bit about the road trip. Later, she went to the hospital for treatment on her muscle pull.

When Miguel reached his apartment, he felt like he was back in his den. He went for a hot shower and was back in La La land.

The next morning he planned to go to the dentist for

his out of shape tooth. Somewhere down the line, the trip did bring a mixture of emotions and was quite a hand full, he wondered.

He went back to work the next day and found it strange as he had his tooth awkwardly carved. The following day on his way to the dentist he thought about Ria and texted her, but she did not reply back.

Ria replied later, as she was busy with her packing. She was heading back in a few days, so she had planned to meet him and Ira for coffee. It seemed that the trip did turn out to be a good holiday, considered Ria. She was going through pictures on her camera and remembered every incident benignly.

*****

Ryan was watching videos of the slums on YouTube and his idea of a road trip was not his cup of tea. The concept of the trip was getting him worried and as for some people the road trip brought about a new moment to cherish.

Whilst on the other part of the world in London, Ryan and his colleague Austin were in preparation for their campaign and trip to India. They were to leave in two months and had so much to prepare. Uncle had suggested Ryan to stay at his friend's home for a few days.

On the other hand, Genelia was caught up with projects and quizzes. She had one semester to complete her Fashion Communication Degree. She was involved with her tutoring at home and was finding it a trouble dealing with her mother's unpredictable temperament.

Ria had re-runs about the scene between her and Simmy. With the help of Denise and her educational course she was able to divert her mind. She acknowledged a new friendship with dignity.

The feeling of suffocation during the road trip changed her mind. The road trip was entrancing, memorable and a great detox of thoughts. Perhaps it was a gateway to a new beginning or yet another bang with a huge problem, pictured Ria.

12
CHAPTER

Slums, Sanitation and Sex

Genelia gets all set with her new project that she was dreaming for years. She embarks on believing in the significance of maple leaves. Ryan begins his new journey to a new experience. Ria's fate opens more ways to beguiling opportunities.

Genelia was bombarded with work and confirmed an appointment with the marketing manager at the Tourism Authority of India. There was a campaign on progressing Sanitation in India at the same time working on increasing the number of evacuation centers, for victims of natural disasters. After what occurred in 2009 and 2010, it was a year for taking precautions. He was looking forward to be part of this campaign. Perhaps this was a way to start grooming my dreams and making it come true, considered Genelia.

Ryan received his confirmation of the programme route where he would start his journey in India. Photography was not a piece of cake. It was more like capturing a story, emotions and a message into a photo, Ryan thought. He was glad to be part of the campaign fighting poverty, promoting hygiene and a safe sex society. He hoped he could capture special moments from the slums and make a difference for their betterment.

He received an email from the Slum Rehabilitation Society. He was to be in Bangalore in a month's time. There was a conference and participants were put in teams. It was an event and an expectation for a career fulfillment for many.

He spoke to Uncle about it. Uncle told Ryan, "You could visit my friend in Mumbai. She is my old friend who is a famous TV host and jewelry designer. The last time we met was about seven years ago. She was here with her daughter Simmy. She had her jewelry exhibition. Oh by the way, - I remember correctly, she also has another daughter named, Ria. I will let her know that you are coming. She will take good care of you and Austin."

Ryan showed Uncle the list of the places he had to visit. "Conferences were taking place in some major cities. We have to cover about 200 slums in four months. It is quite a job! Other cities are covered by other photographers. I guess we might be in India for about five months," briefed Ryan.

Later that day, Ryan had a word with Austin and they were prepared to leave soon.

The day had arrived and they reached Bangalore International Airport. They were impressed with the facilities offered and were escorted by the staff from the agency handling the campaign to their hostel.

Austin and Ryan were aware this was not an ostentatious trip; however, it was an intensive course to see the reality of the unprivileged people who still knew how to smile and survive.

Ryan arrived to his hostel, which was evidently unlike London. The unfamiliar fragrance of people, land and food around the hostel was something he had to get used to. He freshened up and got ready for the awaited conference.

Many delegates from overseas and photographers from various countries and many volunteers were part of it. They were given itineraries, introduced to their teams, and were assigned tasks for every city.

The next morning they had started to visit slums and the reality was pinching everyone. Ryan was shocked at the standards of sanitation of slums, hygiene and medical facilities were minimum and none in many.

In one of the slums, a widow had twins of the age six. She lived in agony. The twins never went to school and helped their mother to wash clothes to earn a living. With the worry of leaving her kids elsewhere the widow could not find any decent job. Her husband was a taxi driver and died of TB a few years ago. After his death, she had to move to the slums when the twins were two years old. Every night was a nightmare as she was finding it difficult to pay her rent and food for the twins.

Ryan could not speak the local language. But he understood it well. Sometimes, he felt helpless because he wished he could do something qualitative for them. He donated $100 for food and the widow was guaranteed free medical facilities for the twins. She was stunned and grateful to the center for creating a project portfolio to facilitate welfare activities.

Two weeks later, Ryan was getting used to the heat and clumsiness of his lifestyle. This was because he was not living in a luxurious way, but with minimal facilities. Nevertheless, he survived brilliantly. He made friends and got to know many people from the slums. Some children went to school and spoke good English that startled him. Austin, on the other hand, felt sick. He was admitted to a nearest hospital in Bangalore for two days. Work went on and it did not postpone for any reasons. A few days later, they were all ready to leave for Lucknow and Gujarat. The heat in the month of June in India was killing. It felt like living in a sauna forever. The consumption of cold mineral water bottles would surely increase, wondered Austin.

Austin was feeling much better, but the heat in India was just too hot to abide. He felt he was getting roasted. Weeks passed and they were going to travel to Kolkata and Rajasthan.

After getting settled, they were introduced to agencies as part of the campaign. They had a welcome party and were briefed with the history of slum areas in the city. It was quite surprising that some of the slums were 150 years old. One of the main problems in the slums was the disease *cholera*. After the presentation was over, the next day they started off their visit to the slums and began clicking photographs.

There were medical camps put up and Ryan was taking pictures of a polluted river near the slum. There was a strong unpleasant smell that made him feel nauseated. He noticed the kids played near a rubbish dump behind the slums. They were ages of about seven to twelve, who were doing silly things like throwing peels of tomatoes and onions to grasp attention.

Two months passed so fast. Ryan was leaving to Mumbai the next day, and remembered he had to call up Ms. Thakkar. He heard a lot about Mumbai and wanted to know what was so great about it. He was looking forward for it.

The next day when he reached Mumbai, he rang up Ms. Thakkar.

She sounded so welcoming on the phone. She had sent her driver to receive them from the apartment where the photographers were accommodated.

As Ryan arrived at the bungalow, he was impressed with the reception he received. The bungalow was not huge, but the well-made interior made it look like a palace. The entrance had a small garden with a fountain, a barbeque stand to the right and a covered parking for three cars. There was a security guard, a video camera at every end, and at the foyer was a European Angelic sculpture that made the grand entrance. Ryan entered the bungalow and he felt like he had entered a fusion of a contemporary- European, spa- like cottage.

Austin did not see the step ahead that led toward the dining hall. He slipped and fell on the carpet. He quickly got up and Ryan laughed, but then he stopped suddenly because he was unsure of how he should be reacting. They paced further. Ms. Thakkar greeted them and escorted them to a private dining hall. The other private dining hall was cozy. He could see the garden outside and on the whole it was assuaging.

Ryan leaned on the small sequined cream colored cushions, feeling quite at home. Ms. Thakkar asked them a lot of questions about their trip, the slum areas, Ryan's Uncle and the diner.

They were offered some appetizers and chilled margaritas. It was the best thing to have during the summer, believed Ryan.

Simmy entered home and called for her mom. She went to the dining hall, was introduced to the young and good-looking men. She found Austin friendly and mesmeric.

She sat with them for a while and offered to show them around. Simmy mentioned to her mother, that Ria was on her way from the airport for some legal work regarding working in Singapore for a while.

Ms. Thakkar said, "I shall see to the lunch preparations. We have a continental buffet today. Indian - Chinese is going to be served, boys."

Austin said politely in his British accent, "Yes, that is fine." Ryan nodded his head.

Simmy showed them their glass house patio near the garden, which was the highlight of the house.

Then they went to the second floor where she showed them the exercise room. It practically had all the equipments needed. Behind the sports room, Ryan saw the sauna and the Jacuzzi.

"Awesome," Ryan said and added, "You don't have to go anywhere. You can chill out here."

Simmy blabbered, "I love it. It felt like living overseas." Austin mentioned, "Even Ryan had his private swimming pool at home." Simmy added, "We do too. It is on the other end of the house."

They saw it. It was surrounded by white walls and a white gazebo which was artistically built next to it. "Ria's room and the library are here. I mean my sister's room is on the same floor. She is practicing dentistry. She likes reading and has a small sit down area. It is relatively peaceful."

They went to the third floor and Ryan could see the rotating video camera. Simmy saw him noticing the camera and mentioned, "We need it. Being a socialite, or associated with media time to time is not easy."

Ryan smiled, and said approvingly, "Yes, I get that."

"Mom's room is on the right next to the pantry. We have a small sitting area and a computer room. It is more like an office for mom and on this end is my room," described Simmy.

Austin smiled. He teased, "You need to breathe."

They all laughed and she blushed. She took them to see the prayer room. The room had colorful, distinctive idols which were quite attractive. Austin eulogized, "Your home is very beautiful and inviting."

"Thanks. Let's head for lunch," directed Simmy in a friendly manner.

Ryan could see the food was well presented. "Oh, this feels like a hotel," Austin said. There were five different varieties of cuisines. Red wine was served by the chef. "So boys, how is the food and - please be frank - I hope our hospitality has made you feel like home," stated Ms. Thakkar.

"Perfect gesture! We feel more than home. Thanks," complimented Ryan. They appraised the tempting meal and suddenly heard the honk, "Ria's here," said Simmy and continued eating.

Ria was tired of traveling back and forth. She had asked the servant, "Good aroma. Why, what is the scene? Is someone home again?"

"Yes, you have guests."

She was quite loud. Everyone heard her comment. She entered the dining hall and greeted her mom. Her mother said, "Yes, we have guests."

"Oops. Sorry!" Ria introduced herself." "Join us," proffered Simmy. Ria sat opposite Ryan and he asked her, "Heard you are doing dentistry. How is that going?"

Her excitement showed clearly in her eyes and in her attitude. "Great! Keeping myself busy for people to have a perfect smile, you see. It is an interesting profession," said Ria. They began chatting and Ryan was talking about the slums, photography and complained about the heat.

Ms. Thakkar watched the way Ryan spoke to Ria. She saw how friendly he was and she seemed to be compatible with him.

She liked Ryan's personality. Very quickly she began assuming things. She was glad that Ryan was from the overseas and seemed eligible. Ms. Thakkar desired Ria to settle down and she could live in her own terms, knowing she was different with immense warmth to share.

Lunch went very well for Ria and Ryan. She felt lethargic as she nibbled. After lunch, she decided to follow up with her work. Simmy took the young bachelors for a drive, bought coffee and left them at the apartment. They made plans to meet up for dinner the next day.

"Well, I can't promise for any absolute plan, but we shall keep you posted for reconfirmation. You can bring your sister along, too," suggested Ryan.

Simmy was up for it and for a change she did not think anything negative nor create any drama.

*****

The evening arrived and Ryan had to visit two slum areas in Mumbai. Austin told Ryan, "Back to work mate." Ryan was busy with his shoots, whereas Austin was taking notes. While taking pictures, someone patted on his back. Ryan was introduced to some volunteers from Mumbai by the team leader. He was mixed up with the names, and accidentally, called someone else's name, and she voiced out, "Excuse me. My name is Genelia, not Preetie."

"Oh, sorry about that, too many people," said Ryan.

"Well no excuses, said Genelia boldly and continued, "I know it can be a load but it can also create confusion in addressing people."

Ryan got this vibe from this intrepid character and hoped she was not part of the team. The team leader said, "These four volunteers will be part of your team. They are doing the toilets and hygiene area."

Ryan was part of the same project. What else would she voice out about? wondered Ryan. Genelia was not there to socialize. She was totally focused and remained quiet. She had told her colleague how lucky she felt to be part of this and how this would give her a chance to do something for the country. They planned and designed the toilet for the slum area.

Austin noticed how the designing and discussions took place and Ryan took pictures of the derelict land chosen for lavatory. Genelia's prime concern was better hygiene for children and women.

During dinner, a tent was set. She took her second serving and Ryan his first. They touched the serving spoon together. Ryan gave her his 'Mind it looks,' and she furrowed her brows. It seemed that a battle was going to arise between the two strangers.

Ryan took some curry and proceeded for other main courses. While eating, Ryan checked his iPhone 4g. He reconfirmed the dinner plan with Simmy.

That night, at the slums, Genelia heard a woman grieving with pain. She enquired about the woman who was going to give birth. She requested the nurses to help her and give her the right medication. A smell of ether came from somewhere, while nurses were quietly handing out the medicine to the patient. Genelia went with the nurses to the tent that was set up for the woman. She wore her mask and gloves to help out. She felt anxious and never knew she would have the courage to participate in this kind of situation.

Luckily, everything was fine and the baby was born. She was adorable, but the problem was that her hands were very strangely shaped. She had eleven fingers and her hands were crooked. The nurses did not have an incubator but had put the baby on a cot with a plastic cover that had tiny holes where oxygen was being put through.

Ryan had come to the other side where the baby was being laid. He saw the quality of medical standards and felt horrible for the baby. He was taking some photos again, and asked the nurse for a better facility for the baby. The nurse was blunt and said, "This is the best we can do with limited funds and as long as the baby is healthy, this is certainly fine."

Genelia went toward that area and monitored their conversation. She acknowledged the matter and requested the nurse to recheck if everything was all right as the baby would not sleep. It seemed she was in some kind of pain.

The mother was unconscious for a while, and the nurse said, "She was a construction worker and helped at the sites." Genelia assumed that the baby was affected with the way the mother did her movements during work. The nurse rechecked after sometime. The child's oxygen level and other organs were normal, but she was still weeping. The baby was sent to the nearest government hospital for medication.

After a few days, it was seen that the baby's structure of bone in her arm was brittle and was concluded to most likely have 'Osteogenesis Imperfecta.' The two week baby had a muscle mass and joint and ligament laxity.

"The mother has conducted heavy work load and the baby needs to be under observation for a month. Conversely, after a few months the baby requires a checkup again," said the doctor to the nurse.

The nurse had shared the news with Genelia and she was gloomy that day. She wished the best for the baby and comforted the mother. It was quite late that night and she noticed that Ryan was also having a word with the nurse.

He told Austin, but no one could do much about it. They carried on with their plan with Simmy for dinner and drinks.

Ryan and Ria had a excellent rapport. They did the hookahs and felt like two long lost buddies having fun catching up. She liked his company.

After dinner, they went to a lounge where Ria bumped into Miguel. He was surprised to see her and asked, "Why didn't you call or text me? The last time we met was with Ira. We are friends aren't we?" Ria had explained that she was leaving the next day.

Miguel texted Ria to catch up at breakfast. He convinced her and decided he would drop her at the airport.

She appreciated his acknowledgement and met for breakfast. Their eye contacts and Miguel's way of flirting with her did make the moment piquant. She was feeling uncomfortable and felt butterflies in her tummy when she was on her way to the airport. She tried her best to ignore that sensation and focused that nothing would happen to make her feel sick and sorrowful. She only concentrated on her career.

"So, tell me when are you coming back? How many years have you left?" asked Miguel.

"About a year and then I'm entering the world of dentistry. I plan to practice it in Singapore instead," updated Ria. She could see that Miguel did make attempts to get to know her more. Sometimes she was unsure of his motives.

"Why? Why not here?" asked Miguel.

"One should be where the opportunity is. So tell me what about you?"explained Ria.

"I still have three or four months to go because I had gotten an extension," prompted Miguel.

"Oh okay, how come?" said Ria curiously.

"Because you're not here," flirted Miguel and there was a silence. They reached the airport and he hugged Ria.

He whispered in her ears, "Safe journey, and think about what I said earlier. Maybe I am serious."

She pushed him away and said, "Bye" and left. She felt coy and did not know what to do about him. She could not tell whether he was he really serious or flirting. Days passed and the situation was forgotten.

A few days later, Ryan was told about the baby's demise. He was shocked. He thought of telling Genelia about it, and he did. They spoke about it, and their emotions for the new born baby were sympathetic. For a change, they did not argue, their plainspoken conversation did bring a balance.

Genelia started asking Ryan many questions about his education and motives of being part of the campaign. He did answer her briefly and asked her, "Are you a detective or a news reporter? You surely have your questions prepared." Now the flame ignited, arguments were swirling.

Ryan asked sarcastically, "Don't tell me you are going to be like a leech everywhere I go now?"

"No, don't worry about that. What do you think? I feel the same way you feel, and for me you are a pest," said Genelia with annoyance.

Ryan listened then argued, "Maybe you are mistaken who is the pest here. The charm is in the communication that is intellectual. That you lack!"

Genelia puckered her brow and cleared her throat, "You know what? You really suck."

Ryan was not bothered. His male ego increased and the sky was the limit. It seemed like the two were going to kill each other someday.

Genelia left and felt on top of the world as she got an opportunity to do some social work.

Weeks passed and Ryan was off to Meerut and Pune. Providentially, he felt the exasperating woman Genelia, was not part of the team which made him feel peaceful.

The weather got terrible in August and Ryan had to shoot during the rainy season. Puddles in the slums were not a good scene. He was so glad to head back by the end of September, but because of the monsoon period; they had to extend for another month. What would happen now? He wondered.

When he reached Delhi, the temperature was about 42 degrees. It was like having a forceful urge to burn your own skin, considered Ryan. He was glued to his work that never ended.

He was keen to see some of the pilgrimage places and know more about India's culture and heritage. He got the chance to see one of the wonder's of the world, 'Taj Mahal,' which was located in the beautiful Agra. He was impressed with the magnificent beauty. The monument was completely made of marble and colorful stones. It looked like a paradise, he thought.   Later that day, he got to see some orphanages and minarets were located at many blocks for security and sanitation purposes.

After visiting Agra, he travelled to nearby slums to

participate in medical facilities for people who were suffering from leprosy. There was a meeting with some government officials to fix the filtration making sure the water available would be clean. Antibiotics were being given to the patients and a six month course was available for people who could be cured from leprosy. With all these volunteering, Ryan felt he was certainly going to become a nurse.

At the end of August he arrived to the religious place in India called 'Haridwar,' where river Ganges flowed. The Ganges River was the greatest waterway in India. Ryan remembered what his Uncle had said, "The Ganges River has a glorious position in the Hindu philosophy. Many pilgrims bathed in the river Ganges." He saw how crowded it was with tourists from around the globe.

The weather was pleasant as it was near the mountains. There was a huge Ayurvedic center where many foreigners stayed for treatments, massages and yoga was practiced daily.

During dusk, when Ryan walked down the hill passing vendors selling variety of antiques and fabrics, he saw someone who looked familiar from a distance. She just stepped out of the Ayurvedic center holding some bags. He stopped for a few seconds, and waited for her so he could take a better look. As she got closer, he was disappointed, it was Genelia. What was this crazy woman was doing here? He wondered.

Ryan left and ignored her. He took some pictures of priests feeding pigeons and children playing with each other. He then heard someone calling his name. He turned around - and came face to face with her. She was also thwarted but acknowledged the moment to greet him.

He stated, "You here. I thought you were done with volunteering."

"Why? You want me out. You don't own this place and you're the tourist here," blurted out Genelia.

"Chill woman. It was just a casual stuff," said Ryan with irritation.

She was yearning to escape from the daily routine and his face. However, Ryan was eager for new sights and

new faces in new places. He was well aware that he had
to juggle his desires with his professional obligations. Both
of them parted away from each other.

He went near the river to get some fresh air and
observed the religious ritual near the Ganges River. He
saw Genelia sitting there. She had bought a small basket
of flowers, lit a candle and let it flow on the river. It was
believed as a good luck ritual, letting evil being washed
away, and improvising the good deeds by sluicing away
bad deeds.

After sending down the basket of flowers in the river,
Genelia took out a picture of maple leaves she had printed
out. She believed that seeing the colorful leaves, brought
her inspiration, confidence and the ability to unify
relationships. She could see priests enchanting certain
mantras to bless people.

Ryan sat on the other corner, that very moment as
Genelia saw the little basket flow naturally, she called
out to him, "You tourist, you want to do this. It is good
luck."

He raised his right brow, "No thanks, I don't believe
in polluting the river and calling it goodluck," and smiled
with ease. She saw him folding his hands together. It
seemed he was worshipping and murmuring something.
From a distance, she found him endearing.

He is arrogant, professional, kind at heart towards
the poor, and prays secretly. But, he could be such a pain.
He could also be like a pathetic red ant bite, thought
Genelia.

Genelia saw him sitting beside the river putting his
feet in the cold water. She then turned toward other
volunteers.

Ryan felt an emotional connection with the place. The
water being chilled felt so invigorating. He began to think
about London, the diner, Uncle and the series of thoughts
came and left. He got up and walked back toward the
camp. On the way, some volunteers called him to where
Genelia was sitting by the steps. He did not look at her
and sat down to converse with others.

She tried to peep and overheard their conversation.

As she stood up, she slipped and was going to plunge into the river. She got hold of one of the volunteer's sleeve, and at that moment Ryan quickly stood up and caught hold of her arms.

She was pressed toward him and could smell his vague cologne fragrance. "I am sorry about this," said Genelia with regret. She pushed him, and rambled away.

Instead of saying thank you, she said sorry, how strange? He thought. Ryan shot near the mountainous area.

A couple of days later, before the volunteers could get back to Mumbai, there were activities prepared to sustain the energy and motives of volunteers.

He strolled down the street to buy some fabrics and souvenirs' for his family. He noticed Genelia coming downhill from the Ayurvedic center. He became intrusive, so he asked her, "How was it?" "How was what?" Genelia placed a question back.

Series of random questions were asked. "Are you ill?" asked Ryan

"Huh!! No, Why? Are you?" spoke Genelia with apprehension.

"I went there to make enquires," justified Genelia. "For what?" asked Ryan.

"Why you asking?" jabbered out Genelia.

"I am curious!" Ryan asked nosily.

Genelia was bugged with his questions and stated something concisely. "Well, made queries about Ayurvedic treatment. I need it for future business prospects," informed Genelia.

Ryan teased, "Cool! Glad you're not dying." He wrinkled his eyes and marched off.

"You're so annoying!" squealed Genelia.

Days were coming to an end. The chosen game for the activity was the most common game, musical chairs. Fifteen people danced around the chairs, until there were only five left. Genelia accidentally sat on Ryan's lap but quickly scooted over to the other chair.

It was surprising, - that the two people left were Ryan and Genelia. They showed attitude, smiled, pushed each other and eventually when the music stopped she stopped for a few seconds. She deliberately let him win. He noticed, but was confused and wondered what the favor was for.

She had poured Pepsi for herself, whilst Ryan received praises and attention of being the winner. He was given a gold medal for participation and looked toward Genelia's direction, but she was talking to someone else. He wanted to ask her, why she stopped?

The leader announced the continuation to the second game. He declared, "The next game shall remind you of high school. It is based on team work and I am sure everyone will enjoy it." He continued, "The game is - Scavenger Hunt."Whispers started and everyone was skeptical about it.

The leader also announced, "I shall be the trump card to help every group find the related items to the three areas: sex, slum and sanitation. Friends, we are all adults here, a little fun will make the activity more entertaining. There will be three groups, and six people per group," instructed the leader.

"The group that wins gets a silver bronze medal with each member receiving a $200 cashier's check. You shall get an opportunity by introducing something new that benefits the slums. You shall be the leader and this is your chance. So who will be the lucky six? All the participants come and collect your chit. Each chit indicates each symbol in relation to the theme of the game," explained the leader.

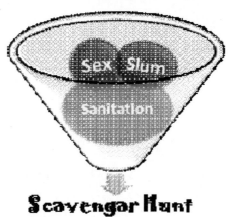

Everyone was stunned with the unusual names chosen. The leader mentioned, "There is a nearby bazaar in this pilgrimage place. You shall get your things there."Everyone applauded and cheered.

The night was suspenseful. Ryan was in the group of Sanitation. He wanted to talk to Genelia, but how could he find the right moment, he figured.

She was pushed to pick up a chit, but before she could open it, she had exchanged it with her friend.

The scavenger hunt initiated an innovative amusement of team building. Personal space was being invaded and enthralled a new reverence.

13

Irresistible Solicitude Saga

Genelia began to feel something strange. Something she had not felt like in the longest time. Ryan tried to befriend Genelia and end the conflict between them. Ria encountered her flashback creating a mental distress that tested her patience level. Her mixed emotions were no less than drinking a strong dose of a cocktail.

The Leader said, "The supplies that group 'Sanitation' needs to find are: *tissue paper roll and sanitary napkins, first aid kit, portable folding toilet and anti-bacterial liquid soap, water purification tablets, gloves and insect repellent, torch and candles.*"

He added, "For group 'Slums' the list is: *lanterns and slippers, water purifier, garbage can, tool kit, telephone and first aid box, and sleeping bags.*"

He continued, "For group 'Sex' the list is: *flavored condom pack, pregnancy test kit, lubricant, aroma massage oil, anti-bacterial hand gel, towel and a bed sheet.*"

"Each group has to find six things. Each segment of this camp has a clue and you have to find your clue based on the list each of you have. You have thirty-five minutes to complete everything. You shall hear a bell. Any member that comes late, is automatically disqualified because we need complete members of the group with the maximum number of items right on this field," described the leader.

Everyone was startled and Ryan found it funny to see Genelia in the group of 'Sex.' She regretted her option of changing the chit. She found it absurd and bashful with the items she had to look for.

The members were given five minutes to decide their team leader and how they would disperse to get the items from different shops.

The souk was a ten minute walk, and the discussion had started. It sounded like a quack here and a quack there. Hearing the whistle blown, the members dispersed and ran back and forth. It looked comical. Everyone showed eagerness to win.

Genelia managed to get the bed sheet and had only fifteen minutes left. She quickly ran into the drug store as she had the responsibility to get the pregnancy test kit and lubricant. She was thinking what to say and bumped into Ryan. He was there to pick up the tissue roll and sanitary napkins. Both of them were in an awkward situation. They were running out of time and asked for the sales man. She went ahead and was stammering when it came to the lubricant. She got the pregnancy test kit and walked ahead.

Ryan looked at Genelia and saw his watch. He had no guts to ask for sanitary napkins. He tapped Genelia's shoulder and with his soft voice he asked her, "Could you do something for me?" He added, "I need sanitary napkins, - I feel awkward asking for them."

She burst out laughing and teased him, "Really? I need a favor, too."They had to be hush about it or else they would be disqualified. Genelia added, "I mean the massage oil...actually a lubricant."

Both of them teased each other, and realized they were running out of time. "We need to speed up," alerted Genelia. They rushed out and ran toward the camp.

She stumbled but got hold of her balance. Ryan waited

for her and asked her while they were running, "Earlier, why did you stop at the game?"

"I never discontinued. You simply won," said Genelia intrepidly.

He grabbed her arm saying, "It is a simple question. I think you're lying and why are you not saying anything."

"Oh, Ryan, why are you so assertive? It was just a game," replied Genelia calmly. She walked briskly. He knew she had something in her mind but why was it bothering him so much, he wondered.

She got there on time and was the first group to win. Ryan was the second runner up as his team member was late.

"The Sex group is the winner. Cheers for them. Each one of you receives an opportunity to do something for your country and certainly your cash checks will be given to you when you reach Mumbai. We are ready to see your business proposal. You have two weeks to show the outline in Mumbai," said the leader cheerfully. It was a moment of joy and a good team work that did break the ice between Genelia and Ryan.

"Why is it sometimes we meet the same person over and over again and - we feel nothing? With some, the first time there is a feeling of a strange connection," considered Genelia. Days passed and the rebellious nature subsided, as if someone just threw a cold bucket of water on both them.

The date was nearing to leave back to Mumbai and Ryan began to miss the whole journey he had for a few months. When Genelia and Ryan got back into their tents, the exhaustion in their nerves drove them to sleep. The next day, Ryan received a text message from Ria.

She had mentioned what a beautiful Sunday it was and candles were lit everywhere to celebrate Ryan's birthday. He was astonished and happy to receive an unexpected message. The message from Ria did bring a smile on his face. Surprisingly, she was the first one to wish him.

What a 23rd birthday? There was no booze, no Mark, no family and of course no girlfriend, he wondered.

Instead Ryan considered this birthday could be special in the slums. He wanted to make this day momentous rather than thinking what he could have done.

Genelia was surveying the area. She began loitering around the slum and took notes. She saw Ryan and peered out at him sneakily. She was wondering why he was smiling to himself. Ryan noticed that someone was around. He slanted his head and saw Genelia. He got up, pretended he did not see her and walked away. He went to a bakery shop, bought a birthday cake, - a dozen bottles of mineral water, plastic cups, and two dozen of barbeque chips. He went to the slum to visit the kids and was so thrilled to share his happiness with them.

Being a photographer, he shot many pictures and gave his camera to the kids to shoot him for a change. They had a great time and the joy on their face was worth watching. Some teenagers could speak English, and they made the attempt to mime in a British accent with him. He laughed, and after a while, he cut the cake with them.

He walked out and Genelia observed him with some children. He was talking to them, and she was snooping around to discover the reason of being too friendly with them. She noticed the happiness on his face was different. It showed his true genuine cheerfulness. His light-hearted attitude toward the kids indicated as an eternal teenager. She hid behind the wall. When they went away, she asked one of the children about the excitement. They mentioned about his birthday.

She went and told the team leader about it. That night there was a surprise for Ryan. Everyone was very cooperative. They wanted to make the moment very entertaining by playing guitar and using wooden chairs as drums. Everyone joined in and created a rhythm. It was flowing so well. He was elated and expressed gratitude to everyone for a great revelation.

He found out that Genelia told the team leader. He thanked her for spreading the news. She was confused whether he pulled her leg or he was genuinely being thankful.

They conversed, and he mentioned, "This birthday

would be special for me." Around midnight, they strolled around the camping site.

They discussed about many things, and Genelia felt he confided in her. She was available to talk, but was in no mood to waste her time to make any friendly conversation with any man. With her past failed relationships, her attitude toward her ambition had aspired. She did not want to be distracted.

She tried to ignore him. But throughout the campaign, she could manage it sometimes and felt her journey had been ill-fated from the beginning. Genelia knew that she was basically running away from her true feelings. She recognized that Ryan was a good man with true intentions, but did not want to acknowledge it.

Before leaving the pilgrimage place, she had a word with the manager to support and permit her to start a branch in Mumbai in her digital library. She had given him her business proposal and he requested for more time to consider the proposal.

After the meeting, Genelia thought about how she deserved to give herself a chance to know people. No one could depend on the past, and falling in love again would be a dream that came true, she contemplated. She loved the romance, naughtiness, classy moments, and those somersault feelings. It was the best thing that could happen to anyone.

However, the twenty three year old took a step back. Ignored it, brushed it away and turned her focus on her ambition. She bumped into him, again. Something natural between them was their chat. The continuous conversation between them was juicy with gossips. When he asked her directly, "Are you dating?"

She was stunned and hesitated to say anything. After a pause she said, "Why? I do date, but not currently."

"I know, Genelia. It's a direct question, but a casual one. Don't be tentative. By the way...can we be friends?" asked Ryan calmly.

"We are!" said Genelia.

"Of course, if you say so. Toast to my new friend, then," cheered Ryan.

"Same to you and goodnight," said Genelia with reluctance.

They parted and went into their tents. Genelia could not sleep and was thinking about so many things. Her mind was like a spider web again. She told herself, "I came here to work and no relationships." That night her abnormal craving for a night snack came back. She got out of the tent around 2am to find something to eat at another tent which housed their pantry.

She had no choice but to have orange juice and nuts. She hated the combination.

Ryan was not sleeping and was going through his photographs. He noticed a bright light and peeped outside. He saw Genelia walking into her tent with orange juice. He smiled and went back to looking at his photographs.

He thought about her. He described her in many ways. She could be strange, but different, cool and annoying, friendly and prudent. She had her charm. Gradually he went off to serene siesta.

The last day arrived and they were all set to head back. By then Genelia and Ryan did become friends. He found her passionate and fanatic.

The flight took off and reached the grounds of Mumbai which was welcoming. He was waiting to share his experience with his family. Time flew and no one could even imagine the earth was spinning real fast. Ryan stayed at the apartment for two days and then shifted to Ria's home for a few days before he went back to London.

Genelia was so excited but felt she left something behind. As usual she denied her feelings and was manipulated with her devilish side. She shut the blinds in her room and began checking updates on Facebook.

Ryan had called Genelia for coffee the next day. They spoke, watched a movie and he tried to make a move, but she always took a step back.

This London dude will soon do his sayonara. Why on earth should I deal with long-distance relationships? She wondered.

He understood that perhaps this needed more time

and how was he going to do it. He could feel that he was growing serious about her and wanted to ask her out on a date.

For some time, he was stuck on a puddle of thoughts and figuring it out. He did not want to take ancestor years to analyze it, but recognized that he should follow his heart.

While Ryan was thinking about Genelia sitting at the Gazebo, Ria arrived as a surprise. He was glad to meet her.

She had updated him that she would be in Mumbai for a few days to celebrate her 25th birthday. Her mother had convinced her to come back for a gala celebration.

"Oh wow! We share the same birthday month. You knew my birthday but I am sorry, did not know yours," sated Ryan.

"That's okay. Your Uncle could not get through you so he sent a message to me. That is how I found out."

She continued, "Anyway, you are coming, and please invite Austin, too. Tomorrow I shall print the invitation cards. You can join me for ideas and perhaps coffee. So tell me how the journey was? I want to know it all."

"Fine Ria, it was juicy- and emotional."He had briefed it up to her and added, "The slums were quite an experience and created a bonding between me, the children and this young lady."

*****

During coffee Ryan had asked Ria if he could also invite his friend, Genelia. He told her that they met during the campaign and became good friends. After Ryan had mentioned about her, she was eager to meet her. It was good to meet and make new friends, she reckoned.

When Ria was sipping macchiato, she remembered how her sister misbehaved during the road trip. She did not want any drama to be repeated on her birthday. She kept her fingers crossed.

Genelia arrived and carped about getting wet in the rain. When she saw Ria, she said, "Oops, I am Genelia."She glanced at Ryan commenting in sarcasm, "Thanks for inviting me at short notice."

"By the way, the rain nowadays has been crazy," pointed out Genelia with annoyance. Hours passed, they chatted, gossiped and Ria asked Genelia about her family. She mentioned about having an older brother who was overseas for an aviation training program in Canada.

She had to head back, so she said with agitation, "I got to go now. I have tutoring today."

"Genelia, do come for my birthday party on the 24th of September. Hopefully, it won't be raining and it was a pleasure to meet you," addressed Ria.

Ryan admired Genelia and did seem to like her more than a friend by the way he looked at her. When she left, Ryan complimented Ria, "You are chirpy, bubbly, sometimes reserved and it is great to hang out with you."

"Oh, Thanks. I know!" said Ria wittingly.

The gorgeous Libran was celebrating her birthday. Wine, margaritas' and cocktails were being served. The party was exotic. Everyone's dress code was Red, White or Black. There was a diversification of things being put up.

At one corner there was a barbeque section where variety of kebabs and seafood was being grilled with different flavors. The other corner had pasta, pizza, Mexican food. The party at the garden outside Ria's home was unlike the usual scene, it seemed like one was in a gala cruise. They even served Chinese, - and lip smacking desserts.

It was disparate to a standard party with spa and a massage corner. Ria's friends could do a foot massage for free. Candles were lit everywhere, music like R&B, Hip-Hop and Bollywood film favorites' were played by the DJ.

For a change, Simmy had written a poem for Ria and the carving was done on a wood decorated with sequins and multi-colored stones. It was very sweet and beautifully written with different colors. Ria was also surprised with a new professional digital camera of Canon. She was astonished and valued the moment.

She hung out with Denise and Dhruv who were officially engaged. The glow on her face was beaming and the rays of happiness sent positive vibes to everyone at the party. She was surveying around and saw Miguel enter the party. She was so happy to see him. He gave her a tight hug, kissed her forehead saying, "Nice weather, and Happy Birthday petite. Wishing you the worldly gratifications and lots of sex in the future," and laughed.

Denise cracked up too, until when Miguel introduced his Canadian girlfriend, Alysia.

Ria was silent for a bit when she heard the sudden news. She was confused with the fact he flirted with her, and then he introduced his girlfriend, she considered.

She wanted to hang him in Mount Everest. She knew men couldn't live without playing with women's feelings. She was glad she never took him seriously but did fall for it eventually.

She tried to be polite and welcomed Alysia.

She did feel strange and her glow was diminishing. She felt that, - whenever Miguel had flirted and showed his overly concerned behavior, she liked it.

The night questioned her again, was he dating because she was not serious or maybe she didn't say anything at the airport when he flirted with her. Maybe he already had someone before. This loser always liked to flirt. Thank God I said nothing or did anything. Why do I feel this mesmeric pull away...again feeling alone, thought Ria spontaneously.

She did not want to ruin her mood so she decided to keep a distance from Miguel. She spoke to Alysia who was friendly and loved eating the ravishing cuisines.

Alysia updated Ria, "I met Miguel at his office. I am doing my MBA internship there and we have been secretly dating for about two months."Ria tried to listen patiently and the grin on her face was being troubled by her flushed emotions.

Ryan was sweet. He volunteered to be the photographer that evening. Wonderful, fun, and wacky pictures were being taken. Birthday wilderness was being captured to cherish forever. He had texted Genelia for being late.

As she arrived, she saw Ryan from a distance and waved at him. She paced toward him with a bouquet of flowers and a bottle of wine. She introduced her brother, Shawn Silveira.

Shawn had arrived for a few weeks in Mumbai to celebrate the festivals of lights 'Deepawali' which was coming up in a few weeks in October.

Ryan introduced Shawn to Austin, and told Genelia, "I shall be right back, need to take more pictures." Shawn spoke to Austin for a while.

Genelia wished Ria, "May this day be the most memorable birthday filled with a rocking bliss of happiness and a cocktail of love and joy."

Just then Ria saw someone familiar coming toward Genelia's back. She was bewildered, but was making sure of her eyes. She was uptight and could not believe who she was literally seeing.

She looked away and Genelia told Ria, "I want to introduce to you, my brother Shawn. Remember, I had told you at coffee a few days ago."

Ria did not look at Shawn and reconfirmed with her about her brother being in Canada. "Yup, he was," notified Genelia.

She was going to get a heart attack. When Shawn saw Ria, the look on his face was blank with a wide smile. All he could say to her was, "Hi, Happy Birthday...nice party."

He was equally surprised and wondered what a small world it was. He saw her enviously and never even imagined he would ever meet her.

Ria wanted to disappear that very moment. Despite the heartfelt entreaties, she chose to ignore her sentiments. It had been long. No contacts and if that were not aggravating enough what did she do wrong that she met him again?

Her mind was spinning. "Oh Lord! It is Shawn, Why? First it was Miguel and then now him. Why?" Her head was repeating this over and over again.

Both of them did not say much or even show they had met before. Genelia left to get some kebabs and a cocktail. She chatted with Austin about new projects and movies.

Ria was completely lost in her own party. She did not know what just happened. All she could think was Miguel broke the news about his girlfriend and Shawn was an unexpected visitor.

She desired a genie to rescue her from the party.

Shawn was astounded himself. He did not even think of ever meeting her. He presumed it was completely over. After almost a year he landed up in her 25th Birthday. Damn, he thought.

Why don't I go for a foot massage myself? Let me take the advantage of this, she considered. Ria went to the corner of the poolside where she had set up the spa arrangements. Respiring, she took her red wine and was doing her foot massage. No one ever knew about her and Shawn, except for Denise.

She wanted to weep. Her eyes were teary and she was trying so hard to be normal. She felt she was crying out loud in her heart. She asked herself, "When people talk out loud someone can listen to them, it is like when you confide or share something with friends. What about when you speak out loud in your mind? Who is listening to your pain, or plead, who is listening?" She conceived, "Is it Karma? Oh crap, I should calm down."

After a few minutes, she thought about it again, who is willing to share the time to listen? Someone get me out of this night? Everything seems to be unfair. Please! She contemplated.

For the first time she was not feeling relaxed while doing her foot massage. It was only an excuse to disappear for forty minutes. Soon the cake-cutting ceremony would start and the belly dancers would begin their show, she recalled. She yearned to be liberated.

The night did bring different moments for the four leading people. Ryan, Miguel, Genelia and Ria. Each of them had their individual desires from life. Their emotions were being mixed well, which was no less than a colorful cocktail.

For Ryan and Genelia some things were blossoming and gearing toward a mysterious ride.

For Ria, it was a small world where old flames ignited.

She was not so worried about Shawn as much as she was feeling uncomfortable seeing Miguel with his girlfriend. She wanted to have wine shots, hoping her mind would not torture her heart.

Ryan joined Genelia for pasta. She could not stop eating and was savoring the pesto black pepper Fusilli. He simply looked at her and thought this was the best day to ask her out on a date.

He escorted her to the Gazebo on the second floor. She loved it. It was made with Italian contemporary décor surrounded by candles and flowers.

The light illuminated the Gazebo with shaded and soft light, making it more evocative and clandestine. The décor of the party went well with the theme of exotic spa lounge.

Genelia wore a white satin sequined dress. Her hair was tied up into a bun, wearing round blue sapphire hoops. She looked elegant.

"Frankly, Genelia we need to talk. I have been trying this for a while, now."

"Why are you hesitant, Ryan?" asked Genelia

"I am not hesitant, but want to make it special for you, so I am thinking of how to do this," replied Ryan.

"Why? What are you going to do?" asked Genelia innocently.

No one could see them, not even Ria. She was right on the other end surrounded by loud music doing her foot massage.

"So what is it? You're freaking me out?" asked Genelia.

"Genelia, this trip was quite an amazing experience. The slums, the rain, the games and even the attitude between us were not so pleasant. It still brought way to new friendship. I would like to move one step ahead. Don't worry, I am not asking you to marry me, yet. Fine jokes apart. Would you go on a date with me?"

Genelia was staring at him listening to every word he said with style, in his British accent. Eventhough Ryan was a little nervous, he expressed the unexpressed emotion. He was so honest as his eyes shining under the stars. She smiled then giggled. She looked at him blankly for a few seconds, got up and stood beside the flower pot to catch some fresh air. Maybe I am being silly, who said this was love. I hadn't experience anything as yet, maybe he wouldn't even be the one, and it was just a date, she marveled. She could sense something so beautiful was in front of her. She saw a handsome man and a perfect scenario.

*****

Ria was still having her foot massage. Simmy called out her name several times, but she did not hear it. So she went over to tell her, "When you are done, we shall do the cake cutting. The belly dancers are here. They will start when you get down."

"Fine, will be there in twenty minutes," said Ria with apprehension.

As Simmy went down, Shawn paced up the stairs. He was looking for Ria. He wanted to talk to her. Then he spotted her. He commented, "Ria, is that you there." She opened her eyes, her lower lip turned down, and she took her wine glass and turned around. She wanted to be salvaged, not be put in flames, she thought.

"Oh, so you are having a massage, remember the time we or I accidentally went into the spa room and you were there. What a scene!" said Shawn emphatically.

The last thing she wanted was a flashback, and then she said, "Yes, Shawn that was a scene. So, how have you been?"

"I have been good. Training can be tough. Seriously, how are you doing? It was a surprise to see you today."

"Why ask now, Shawn. I am absolutely fine. We all have moved on. You have become history for me. Today was a surprise. I guess…we were meant to meet," Ria said confidently.

"I am happy you moved on. That was the best for us and I apologize for not keeping in touch. Anyway, how is dentistry going on?" asked Shawn.

"It is great. I am going to complete it soon and participate in workshops, so there would be a lot of traveling. All cool stuff," said Ria boldly.

"We can still stay friends, right," said Shawn politely.

"Yes we can. As far as I remember, you did mention about always being a friend. I tried keeping in touch but..."reminded Ria with optimism.

Ria thought, she could be friends with all the men in the world. She was happy that he spoke. Even after so long! Destiny got us back to nothing, but a normal acquaintance.

"Do you want a foot massage?" asked Ria.

"Yes. Thanks, but wouldn't mind a shoulder massage for couple of minutes," opted Shawn and added, "Ria just to let you know I am glad we met. It is always for a right reason. I never wanted to hurt you and you were always special and will always be."

"I got that. Thanks for the update. Let's talk about today. Any dating?"asked Ria curiously.

"Well, yes I met someone in Canada. We are getting to know each other. She is nice. I feel the compatibility," conveyed Shawn.

"Good! And perhaps it was better to say a few words to feel at ease, I suppose. I shall see you soon downstairs," said Ria politely. She began to calm down and realized destiny brought the moment to settle down her grudge towards him.

"Thanks and will catch up with you soon," said Shawn pleasantly. While Ria went to the rest-room, Ryan waited anxiously. He waited for a couple of minutes for Genelia's answer.

After some careful thought, Genelia turned around, looked at him and said, "Yes, we will go for a date. It is just a date." He was so glad and ecstatic.

His upper lip raised and he hugged her saying, "Thanks for making this evening more special."

"If I had said no, would it not have been a special night?" asked Genelia.

"No, the night was already special when I saw you, it became more special when you acknowledged," stated Ryan.

She began to blush and said, "Stop, we should go down."

The next thing Genelia knew she was in his arms and his soft lips kissed her shoulders, her neck and her lips. She quivered and he let go.

"What happened?"asked Ryan.

"Don't know, just a sensation maybe," uttered Genelia.

He knew it. She was shy. He kissed her again. He liked the taste of her fruity lip-gloss with a tint of pesto flavorings.

She was surprised and could not believe she actually agreed to it. She sensed she was caught up in inferno. He was so warm.

She kissed someone after a few years and had forgotten how it felt. He was so gentle and it instigated a new feeling. She was glad she followed her heart. He hugged her with so much affection, his hand running on her back and later he took both his hands and put it on her cheeks. They were warm and comforting.

"Genelia, I will let you know tomorrow about our date details. Let's get back to the party," said Ryan. He was swept away with a foretaste of affectionate indulgence and was waiting to tell Ria about it.

Ria opened the door and was stepping down to the party. She had a word with the belly dancers to start their show. She was back with her friends and she sure did know how to poise herself wholeheartedly.

Miguel glared at Ria from a distance. It was a strange look that showed he was not satisfied with something. He went up to her to take a few pictures. He murmured in her ears, "Seems like you and Shawn are tight buddies."

Balance in life was a tricky thing. Every time she thought she had a solid position it had a way of throwing her. She stared at him and said, "What are you talking about? You are thinking too much, I guess. Shall we cut the cake? Mom is waiting, too."

She acknowledged Ryan's benevolence, "I really appreciate your help, photographer."

"No worries. It is my pleasure, and by the way she said yes. Genelia and I are going on a date," updated Ryan cheerfully. Ria was baffled and pleased for Ryan at the same time. What's happening here? She thought. She was receiving news after news, like a thunderbolt was falling over. She squeezed him saying, "Cool."

"Tomorrow Ria, I will talk to you about it. Your party is rocking. Something is in the air. It kind of worked out. I did not want to be repentant about not asking her out, since I really like her," said Ryan.

Ria began talking to Genelia. She liked Ria's nature and passed a flattering remark, "I am glad to have met you. Very rarely I meet people who are themselves and of course fun to be with."

"Ladies and men, fine, friends and sexy ladies...we have entertainment tonight," announced Simmy. Everyone turned back and the belly dancing continued.

"It seems like the artist put every color on the canvas following every beat. This is awesome!" commented Ryan. The rhythm of music captured everyone's emotion and attention artfully.

She turned around and saw Ryan and Genelia talking to each other. Shawn was talking to Austin and Miguel was standing alone beside the kebab corner. She was wondering where the Canadian babe went.

She asked him, "Why are you here? Join us there."

"It is fine. I am cool here," said Miguel.

"Where is Alysia?" asked Ria.

"Oh, she just left. She had other formalities," said Miguel.

"By the way, she is pretty and quite friendly," praised Ria.

"Thanks, but I did not ask," said Miguel insolently.

Ria was already having a challenging night and without a pause she said, "What is wrong with you? Did a ghost just settle in your brain? I have noticed you have been weird."

She turned back, looking in front and Miguel caught her arm apologizing, "I am sorry. It's your day. You deserve the best."

He stood with her and did not want to create any scene that would upset her. He wanted to tell her that he overheard the conversation with Shawn.

He began to feel strange even knowing he was already

dating. Let's see how this irresistible saga would continue to haunt us, wondered Miguel.

The night is mystifying and I am feeling puzzled, contemplated Ria.

Sentiments, adoration, confusion, and ambition of making life meaningful was all seen and felt that night.

Genelia was mesmerized by Ryan. She felt the somersaults after he asked her out. Her mind was going 'Twing Tang, Twing Tang repeatedly.'

14

The Irresistible Saga Continues

Miguel volunteered to dance with the belly dancers. The cake was cut, confetti was in the air, and the air was getting breezier.

The DJ started off with some peppy songs. The party went up to four in the morning, until it started pouring. Miguel confirmed coffee with Ria the following day.

Ryan was already thinking how he could make the evening special for Genelia.

That night Ryan had asked Ria for some places that would be memorable for a first date. She recommended a five star meal, gave him her discount card and allowed him to have the driver for their night. Ryan was excited. He bought a stylish candle holder for Genelia and was planning the rest of the evening with elegance. On the other hand, Miguel was waiting discreetly to catch up with Ria.

After work, he told Alysia that he had to meet Ria for coffee at six. Alysia kissed him and continued with her work.

When Miguel met Ria, they spoke about many things.

"I acknowledge the gratitude for making it yesterday," expressed Ria.

"Ria, I have something to tell you. Yesterday, I overheard everything between you and Shawn. I was looking for you and when I walked up to the pool side...you know. Why didn't you ever mention anything?" asked Miguel.

"I was not supposed to discuss past relationships. I mean, I don't think it was important to speak about my personal relationships that were history and share it with you," remarked Ria.

"Why?" Miguel insisted.

"You have never said anything about yourself. We are good friends, not best buddies or let's say I did not feel comfortable about it," said Ria deliberately.

Ria was just releasing her frustration. She realized she was being a 'J.' She usually used 'J' as an initial that symbolized *Jealousy*. She created that short term when she was in high school. She would love to share with Miguel, but did not find the need to do so. He listened to her curt comments attentively.

"I am pleased that we are atleast friends, being close buddies will be shaped someday," anticipated Miguel.

She emphasized to Miguel, "Yes, maybe. You shall be leaving soon, too. Anyway, how is Alysia?"

"I don't want to talk about her right now. She is fine," uttered Miguel.

Ria got up and sat next to him. She told him briefly about Shawn and he spoke about work stress. He watched her speak and did feel something for her but could never figure it out. He could not get his eyes off her.

So for the time being he ignored how he felt. The game was going to be interesting, he thought. Then he realized, why am I thinking about all this? Alysia is who I should be thinking about, and smiled.

"Ria, it was good catching up. I shall make the most till I am here." He hugged her tightly for a few seconds and told her, "You smell good today."

She pushed him away and demanded in a jovial manner, "Go have dinner with Alysia." Her windows of the heart were sealed temporarily from feeling anything romantic.

When she was home, she had mentioned about coffee with Miguel to Ryan. He was ready to leave for his date and wanted to make the moment extraordinary, unique and unforgettable.

When Ryan left, she went for a hot shower. She turned with a start of consternation to find her worst fears realized. She was driven back to her flashbacks at the party, and was thinking about Miguel. She promised herself - that she would be happy for others.

Perhaps this was all meant to be, she wondered. She made good friends and they met their special butterflies. She named their companions, butterflies. She indicated a companion as a butterfly because of the vibrant aura and love he or she would bring into his or her partner's life. With that moment, everything is magical, emotional, and worth every pain of pleasure, she thought.

She was smiling as tears rolled down her eyes. She considered focusing only on her career and was never making a U-turn. She knew she was alone, but not lonely. She decided she shall get back to Singapore in a few days and work on the workshops.

Temporarily, Genelia was meeting Ryan directly at the venue and felt shy and edgy. She hoped the night would be yuppie and yummy. She was surely getting naughty in her thoughts.

She waited in the lobby swinging her phone around. Ryan was a guest. He would be leaving soon...no point taking any risk for a new adventure, she contemplated.

She heard an inner voice telling her, "Life is an adventure silly. You are always at risk. One must take pleasure in the menace. If you did not want to take any danger, what the hell are you doing at the hotel lobby right now?"That inner voice did bring the practical thinking in her.

In the spur moment, Ryan arrived with white and yellow flowers. He did not want her to misinterpret anything as yet, so taking it slow would be the best thing to do, he considered.

He wore a black shirt with a maroon tie and Genelia was wearing a lilac halter dress with lace surrounded at the end of the border. The lilac halter dress was below her knee with side slits. She looked chic with panache, he thought.

He gave her the flowers and accompanied her to the open air terrace restaurant. Being on the 20th floor, the view from the restaurant was spectacular, and dazzling. The entrance of the restaurant had two giant blue and white crystal chandeliers.

As they entered, the color of the lighting changed dimly and slowly into four colors of yellow, light blue, pink and white making the restaurant look like an oil painting. The weather was pleasant so they sat outside.

They ordered chilled white wine and fried ravioli chips with the cream of lobster dip. It was the specialty of the place. The second appetizer Ryan ordered was an almond mushroom fish cake with avocado dressing served with potato wedges that was suggested by Ria.

They spoke about the campaign and their experiences of being part of this social crusade. "Hey Ryan, the fish cake is scrumptious. I like the taste of almonds," complimented Genelia. Ryan noticed the joy on her face when she saw food.

"You were saying about your diner. Cool, people in London also love Indian food. So, how often you ate at the diners?"

"Actually, I hardly eat there. I eat at home, or sometimes with my close buddy, Mark. We have our beer days and talk about stuff," stated Ryan.

At some point there was a pause. Genelia was out of words and wondered what to say next. Then they both popped a word, Genelia with movies and Ryan with sports. They laughed and spoke about both the aspects.

The appetizers were filling, so Genelia opted to order soup and Ryan ordered something with fish. It was a coincident that he spoke about Mark and he called. Ryan spoke to him for a bit but did not tell him he was out on a date. He thought of updating him when he got back.

Genelia popped a question, "So anything exciting cooking for your future plans?"

"Interesting question, I am figuring it out. There are some plans, but it is good to go with a flow and it is better not to have any advance planning. What about you?" expressed Ryan.

Genelia thought that was informative, and confided, "Remember, I had told you about a business proposal in Ayurvedic medicines. I have passed with my comprehensive exams and now I have plans to open a small Ayurvedic treatment boutique associated with an educational digital library by next year 2011."

"That's interesting! I'm looking forward to your creation," said Ryan.

"Yes, me too," pointed out Genelia. They cracked up and Ryan praised her with a great sense of humor.

As their date was coming to an end, he studied her with quiet insolence. He wanted to ask her if their relationship would be able to continue further and considering it being long-distance.

Genelia looked at her watch. Eventhough she was having a good time, she was feeling sleepy. She yawned but luckily Ryan did not see that. When he drove her back home, he was thinking of his question. He wanted to continue this moment of happiness.

He liked watching at her chatter. She was glamorous, insightful and talkative. All he could think was, "I like you a lot and I think I am going to fall in love with you. He did not say that aloud knowing Genelia would freak out.

She got off the car and told him, "I had a great time and thanks for the dinner." He gave her the candle holder. When she opened it, she was fascinated.

She thanked him and complimented, "Wow, it is really good. Thanks again," and hugged him goodnight.

He did not let go off her, although she wanted to leave.

"I have to ask you something. Don't be nervous. Calm down, and let lose a little sweety," said Ryan calmly.

She felt ticklish in her left ear, so she shut her eyes. Ryan added, "I really like you. What do you think if we carry on further? I know you might be thinking negative about long-distance, but today technology has become so friendly for couples, too. We can definitely work things out."

He slowly moved his head upward and kissed her cheek and let go off her. Genelia's eyes were still shut. "Tell me what's on your mind. I really want to know," asked Ryan with apprehension. She opened her eyes and was silent for a few seconds.

"I need some time to think about this," appealed Genelia. For that moment she never thought Ryan would ask anything like carrying it on further. Her past relationship broke up because of long distance.

She added, "That is so sweet. I know you are leaving in three days. I will let you know."

"Please let me know by tomorrow evening. This is the moment where we can't make hasty decisions but we can't take too long either. Even the three days left, I would like to spend every single day with you," requested Ryan.

"Ryan, it is not easy to maintain long distance. Even though there is technology, phones and stuff. My last relationship did not work out because of this," addressed Genelia.

"Well, I am not concerned about what happened in the past. Maybe he did not like you enough to want to make it work. I feel we are different. We are not kids, and no pressure sweetie. Think about it," said Ryan affectionately.

"Thanks," spoke Genelia with irony.

She kissed him goodnight and did not want to be condemnatory. She was definitely going to think about it.

He sat in the car and he was wondering what she would say. At that point he got upset that she was ready to consider it history. Conceivably, after having time to think she might change her mind.

When Genelia was in her room, she felt like she wanted to throw up. She was feeling so heavy and anxious. "Who said making a decision less than 24 hours was not hasty? It is," she was thinking out loud.

She felt the pressure and could not sleep, so she went for a drive. She switched on loud music and was having her midnight snack.

She thought continuously and sensed her head was going to explode only thinking Yes or No. She felt like she was becoming a thinking machine, which was soon overflowing. She did not know what to say. She did like Ryan a lot, but feared that if she said yes, then she would lose all her ways of fulfilling her ambition.

Tick tock, tick tock. The time was flying.

In contrast, for some people simply saying yes or no was so hard, and for some people dating was fun, a hang out, or even having sex was a casual thing in a relationship. As for Genelia it was so difficult. She felt she was going to choke.

Similarly, Miguel was not that person who would think of commitments. A full-time pledge was just not in his books. Nevertheless, he knew one thing, if he really fell in love he would never fall out of it. He and Alysia had dated for two months now. He liked her and knew he was enjoying every bit of it.

Hours passed and Genelia had to meet Ryan for coffee. She was so sure she would say no and stick to that. But when they met, he looked so hot with slight hair on his chin. He wore a white t-shirt and blue denims. She predicted he did not shave as he was so eager to know what her answer would be. It was obvious to her.

"So, Genelia how are you? Slept well?" asked Ryan flirtatiously.

"No," Genelia answered.

She wanted to smack him for making her feel so uneasy. But she tried to be polite as she was going to say no. She was at the crossroads and did not want to make any wrong decision.   Genelia continued saying, "I had some stuff to do last night and also met a friend regarding discussion about some project."

"Oh, don't tell me at midnight you were over a friend's home. Wow you're assiduous," teased Ryan.

"What's that? Sorry please use simple vocabs," taunted Genelia.

Ryan did not clarify about the vocabulary. He got up to buy coffee and a walnut brownie. She could not even eat and waited to run away from there.

He brought the coffee and sat next to her. His cologne fragrance, his arm brushing hers and his eyes…how could she say no? He did not ask her anything as yet. He filled her in about Ria heading back to Singapore in a few days. Austin was leaving that night and he had delayed two days, so that he could spend some time with her. From the way he spoke, she felt too mean and excused herself.

She went to the rest room and felt like banging her head on the wall. She took a deep breath and was back. She was twirling her hair and listened to Ryan talk.

He held her hand. She ignored both the reprimand, and the way the slight growl in his voice touched something deep within. She felt goose bumps, and her heart's pulsation started increasing again.

"So, what have you thought Genelia?" asked Ryan.

She looked away, and he came closer, putting his right hand on her shoulder giving her a side hug. She could not resist…she controlled so much and said, "No -

I really can't do this. I mean we can," said Genelia restlessly.

Ryan said timorously, "You are confusing me, and remember I will still be here for you no matter what."

After a pause, Genelia confessed, "I say yes, Ryan. I was going to say no, but couldn't."

Out of happiness, he conceded, "You're serious! I am lucky today, then." He kissed her hand. He added, "Now these few days are for you my baby."

She ignored her negative thoughts and appreciated the moment. They went for a movie, and savored typical Indian cuisine. Genelia took him for a tour around Mumbai for a few days.

Whilst Ryan was happy dating, Ria was making a few phone calls. She had planned that when she returned back to Singapore; she would come back and participate in the workshops in Mumbai itself. Ria believed, sooner or later Mumbai would be her permanent address. It did not matter if one did not meet the true companion. What mattered the most was running away from the situation. She did not want to do that anymore.

*****

Ria contemplated many things and wanted to manifest life on her own terms. She was notified about the workshops going to be held at schools, universities and villages in Mumbai. She had a meeting with the executives who were arranging a dental conference for dental hygiene.

During her break she came down to the coffee shop with some executives for lunch. As she entered the lift she saw Miguel. She could see him smooching Alysia.

She was stunned and looked away. They were so into each other, she wondered. She had no clue Miguel worked in the same office building. He stopped when he saw many people entering the lift. He also glanced at Ria, but she was looking at another direction.

Miguel wondered, why didn't she say hello?

Why do I have to see this? Thought Ria. She sighed and got out with the rest.

Miguel called out her name. She turned and excused herself for a few minutes. "So someone doesn't want to talk," criticized Miguel.

She looked away and said, "Please keep your romance out of the lift then. I did not know you guys work in this building. Anyway, I really have to go, have a meeting so will see you later, enjoy lunch." He simply saw her leave in a hurry.

After lunch, Ria went to buy peach lemon tea. She saw Alysia smoking and talking to Miguel. A few seconds later, they kissed and parted. He went back inside the office building.

Ria had entered the supermarket. She bought the peach lemon tea and as she walked out of the store, she bumped into Miguel.

"Hey petite, watch for yourself - and are you okay?" inquired Miguel with worry.

"Oops, I am fine and in a hurry. See you later," said Ria hesitantly. She paced toward the right, he moved right, she turned left, he moved left. Ria got exasperated and said intrepidly, "Stop it okay."

"Hey, want to meet for dinner tonight?" asked Miguel.

"No, you don't have to make plans only when you see me. I am busy," said Ria bluntly. She did not know how to react to him.

She was trying to be happy for him, and wanted to be left alone, not being a sandwich between him and his Canadian babe.

She was back in her meeting. Miguel had texted her, but she did not reply to him. He called her twice and she did not answer. The meeting went on for a few hours. She enrolled for the programme and was leaving the premises.

When she got into the elevator, she was glad she met no one. She paced briskly and waited for her car outside the building.

While waiting for her car, Miguel got out of another elevator. He could see her walk so fast, so he ran after her and called her, "Ria."

She did not hear him. He caught hold of her hair, and she turned around wondering, which weirdo it was?

Ria said brusquely, "You couldn't just be more violent. Why are you pulling my hair?"

"I am sorry. I was in a hurry...you leaving?" asked Miguel.

"What do you see? I was just getting into car," spoke Ria frankly.

"I need a ride," he blurted out.

"Fine, where to?" said Ria.

"Let's sit. I will tell you," persisted Miguel. He did not know where he wanted to go. He wanted to pick a fight with her for ignoring his call but when he saw her - he said nothing.

He sat with her in the car and told her, "I need to buy something for Alysia. I need a ride to the nearest department store. Thanks, you're so kind."

She wanted to vanish but couldn't.

"How was your meeting? What's the scene?" asked Miguel.

"Nothing much, I enrolled for the dental and hygiene workshops that will be held in various cities in India.

Besides, what are you buying for Alysia? What's the occasion?" questioned Ria.

"No occasion. When you like someone, you like buying gifts. You know it comes from within," described Miguel. He felt silly telling her that. At the same time he did not want to say much. He just wanted to spend time with her forgetting the rest of the world.

Ria looked away because she could see his flirtatious eyes. Miguel was coming closer. She turned her head and watched him admiringly. She tried to be normal and asked, "How come you are sitting too close to me? Scoot away!"

"What's up with your strange behavior?" asked Miguel.

She complained, "Damn, it's raining, oh the traffic." She could not understand why she could not sit next to him when she was alone with him. She felt so uncomfortable.

"You are too quiet. So do you want to grab a coffee? It is raining, there is traffic and looks like I have no chance to reach the shopping mall. We are simply stuck in the rain, Ria."

"I don't want anything," said Ria crisply.

She took out her shawl, wrapped it around her, and shut her eyes pretending she was going to sleep. He looked at every move, and was just staring at her with ardor. If he really did feel something for her, what was he waiting for? He wondered.

Miguel remembered the first time he met her when they went for the road trip. The big scene between her and Simmy was an over rated drama. Then he stayed back with her. Today, the prospect was similar; he saw her and was doing crazy things again.

The traffic started moving slowly and Miguel was getting agitated. He tapped her shoulder and said, "You are seriously sleeping. We are going for coffee, and don't be boring."

She thought she was never boring, but being with him made her behave in that manner. She went with the flow.

After the traffic was moving, the driver stopped at the nearest café. While Miguel walked back toward the car with two cups of coffee, a man with the motorcycle drove passed him. Water was splashed on his jeans and the coffee fell.

Ria laughed out loud in the car. Eventually, she got out of the car and went out to buy another cup of coffee with him. She got wet in the rain. She paced toward him, her hair slightly getting wet. Miguel was admiring her.

"That was a big scene out there, Miguel. You looked liked this child whose ice-cream fell and was feeling devastated," teased Ria.

"Oh, so you were watching the whole scene. I thought someone wanted a nap," spoke Miguel with a sly attitude.

"Well I thought someone said I was boring," said Ria giving a cheeky smile.

They bought the coffee and drank it looking at the rain drops falling down the window pane. Ria's mood was pleasant. She laughed, made fun of other people getting wet in the rain.

"Ria, come with me for dinner after this or may be a movie," invited Miguel. He was simply speaking what he was feeling.

She panicked and asked hastily, "What? Are you crazy? What about your Canadian babe?" She instantly realized she should have not brought up Alysia and walked out of the café. She could not help it.

He followed her and was surprised with her statement. "Where did that come from?" asked Miguel.

"Slip of tongue. Just a casual comment," said Ria.

"No, you definitely meant something. You're sarcastic. I noticed even at your birthday party you were different and not very pleased," commented Miguel.

He came closer and peculiarly adding, "What it is? I feel and I know you're feeling something. You get snappy and then go silent. Seriously, what is it?"

"Stop assuming. I think we should get going. It is late and I have loads to do," spoke Ria candidly.

She took a few steps ahead and he pulled her back. She fell backwards on his chest. She hit her head hard on him. "Ria, why is it today I feel it is a very eccentric and discomfited day for both of us. I guess not even today, but ever since we met, something has been different," depicted Miguel.

Her heartbeat was thumping so fast, nothing like this happened before, not even with Shawn. Ria was out of words. She was hoping everything got back to a normal state. Unexpectedly, Miguel eulogized her saying, "You are pretty when you laugh. I am not joking or flirting. You are what you are."

Luckily the rain had calmed down, so why not Miguel's behavior, considered Ria. She felt awkward and told Miguel, "I need to head back home."

"Really, what about for a change you don't rush back and do something for you," said Miguel.

"What do you mean, Miguel?"

"Have you ever thought of having a relationship after Shawn?" inquired Miguel.

"Well, Umm…not really, why?" said Ria suddenly. She was not feeling too good about his actions and questions.

He slowly held her wrist and was looking down toward her eyes. Ria was avoiding eye contact, and was trying to get him leave her wrist. But he was gazing intently at her eyes and movements. She did not understand why he was not letting go.

The rain had stopped. The cool breeze was blowing through Ria's hair. The cold water was running through her feet, and there was a drop of water trickling down her face.

Miguel left her wrist and gently brushed his finger on her cheek removing the water drop. Ria was still avoiding any eye contact.

Then for a split second she looked at him, only that one second, one look, one moment of feeling so close to him. She was battling with her emotions.

That whole situation and moment may have seemed wrong because he was dating. He had a girlfriend. But still, it did not bother her, she could not resist, she did look at him. His firm physique, his expressive eyes, and noticed that he was coming closer, tilting downward.

Oh no, is he planning to kiss me? No, this can't be happening…thought Ria.

She moved one step backward, and felt his hands behind her back. He was drawing her closer to him. She wanted to kick him or pinch him but she could not move. She felt she had frozen at that moment.

Momentarily, their lips brushed a whispered hint of a touch like a butterfly's caress. He pulled back slightly looking into her eyes and she could see a glimpse of the devil in disguise.

She moved her face away. Miguel touched her warm face and leaned back toward her lips. Her eyes were opened, she wanted to scream, his eyes slowly shut, and he kissed her gently making her eyes shut.

The kiss lasted for a few seconds. His touch was surprisingly gentle, no more than a brushing of two fingertips that made brief contact with the side of her face. Later, just a touch on her soft cheek that trailed lightly down her chin and then withdrew.

Miguel was a good kisser, considered Ria. She felt she was in no position to feel that way and flatter herself. Even while the prevailing belief, she had to block out all other sensations.

She gasped aloud and jerked away. She pushed him. "You have a girlfriend. Oh no, and you are cheating on her," said Ria regretfully.

"Ria, I am not cheating. Umm...yes. I am so sorry. It was perhaps just a kiss," said Miguel unexpectedly.

He did not know what he was saying. He had gotten barmy and was truly being wacky. He felt a strong connection toward her that he had no control of his words.

After hearing what Miguel said, Ria felt the kiss took her self-esteem, and her guts away from her.

"Miguel, this was so wrong. You are strange and I was a fool. I should have..." and added, "You're not coming with me. Find your way back home or Timbuktu. It's your problem, you weirdo."

She ran toward the car leaving him behind. She felt idiotic and did not know what happened to her. She could have just stayed back in the car.

It was so courageous to plan to come back here and now I feel I put myself in the rubbish dump knowing that there was garbage. What was I messing with, my heart, she thought.

Miguel saw her leave. His ego had diminished and the culpability was looming. She was right! I am a crackpot and shit...marveled Miguel.

15
CHAPTER

The Wishing Well

Ria and Miguel bounced to a new problem. Ria wished if she
could redesign her life patterns. Genelia began to face the
reality and tried her best to fulfill her mother's desires. Ryan
heads back to London and faces unexpected silence and
difficulties.

The moment of an eternal and a faithful mistake surely
brought Miguel into a hot soup. He was left in the middle
of doing something he was not supposed to.

Ria was in tears of happiness, she wished. She knew
Miguel was dating and got attracted to something that
was never going to make sense, she believed.

She was carried away in the moment of adoration and
couldn't resist a charming man. The kiss with a warm
questing tenderness persuaded her – for the barest of
moments – to indulge in a moment of a fairy tale world.

She hated the feeling of letting go off someone whom
she thought she had feelings for. She contemplated with
thoughts that everyone always wished, hoped, and had
longed for all sorts of things. But who knows where the
wishes fell into. Which kind of well: *the forgotten well, the*
screwed up Karma well, ask again next life well, the delay well or
the make true well.

Where did my wishes fall into, or did anyone know about my wishes? Was anyone taking an account? What about any good deeds I ever did? What could be the results? Perhaps my hopes or wishes fell into the delay or forgotten well, wondered Ria.

Usually she was a logical person, and so when insights came her way she had a doubt of her validity. She was hoping not to fall into the trap and felt devastated. The feeling was predominantly strong. She knew it, life wasn't always that predictable, or else everyone would just get what they wanted, anytime. She had to trust her instincts, and enjoy the pleasure that did come her way for a short period of time. She was still where she was, and realized she was going to Singapore for a while before the workshops started. She needed a change, she believed.

Miguel needed a transformation at that moment, too. He messed up big time, he thought. He waited there for a while and bought another cup of coffee. He took every nip of it regretting how he hurt her.

He stood there for a while feeling perturbed. He could not get a taxi, so he got into the auto rickshaw. The faster he wanted to reach his apartment; it was delayed because of the traffic. The driver tried to change lanes so he could get to the destination on time.

Miguel sent a long text message to Ria: *Please don't torture yourself for something that did mean so much at that moment. It was a moment of bliss and unity of people who realized something was missing in their life. I am sorry if I offended you, ur friend alwayz, Miguel.*

He wanted to call her after a few days, considering everything would be fine by then. Ria sent him a text back: *A bad mistake! Will meet you before you leave to Chicago...let's see*

Why I even replied to him, she thought. She felt she saw a ray of hope, but everything turned into a wet blanket. She tried to be neutral but couldn't. Miguel sensed Ria's reactions by the way she texted back. He was relieved that she did text back. He knew what he had told her was different from what he felt.

The breeze was so pleasant. He shut his eyes, and all

he could think of was Ria. He did feel blameworthy, but at the same time the pleasure and sensation of a new emotion had risen. He could not distinguish it.

A few minutes later, the driver had to make a u-turn. He did not notice a truck coming his way.

Because of poor judgment, there was an accident. The auto rickshaw over turned. Miguel flew out of the auto rickshaw and slid. The driver hit his head and leg badly. Miguel hurt his left arm shoddily and there was a loud sound of his bone cracking.

Fortunately, the police had arrived on time and took a statement. The truck driver denied his fault, and with the delay of ambulance, Miguel became unconscious for a few hours.

Hours later, he gained consciousness. He was having difficulty in moving his left arm and his legs. He was in a state of shock and confusion. At that moment, he felt the kiss with Ria was a bad pay off.

He was glad he did not turn blind or deaf. He told the nurse to call Tanish, his cousin for further formalities. Miguel had his health insurance covered. The doctor discussed his issue and informed him, "You need complete rest, as your spinal cord seems to be affected. I am sorry to say but your left hand is semi-paralyzed. You may feel the numbness right now, and we shall see what treatments can be done to ease the pain from the accident. You won't be able to move your left hand the way you used to. It will take a lot of time to heal. By the way, are you a left-handed person?"

"No, but this is bad news," startled Miguel and asked with fear, "What about the driver, is he fine?"

The doctor said, "His right hand was amputated. He is under observation and is doing fine." Miguel assumed that the doctor was crazy with the way he described everything so casually. That man's hand was chopped, and he says he is fine. What a jerk? considered Miguel.

The doctor continued, "The driver will be able to get back to his routine in a few months. He will be shifted to the government hospital in two days. Let's continue with you now."

Miguel was speechless and confounded. The blunt nature of the doctor made him miserable. He was given pain killers, so he could sleep for a few hours. When he woke up, the doctor reported, "You are lucky. You are alive and can still do everything independently in a couple of months.

"I was leaving back to the States at the end of October," said Miguel.

"Young man, your test reports say that for now you need to be here in the hospital for two weeks because of your legs and you can slowly start walking using a walking stick. That should take maybe a month or two. You need to wear a cast on your shoulder for the bone, and need therapy for your back and legs. This will take a couple of months," the doctor said with care.

Miguel was disheartened. He did not want to stay too long in India anymore. The thought of Ria, Alysia and his accident made him aloof.

Two days later, after careful observation and tests, the doctor informed, "After three to five months of therapy you shall recover from this. As for your legs, you need physical therapy. There is a knee swelling and some internal bruises."

He heard to a chain of injuries that got him feeling giddy. He puked.

"Don't worry. You will be able to walk again in a few months, and possibly you shall be jogging someday, soon," pacified the doctor. Miguel had undergone a surgery and after a week from surgery his physical therapy had started.

With regular therapy, two weeks had passed and he was enduring with the thought to walk again. Tanish arrived. He was so happy to see Miguel getting in good shape. All the other days that he visited, he noticed Miguel being quite temperamental.

Tanish was told that Miguel's blood pressure was quite low. When he opened his eyes with trepidation, everything looked blurry and slowly things began to come into focus. He asked Tanish for a favor, "Please don't say a word about this to anyone. It has been two weeks and I am alive. I mean you have told my parents that I had a small accident, and I am fit and fine. Stick to that! I don't want any chaos as mom seems to be fine when I spoke to her. Tanish I am in an awful situation. I feel messed up and I just need some time before I start to socialize." His teary eyes showed the pain he was going through.

Alysia called Miguel as she waited in his apartment thinking he would be discharged. Tanish told her the situation and she went back home. She said she would visit him the next morning. Miguel found it strange as she could have come to spend some time with him at the hospital, he wondered.

*****

Conversely, for some people happiness was just sweeping their feet. Emotions of being flirty, playful and naughty were soon coming to a break. Ryan was on his way to the airport with Genelia.

She felt so low and an awkward sentiment was troubling her. When she had said yes, she thought in a matter of few days he would leave and she would break it off. However, this time she was sure she was in no position to utter anything. She had developed feelings for him.

She was actually falling in love. She and Ryan named, 'Long Distance Relationship, the LDR.' She was never good in handling an LDR, for this one, she wanted to give it a shot, why not, and how bad could it be, she thought. The only option she wanted was yes, yes and yes.

Ryan got out his luggage, and asked Genelia, "Want to have some cozy time at the café?" "Sure," she agreed.

The growing heat and pain of him going was beginning to hit her. She was feeling sick, very warm and felt like she was having a migraine. Genelia got the cappuccinos and sat down. She noticed Ryan looking at her, he took out a CD and told her, "This is a DVD, whenever you miss me, watch me."

"Wow! This is cool, Ryan," cheered Genelia.

He added, "LDR's can be a pain but there are so many

ways to make your loved one feel special. Oh, by the way, some tips were taken from the internet," and he winked.

Genelia blushed and with her soft voice she said, "That's fine, atleast the effort is certainly appreciated. Ryan, how long is the video?"

"Watch it and find out, Genelia!"

"By the way, we are going to have a date every week. Simple, we shall meet online, eat and chat together. The rest is a surprise," explained Ryan.

Genelia could see the effort being put by Ryan.

"I am so glad I came here. These are my contact details. Oh, take this, this is for you too," said Ryan enthusiastically.

He had bought her a crystal pendant with a silver chain from Swarovski. He came closer to her and put it for her. She felt a ticklish sensation.

He was taking every glimpse of her. She radiated an astonishing sensuousness of such a degree that he just could not take his eyes off her. She looked pristine, cheerful and pure. He hugged her, and she wanted to cry for a change. His love for her was so cute. She could not express anything but felt she was already missing him. They both looked at each other. Their mutual visual interaction became intense. Passion swelled swiftly. Her eyes became teary naturally and she confessed it, "I will miss you."

She added, "I like the idea of dating every week. I shall watch this DVD often. We will call each other atleast once daily," and she stammered saying, "Never imagined that such a trivial experience would give me so much pleasure into my life. Do you remember the first time we met? I so wanted to kill you. But today, I feel I have been mesmerized with the genuine sensation of...a strong liking."

Deep down, she learnt that there was an invasion of her private space. But she did not mind sharing her space with him.

She became all quiet. He had to leave. He took his stuff and they did their goodbyes at the café. He kissed her cheeks and left...leaving her in deep shit trouble.

Now a volcano would erupt for both us. How would we handle the LDR? That was something to see in its own time, considered Genelia.

Genelia quickly took a tissue paper and wrote a short note for Ryan:

Hey there, it's me...Thanks again for the wonderful and enthralling experience. I enjoyed it thoroughly. I feel in synchronization with myself, each day that was spent with you was positive, fulfilling and worthwhile. Thank you for bringing this moment into my rocking life, now it is wacky too. I know I wanna say much more, but save more for the date we have soon...takecare and miss you...me

She ran out of the door, and slipped through the crowd, and saw him. She managed to find him. She patted his back just before he entered the airport and gave her first ever love letter on tissue paper. Ryan took it and was smiling all the way. He went inside, quickly read it and called her, "See you soon! We have our first LDR date very soon...kisses to you," and he disconnected.

Genelia left the airport with a new set of activities yet to play in the following days.

Every day was a new challenge for Genelia, Ryan, Ria and Miguel. Every time the cocktail was over, it felt the glass was refilled with new flavours.

Every day when situations could be handled, a new emotion was developed.

Miguel tried his best every day. He faced a new sentiment, until when two months passed. By then he was back at his apartment. He called Ria several times with his new number, but there was no reply. He just wanted her to pick up the phone, even though he did not know what he would say, but knowing that she was fine would give him the complacency, he considered.

During the past couple of weeks, Ria had been busy with her first ever dental workshop training for grade three students in Singapore.

She did have thoughts and visions of Miguel time to time. She had received unknown calls but assumed it was Simmy or her mother. She wondered why Miguel never called her and thought he probably left back to Chicago.

She had her flash back about the kiss in the rain. It always made her feel good and brought tears of an awful pleasure she could not feel for real. It was not like she never kissed before, but with Miguel she felt different. This time she was never going to text him about anything. She assumed he was still dating Alysia and were happy. She had nothing to say and preferred to focus on her dentistry.

Ria's mom had visited her in Singapore. During tea, she had mentioned about allocating assets. She was told that 60 percent of the property and business would be given to Simmy and Ria had the rest of the 40 percent. Ms. Rashida Thakkar was proud of Ria about her career.

She had a friendly chat with her and added, "Simmy is not like you. She would never be able to make something qualitative out of her life. I will always love you and Simmy. Parenthetically, you may have forgotten, but when you were young, you were really good with art, just a thought, why don't you also share some ideas or designs in the jewelry business? Sooner or later, besides dentistry you will also be part of the jewelry business. Simmy will be doing some managing part. You know her dictatorship! You can be responsible for design and marketing. Don't worry, both of you would be the bosses of your job. Think about it, this is a huge decision and if you start slowly you shall understand it and you never know you enjoy it."

Ria was thinking what her mother told her and freaked out. Designing for jewelry and cleaning teeth were two different worlds. She recalled a conversation she had with Denise months ago. Denise said, "People say, when you do so many things you become the Jack of all trades and the Master of none."

However, Ria disagreed, she argued, "How about thinking it this way? What if you are excellent and know very well how to handle many things you're good at. One is good at it because of the special talent. Then one becomes the Master of those multiple things. What if you are good at doing many things? Who cares? It is a win-win situation. There is a benefit from both sides."

When Ria remembered that conversation, she gave it a thought. After the training in Singapore, when she would be in Mumbai for the workshop, if she could squeeze some time, she would initiate some creative output in jewelry designing as well as continue with the dental training. She gave herself the credit for becoming a Master someday in mastering the two professions.

She did not think about Miguel at all because of her hectic schedule.

Miguel was very much busy in his life, trying to get back to routine. When Alysia returned from work to Miguel's apartment, she was excited and hugged him. She kissed his cheeks and sat on the carpet. She saw a sex video near the television.

She asked Miguel, "Why do you have that?"

Miguel replied, "Sorry, Alysia. It's not mine. It must be Momo's, you remember the strange journalist from France. He must have forgotten it."

"So, you haven't watched it," asked Alysia jovially.

"Nag, nag, nag, don't you have anything better to do? No, as you know I was having the time of my life after the accident," replied Miguel cheekily.

"Whatever! You want some wine? I have also brought pasta. We can have it for dinner and perhaps watch a movie," offered Alysia.

Miguel drifted away from any input. He had wine and the pasta.

He tried to take continuous steps, but could not. He was struggling and tried to balance using a walker. When Alysia was getting closer to him, Miguel switched on the TV.

She admired him for a moment. His arms always caught her attention, and even relaxed his biceps looked powerful.

They kissed and while lying on the carpet, after kissing her, he stopped. For a moment he completely felt out of breathe and thought of Ria.

He could hardly move his left hand and his legs. He gave an excuse and told Alysia, "We can do this later. Perhaps, after a month I would be better when I can actually move my left hand." He gave her a kiss and added, "You want to go out for a while?"

"Sure, we can," said Alysia.

He was taking steps warily and thinking about Ria again. Alysia was holding his arm thinking about her relationship with Miguel. She did not want to be a baby-sitter.

She was silent. As they strolled by the beach - she could feel that at that moment nothing seemed romantic anymore after the accident. She remembered how they flirted a few months before, and started dating. It had some spice in it, she contemplated. But now she had enough of drama. Eventhough she still cared for him, she wanted to end the relationship.

He saw the waves not feeling good at all. The accident had changed his life completely. He was seeking answers to his motives.

"How are you feeling?" asked Alysia.

"I am getting better," responded Miguel with a smirk.

He wanted to feel the freedom back in his life and mention what had happened between him and Ria. It was better I say nothing and try to forget what happened. Can I actually forget? wondered Miguel. He wanted to take everything back in control of his routine.

After some time, Miguel told Alysia, "Well, we have been dating for a while, and sometimes I feel we are not heading anywhere. I mean it is not like we have a future to this."

Alysia shared her view, "I am glad we are talking about this. I don't see it progressing anywhere either. I need to do a lot of things in Mumbai. I have found a good friend, and you have been an encouragement in my life. Seriously, I am young doing my internship and I have a long way to progress. Recently, I have signed a few modeling contracts and do consider potential there, too."

Miguel listened carefully, and added, "I am happy for you and it is good you know what you want. I have to get back to the routine and will be going back home. I miss Chicago and my family. We can always stay in touch."

He was not surprised about the breakup. He had enough pain that he did not find this a misery. Precisely, he was glad to meet a person like Alysia. She was young, vibrant and humorous. "So, when is the first shoot? Best of luck," encouraged Miguel and hugged her.

She rested her head on his shoulder and they sat down looking at the waves. "When I call you, do pick up my phone, and we shall catch up. We will still do our movies or lunches if you are still in Mumbai," recommended Alysia. At one point, there was a breakup and the feeling of liberation, considered Miguel.

*****

Genelia did have her dates online. She had never done something so dumb but cute before. She got her food in her room like other weeks, lit candles around and chatted with Ryan.

She wanted to share certain things with him, but did not know how to tell him. She found it difficult to do this. She wanted to share how she was coping with her mother's temperament. She felt embarrassed to share this and felt maybe after some time she would let him know.

So far her dates online were going well. She began giving excuses and missed it sometimes. She graduated and focused on her business plan. Too much was running in her mind.

Shawn had left back to Canada, and Genelia's mother desired her to get married to a nice Christian. One day, as she was writing her business plan, her mom stormed into the room, accusing her for being irresponsible about her life. The whole bombardment was coming up almost every day. She knew her mom was going through menopause but this was certainly out of control. She cared for her mom but could not see any reason for her harsh comments.

Genelia was emotionally breaking away. She could not even share about her business plan with her, or say anything about Ryan. She tried every possible way to maintain harmony with her.

The moment she arrived home she felt she was in this silence shelter where everyone was doing their own thing.

She was a zombie at home, figuring where she stood and how her life would be meaningful when she had an uncooperative mother.

After trying to speak with her dad a couple of times, he finally listened to what she had to say. "I don't want this whole thing to mess up. Dad meeting any kind of therapist to share her problems may not be too bad. Perhaps meditation or even yoga would do. Life will be different with a new perspective for her," requested Genelia with empathy.

The whole discussion with her dad was like talking to a wall. When she was home, her mother had self-created another problem. "Genelia," called her mother and added, "Aunt Rosam has sent these proposals for you. Have a look at these three proposals, their resume, and pictures. One more thing, they are interested in meeting you."

She was stunned and asked, "What is happening? When did this happen? Why are you so pushy and annoying these days? I am not a child. There is always a right approach to this. This is unfair!"

She wanted to faint. She was thinking of Ryan, her business plan and wondered what was she going to do with this problem her mother created? She fell in love with Ryan but was still unsure of the future.

After the argument, that night Ryan had texted her, but there was no reply. He had called her a couple of times and no reply again. He even sent her an email and doubted something had happened. He wondered what was going on.

He knew LDR's could be a pain for Genelia, but it was not too bad. She had missed out on the weekly dates sometimes. He realized that it had been about three months since they were dating. Maybe I am thinking too much. Perhaps she was busy, he assumed.

He got worried, so he called Ria in Singapore. He spoke to her about Genelia and was relieved that she would be going to Mumbai in a couple of weeks. She could meet up with her.

Genelia had sent a text back to Ryan, telling him that she was busy with guests and the business plan. He was happy to know she was fine, but felt something was wrong.

Weeks later Genelia received a text from Ria that she was back for a while and wanted to meet up. They met and Genelia told her everything.

"Please don't say anything to Ryan. I am figuring this whole thing out. What do you think? What should I do?" confided Genelia.

"Me and relationship advice, seriously, tell him the situation. He deserves to know that you have been keeping busy with many things and your mother's proposals for you. He understands, maybe he figures out what to do. In the mean time, for the sake of courtesy and respect of your parents you need to meet them. Tell him you're helpless and got to do this or be brave enough and tell your parents about Ryan. You got to be fair, Genelia. Yes, also tell him about the plot you plan to buy on loan for the business set up, too. Sharing is important and you never know it brings good results," expressed Ria with optimism.

"Thanks so much. I know sharing is important. I want to speak to Ryan about so many things but sometimes I feel this is as far as I can go. I do tell him almost everything. Why not this?" admitted Genelia and added, "So how are you and everything? We have been discussing me, and now you."

"Everything is good, busy with work and now designing for jewelry," revealed Ria. "Need any help let me know. I have been a fashion student," proffered Genelia.

"You're a life savior. I sure need loads of help with graphic designing," spoke Ria approvingly.

"Great we should meet up more often, then," said Genelia.

Ria did not bother asking Genelia anything about Shawn. She did not want to create anymore stress in her life.

Genelia eventually met up with the three prospects in two days. She was overwhelmed with the whole thing. One fellow was shorter than her. She wanted to laugh so much, so that one was deleted off her list. The second one did not support the idea of her business plan and wanted her to marry within two months. Genelia knew that this was certainly not happening. She had a life she considered and deleted him off the list, too.

When she met the third one, she found him interesting. She met the third prospect the second time for coffee. At one side she kept receiving text messages from Ryan because he was so upset with her and coffee with another person whom she thought she might be married to, got her frustrated.

Genelia shared her future plans with him. He agreed and seemed quite cooperative about it. She was doomed in confusion. She was thinking, London or Mumbai. The third prospect was an IT guy, made good money, and was twenty seven years old who agreed to support her with her business. She considered, if she said yes to him, was it because she liked him a lot or was it because he supported her business plan? She gave it a careful thought for a few days.

Genelia met him several times sometimes for lunch or coffee, and thought of breaking up with Ryan before the New Year celebrations for 2011.

She did not want to prolong it before something worse would happen. She preferred staying in Mumbai to establish her dream project. She went to the church for a while and decided - this is it, my life with the IT guy and my business.

She adjudicated she was going to talk to Ryan. Let me cross out a few more days on my calendar and gain the confidence to speak to him. She did not want to hurt him and felt mean to end a pleasant relationship. She needed time which she did not have.

Time was running out for Miguel, too. He had been crossing out days, until he could finally get back to Chicago. He had a strange experience with relationships and missed home. The doctor told him to exercise and if his backaches got better he could travel. However, after days of therapy he could finally walk without the walker.

He began going to the beach every morning for his

regular exercises. It made him feel energetic and active again. He wanted to show his mother he was fine and how much he missed her and dad. He was also reluctant to speak his mind with Tanish about Ria. He would be stunned, he pictured.

It was always good to release stress by speaking what is on one's mind. Genelia did the same. Ryan was finally blown off on his date online when she had said it was better they broke up. She meant every word she wrote to him three months ago and still felt happy talking to him.

"We both mean the best for each other and there was no doubt about that. Again, how long are we going to do the LDR, three months, six months, one year, and then what?" said Genelia apologetically.

"The whole point is dating and time will tell. You can't jump or analyze anything. You want to break up because you love someone else right now, right. That's why you're planning to marry this person," said Ryan with resentment.

"Ryan, there is so much more to speak about us. I don't really want to do this and I know you are not ready for any commitments as yet. I simply can't do long distance. Sorry!" Genelia disconnected and went offline. She cried and felt she broke her own heart.

She had nearly found the dream she searched for nightly, the dream that took her back to a time when another deep voice carried itself through her days and kept her secure in the comfort of its presence-the voice that protected and loved her for the past three months. The voice that was gone forever except in that special world of dreams. A rude shaking threatened to end her revere.

Was he even ready for a commitment? Every time we spoke about marriage he spoke about time. I feel I am satisfying my mother's wish and sacrificing my dream to be with Ryan because of time. This is suffocating, she thought.

Ryan read the note Genelia had written on tissue paper. He was dazed, and angry. He was really hurt by her.

On the other hand, Ria contemplated if she ever bumped into Miguel, what would she say? She remembered him saying that he was traveling back in two months and he never called nor said anything. She presumed he was back in Chicago by now.

Moreover, Miguel wanted to meet Ria at least once to apologize and tell her how he truly felt about her. He desired to speak to her atleast once before he left.

Each of them wished for something, hoping it came true.

16

CHAPTER

What Do We Qualify as Meaningful?

Genelia looked at the Maple leaves and felt calm. Her belief in the beauty of maple leaves had spread to her dear ones. When Ria felt the glass was empty, a new cocktail was needed to be refilled. She wanted to sip the blend of different flavors that brought a colorful beauty in the drink. Ryan and Miguel took a step ahead and captured the essence of sensibility by making their life more meaningful.

Ryan was freezing. Who says winter can be soothing and a fun weather? He thought. He was completely lost after the breakup with Genelia. He did not even want to celebrate New Years with anyone.

Aadil managed to convince Ryan out with the family atleast up till the countdown. He kept staring at his phone hoping it bleeped. But nothing happened, so he texted Genelia: *Wishing u a bright and happy New Year 2011.* He waited for a reply from her.

That night as Ryan was heading back home, he saw many teenagers and young adults snuggling and their joy reflected their inner happiness.

He looked at them and murmured sorrowfully, "They are unaware of the reality of really wanting to be with someone. Good to be at the age where cuddling and kissing was merely an ecstasy. Oh, Genelia I miss you."

Genelia had to figure out how she would deal with the emotional turmoil she faced. She was watching the DVD Ryan had given her at the airport and during that time she received a text message from him. She replied and wished him the same.

She felt so sad that night, too. She thought her parents practically came out of the 19th Century. She tried to say a few words to her mother, but she had put on a helmet of ignorance. True, mothers did know it all, but they are human, too. They make mistakes. When children mature, you can't play that attitude of I know it all game, all the time. Children become wise, and are smart enough to make their own decisions, believed Genelia.

She did not know what to do and how to speak her mind with her mother. A month later, she had to put her foot down. She knew she had to face and confront with a melodramatic character that she really loved but could not help it. Before Genelia could speak to her, she planned to meet Ria. She wanted to discuss some things with her.

They met up for coffee. They discussed designs for jewelry and Ria managed to finalize four designs to show her mother. Genelia also updated her about her break up. She mentioned to Ria, "I miss Ryan sometimes. I feel I did a terrible mistake. Now, I am finding time to speak to my mother about my business plan."

Ria gave her moral support and stated, "What you are planning to do is great. Don't do something silly to regret later."

Days passed, Ria got busy with her two worlds - dentistry and jewelry designing. She moved on. She wondered the best option was to get out of a sticky conversation.

*****

Alternatively, Miguel was in the middle of trying to lift his coffee mug using his left hand, but the coffee mug fell. He could not lift anything at a higher level using his left hand as yet.

At work, he had finally signed the contract for a transfer back to Chicago. His reality was back and regarding relationships they would work in their own time if it had to, he contemplated.

Miguel was looking out the office window analyzing his life considering, it is true...no one knows what life holds for you, what may be meaningful for you may not be for another. Different people would take career, love, fame, status, education or even looks very substantial in different ways. But who knows what we actually qualify as eloquent. He was yet to define that?

His thoughts wondered around about how life became cloudy and blurry. At that point we all need the wind wipers to reassure us that everything would fall back in place so that we could be in charge of things happening in our lives, he wondered.

Similarly, Genelia felt equivalent to Miguel when it came to her emotions. She shared the same space when it came to making things meaningful and positive again.

It had been a while when Genelia opened her book that had pictures of maple leaves. While she was taking out old books, she came across the book and sobbed.

After weeping for a while she felt like someone patted her on her back saying, "Follow your heart and give it a shot."She turned around and saw herself in the mirror. She knew it was her inner voice showing way back to positive thinking. She could see a ray of hope and the true meaning of life.

She did not want to become a zombie or a loser. She was definitely going to do something about the problem she faced. She went on Twitter and uploaded a picture full of maple leaves.

She thought of speaking to her mother as soon as possible. But every time she took the courage to say a word, she stepped behind and two months had passed by. Her mother was not so convinced about her business plan, so she considered discussing about it later, again.

In the mean time, Ms Thakkar had planned to go to

London to visit Ryan's family and have her jewelry exhibition with Simmy. Ria was busy with her workshops in Mumbai and focused on what she reflected was important.

Ryan texted Ria on and off updating her about life and work. She knew he missed Genelia but she never wanted to be the agent for anyone's love affairs.

A few days later, Genelia called Ria asking her if she wanted to go watch a fashion show. She had received free passes from her friend and thought this would a break for both of them.

Genelia had signed the deal for her plot and could not wait for that day assuming it would take atleast a year or two.

In the interim, Miguel was glad he was feeling much better and on the same day while he was making noodles, Tanish came over to accompany him.

"I had come here for just a few weeks, and now it is a year," expressed Miguel sensitively.

Tanish had asked if Miguel was interested for another road trip to light up the moment. Miguel totally declined the offer genially. "It is all cool, Tanish. Maybe a road trip after a few years when I visit again," joked Miguel.

Tanish spoke sympathetically, "You are not only a great cousin but a great friend, too. The fashion tomorrow should be fun. You can do your work and I shall flirt." They ordered pizza and played computer games.

*****

The evening weather was similar to Ria's disposition. That day, she ate Chinese food for dinner with Denise. She looked forward for their wedding in a few months.

"Since you are ready and we are having dinner, here it goes! I have got passes for some fashion show. I am going with Genelia," informed Ria.

"Yes, you had mentioned. Good sweety, you need it. Have fun and try to flirt around. I have things to do. Besides, you need some time off from dentistry and see the fashion world," refused Denise affably.

After dinner, Genelia called and asked, "Ready, will pick you up in twenty minutes." "Sure," said Ria.

Likewise, Miguel was also getting all set and Tanish helped him to put on his tie for the fashion show. Miguel had a meeting with some fashion designers for an advertising campaign.   He told Tanish, "Hurry up. We have to go now. We have to be there by eight."

Sometimes destiny played an outlandish fixture. Ria and Miguel were going to the same fashion show but no one knew if they would meet.

Miguel got there just in time. Maria, the journalist spoke to him, "Hey, sexy, something wrong. Who are you finding?"

"Hi Maria! Where are the designers you had mentioned?" asked Miguel. He noticed that there were photographers and media crowding the designers for an interview.

Maria continued, "Had heard about the accident, you are looking good and robust as always."

"Thanks Maria. You have always been kind and thoughtful," acknowledged Miguel.

"What's up with life and work?" asked Miguel.

"All good! So you are leaving back to Chicago. It was nice to correspond with you. Have news for you. I am four months pregnant and I am so excited," said Maria.

"Congratulations! You shall be a great mom," said Miguel flatteringly.

He turned around and saw two designers coming toward him to discuss about the campaign. Maria could see that, and she told Miguel, "See you inside at the show. My crew is backstage. When ready, tell me, they will speak with the designers." Miguel nodded and had a word with the designers.

He was back into action. He did not lose his charm and negotiation skills. As he went inside to watch the fashion show, he felt something was missing, but did not know what. He sat on the first row toward the left with the VIPs. Tanish sat next to him and was awed by the glamour.

Whenever a hot or a sexy chick came out, they looked

at each other, nodded and smiled. It was their code language saying, she is worth a try. Tanish loved the stunning women but stayed away from them.

He once told Miguel quietly, "These chicks are risky business. Some don't even come with subtitles. Eventhough they are hot and sizzling beauties we need to stay away."

In contrast, Ria was sitting on the third row toward the right with Genelia. "This is good. I love all the outfits," said Ria.

"Yes, they are so cool," agreed Genelia.

"Hey Ria, there is an after party with the VIPs, want to go?"invited Genelia.

"No parties," refused Ria.

"Hey! Just an hour and this does not happen all the time. We will go and you are coming. Loosen up a little, you know wine and shine," said Genelia enthusiastically. Ria agreed and enveloped the moment with joy.

Ria and Miguel were nowhere near each other.

After sometime, Ria had enough of the glam and noise, she got up quietly and told Genelia that she was going to the restroom. She passed the leading designers, models, celebrities and got her way out.

In the restroom, she was thinking and feeling gloomy. Then she marveled with the fact that she deserved happiness, too. Why on earth was she staying away from fun and only concentrating on work and missing Miguel?

She got out, and accidentally bumped into a model. She apologized and paced toward the hall. It was crowded outside as many people were speaking with the media.

Ria entered the hallway, and a few meters behind her was Miguel. He had to speak with his colleague about some work and was going back toward the hall.

As Miguel walked toward the hall, he stopped by to talk to Maria. He chatted away about the fashion show and the upcoming collection since he would not be there to see it.

Ria was about to enter the ballroom through the wrong door and Miguel was also heading back to the hall. She realized and quickly moved herself out of the crowded area, and went through another entrance back to her seat. There was no such scene of them bumping into each other and missed each other by a two meter space.

Finally, the show was over and the excitement to the after party was declining, Genelia was not in a very good shape but still tried to have some fun.

On the contrary, Miguel wanted to get back home but had to go to the after party and Tanish was excited to see the models. He told Miguel, "You are leaving soon, man. Let's have some fun and we haven't hung out for a while."

Miguel supported the idea, "We are going anyways, but after that if you want to stay, you are on your own."

He felt his life seemed dysfunctional. He took a glass of champagne and with every sip he remembered Ria and the journey he had in India.

When he surveyed the party, he could see a young man battling to move his left hand and being able to stand again for long hours. The accident had changed his passion about life.

In the other end of the party, Genelia was in the balcony looking at the buildings around Mumbai city and missed Ryan's warmth and love. She wanted to call him and ask how he was doing. Until she did not break up with her potential proposal she would not be able to get through, she considered.

Sitting opposite her was Ria. She felt she was hiding herself behind her career and was beginning to close the chapter to romance. Some models came out in the balcony to smoke and they ended up flirting with Ria and Genelia.

Ria got snacks for them pretending she knew everything about the house and Genelia played along. They knew the models were looking for a one night stand, so she humorously ignored their indirect offer.

Ria had burst out laughing. "Hey Genelia, looks like you drank a bit too much." By then the three models had gone. Genelia's eyes were teary and she spoke to Ria about Ryan.

Miguel was nowhere near them. He was out in the dining hall talking with his colleagues and Tanish. Even being in the same party he did not have a glimpse of Ria.

It was so crowded and the penthouse was big. Ria and Genelia got out of the balcony and entered the dancing zone.

Ria was already exhausted and mentioned to Genelia that she would wait for her at the lobby.

As she walked out she bumped into Tanish. She did greet him and he was tipsy. "I got to go and we shall meet soon." She wondered if Miguel was around. She quickly surveyed the place but did not see him.

Genelia got out of the smoky room, grabbed a glass of chilled water, and took the glass making her way out of the crowded party room. She brushed Miguel's arm but they did not look at each other.

After a few seconds, Miguel turned around and he saw Genelia leaving. He recalled her from Ria's party but never made the initiative to go up to her. After a while, he told Tanish he was leaving.

The night was ironic and it conveyed an indication of more drama. Tanish had mentioned nothing about meeting Ria.

Genelia had some snacks in the car. She shared it with Ria and mentioned about her crazy desire for midnight snacks. The breeze, fast car drive and loud music were a stress buster for them.

The next morning, Miguel developed a routine for exercising and keeping fit. Every morning he went for a walk, did some stretching, listened to music and read his newspaper at the park beside the beach. He felt like a normal soul again.

Harmonizing and feeling lively was what everyone desired. In the other part of the world - Ryan was balancing his routine. He was almost done with the jewelry exhibition Ria's mother had at the party room in the diners.

After the exhibition, Ryan bought a can of beer and went for a walk. He missed Genelia deeply. He was trying to remember the exact words she said before break up. She sounded so confused and abrupt. Eventhough some things might have been sensible for her, it was not for him. Suddenly he had the urge to meet her. He had never felt like this for anyone.

He yearned for a fresh start back. Genelia was the same person he loved, so he geared up his self-belief. This is it. I am calling her, he thought.

Ryan took out his phone and called her a couple of times. But Genelia did not answer. He was disappointed. Perhaps this was a sign of some sort, he presumed.

After a couple of hours Genelia saw the missed call, but she did not recognize the number. She assumed that maybe it was from London, but wasn't sure.

For a moment she thought it was Ryan, and then she assumed, what if it was not. She wanted to erase the thoughts of the awful night she broke up with him.

The next morning during breakfast she told her mother, "I am not getting married to this fellow. I can't do this. I only said yes because he was going to support me for my career. I mean this is absolutely not fair for both of us. Ma, I don't love him and tried but can't get married for you. It has to be for the right reasons, and it's a no."

Genelia's mother heated up.

After being quiet for a long time, she continued, "Ma, listen to me. You are making marriage dreadful for me, okay. I don't want someone in my life, I need that person. He should be my passion, humorous, trustworthy and respectful. This depicts pleasant and genuine happiness. I tried to talk to you, but you never seem to understand. I broke up with him. Shawn moved on, and now you made me the punching bag. It is absolutely unfair and hurtful putting me into situations. I am glad you supported me for my business plan, but can't do this crap anymore."

Genelia got up from the seat and added, "You have to get over finding faults and seeing the negative in everything. Please!" She stormed away. She locked herself in her room, and wept all day. Genelia's dad heard the whole thing and tried to comfort her. She was relieved that there was an end to fakeness.

*****

Putting an end to something that indicated no light of sensibility and fervor was the best preference anyone could make. Ria had put an end to her thoughts on romance. She went to the beach every morning for meditation and yoga as part of a routine she developed for a while. She felt so serene and loved the quality time she had with herself.

She was on top of the world when she saw the waves and admired the beauty she saw every day. She heard her phone ringing and took it out from her bag. It was Ryan.

"Hi Ryan, been a while, how are you?"

"Not too bad, Ria. So what is the time there? It seems quite late."

"No, I am at the beach for yoga. So tell me," asked Ria.

"By the way, I was thinking to visit. I am trying to get tickets," said Ryan enthusiastically.

"Nice. You miss me and of course India, right," teased Ria.

"Well, yes you are right. It has become more special for me. Honestly, I want to visit and give a surprise to Genelia. Things are kind of over between us, but I want to give it a shot for the last time," explained Ryan.

"Great! It is always worth and you never know. Don't worry and see you soon," encouraged Ria.

Ria was so happy for Genelia. Perhaps the surprise visit would do all good and they would live happily ever after, she considered.

Moreover, Ria and Miguel began sharing a similar activity with similar timings, too. But they never bumped into each other.

Three days later, Ria did her regular workout. She was engrossed with her music while she was doing yoga.

At the same time, it was also a regular routine for Miguel to take his walk. That same day, after an hour, he listened to loud music and came to the beach for a brisk walk. He strolled ahead, then paused, went backward, and saw Ria.

He was thrilled and his heart started beating faster. He took a few steps toward her, then turned away and walked ahead a few steps.

He realized that this was his chance to see her. He knew he would call her before he left, but the whole point was, she was right there, he thought. He waited for this day for so long, so he turned back and paced toward her.

Ria did not know anything. She was meditating.

While meditating, she had put the scarf on her face and with the breeze Miguel caught a glimpse of her. He smiled and could see the calmness on her face and the comfort as the sun's rays were shining on her.

Miguel gazed at her for a couple of minutes. He stood from a distance and could see every move. After some time, Ria slowly opened her eyes. She did her stretching and wiped her sweat. As she got up two dogs came running toward her.

She screamed so loud and when she turned around Miguel was right in front of her. Alright, I am going to get a heart attack. Why do I have a shock all the time? First the dogs and now Miguel, she thought. She continued screaming and after a few seconds the dogs ran away.

Miguel told her, "You sound like an ugly duckling, quacking - The dogs are gone! Well, take a deep breath."

She just stared at him for a few seconds thinking she had gone crazy. "I thought you left to the U.S?" she blurted out.

For a few seconds both of them were speechless and Ria looked away.

"Looks like you wanted me to go back so soon," said Miguel disdainfully.

Ria was already in a different state of mind as she was stunned to see him. She wanted to meet him, and when it did happen, she was speechless.

"Say something or are you going to be mute?" insisted Miguel.

She turned around and said, "It was good to see you. Random, anyway, I really have to get to the workshop."

"Sure, Ria, after we have had a few words. I have wanted to say this for months but have ignored the facts and have always been pragmatic. Today, I believe in fate, and yes we all get a chance to clear out things once, for me it is today," said Miguel assertively.

She simply looked at him, and felt uneasy. Her heart was beating so quickly, she wanted to run away. She noticed he wanted to talk so eagerly.

"I must really go," said Ria hastily and she walked a few steps ahead.

He held her arm and said, "Listen, I have something to say. It is about us."

"Well, there was never an us," said Ria emotionally.

He added, "I broke up with Alysia, if that is what you want to hear?"

"No I don't want to hear anything and what makes you think that," asked Ria.

"Ria, what happened that day was absolutely the right thing. I have been thinking about you every day. I knew something was wrong with me the day I stayed back with you during the road trip. I know you feel something too, but you never mentioned or let's say you suppressed your feelings," spoke Miguel empathetically.

He came closer to her, held her right hand and said compassionately, "Ria, we really need to talk, please say something."

"Miguel, I don't know what to say. I am astonished. Well frankly, something has been wrong and bizarre after I have met you. Whenever I fix something, a tornado starts to arise. So tell me, if we never met here coincidently you would have never even said a word, no call, absolutely nothing, why? This is what I despise. Why men don't try or even do anything? Even in the world of modernization, it feels nice and warm when the man makes the move. At the end of the day, the ball is in the man's court, because he can make out if the woman likes him, too. But no, men chicken out. I had a great morning and you ruined it," said Ria despondently.

"I did call you a couple of times. You did not pick up nor reply to the calls. I was even thinking of confessing about my feelings toward you with Tanish. But, man you love me so much. You're so upset and I love you, too," said Miguel benevolently and hugged her using his right hand so tight.

"Let go off me, I can't breathe," emphasized Ria. But

he didn't. Slowly Miguel let go off her and they walked by the shores. He apologized and promised he would make it up to her.

Miguel begged for her forgiveness and told her, "I was going to call you for sure before I left." He confessed that he had fallen in love with her and the day he had realized it, it was driving him insane and thought he would get retarded some day. While he was confronting, a volley ball hit his head.

He turned around and passed it using his right hand. He seemed to be different and she noticed that he was a little slow. She asked him curiously, "You seem to be a little slow…"

"Now you are being observant. The past few months, I feel delayed because of an accident." Miguel told her everything he went through after that one kiss.

She was rapturous and felt the guilt. The compassion for him had never subsided. She told him, "I am sorry. I should have picked up your phone call. I did not know who it was, since it was another number. Umm…I don't know where to start." She had made assumptions and did not know exactly what happened.

"I am sorry. It didn't matter how many times I'd apologize. I know I was wrong."He kissed the top of her head and held her for a moment and confessed again, "I love you a lot, like a lot," said Miguel avidly.

She wondered whenever I think of him or see him, I can't help it, I smile. He is so sweet and mystifying. She felt that her wish was answered and it was not ignored. After all the wish well did exist. She could feel the cupid granted her happiness she deserved.

She returned his passionate kiss with honor and said, "I love you, too." She was so happy and she pulled her hair aside, nibbled his ear and kissed his cheeks.

She had to rush back to her workshop.

That evening, Ryan called. He had already reached Mumbai and wanted to see Ria. She was anxious to share the news to Ryan about Miguel but waited until she met him. She was surprised by the magic, destiny offered when one felt like a dying hope. Destiny just snaps and puts you in an awkward situation and everything gets right, feels right. Perfecto! She marveled.

Finally, she had spoken it out loud. - Ryan was happy for her. They went for a ride and spoke about so many things.

"Honestly, I don't know details about Genelia's proposal. I have not met her for a while. But you have to try and don't chicken out. You never know she is waiting for this moment or maybe she did make a right decision. Either way you will find out after meeting her. If it does not work out, it simply does not. You move on and shine again with someone else I guess. Goodluck!" lectured Ria with concern.

"I have a plan. I want you to call her somewhere she has no clue and won't suspect anything," suggested Ryan.

"Where and which place would be different?" asked Ria.

"Call her to a zoo," suggested Ryan.

Ria asked feeling surprised, "What? Seriously! That is strange. You are going to speak to her in front of all the animals and birds."

"Ria, that's not funny. She won't suspect anything. I need you to get her there," requested Ryan.

"So someone will be all so romantic in front of the lion, tiger, elephant, zebra or who knows the parrot," said Ria merrily.

"Shut up and don't be a bugger. Please appreciate my creativity," said Ryan in his British accent. "This is so incongruous," said Ria and smiled.

Ria called up Genelia and said, "Hi, it has been a few weeks and I am in the mood to do something different and inspirational. I need a change and want to share about many things with you. Do you have any suggestions?"

"Nice. How about bowling?"

"No," replied Ria.

"Spa," said Genelia encouragingly.

"No," replied Ria bluntly.

"Final suggestion! Bungee jumping!" Genelia taunted.

"No, with that I will throw up," replied Ria disapprovingly.

"Let's go to the zoo," recommended Ria.

"A zoo! Seriously, I was going to tell you to pack your bags and go to Alaska, but zoo..." asked Genelia astonishingly.

"Come on, it is not that bad. I will pick you up at nine. Thanks," said Ria convincingly.

"I am not fond of going to the zoo. You know the animals are caged, but will go only for you," said Genelia. What a nightmare? Ria has a strange taste, she wondered.

Ria had updated Ryan and he felt his journey was like an adventure.

She supported him and added, "Getting her to the zoo was a great job done. So for now, good night! I have a date with Miguel tomorrow...am so tickled."

The next day, at the zoo, Genelia was feeding the crocodiles and was so scared of being eaten by them. She saw Ria not doing anything that she said she wanted to. She was annoyed and eventually Ria did feed the chimpanzee and elephants.

Ria updated her about the relationship with Miguel. Genelia was surprised with her romantic story and cheered for her. She looked away and was upset seeing some animals being in bare cast iron. It was preposterous. Ria thought of diverting her mind and took her to the underwater aquarium.

"Later we can go for an elephant ride," remarked Ria. Ryan texted her and told her to accompany Genelia where the starfish were.

Genelia admired the multihued fishes, took pictures, and was going to go to the small room where the colorful starfish were.

Ryan had tipped a big buck to the security for keeping the area sealed for one hour. He wanted to propose and confide to his girlfriend.

After Genelia and Ria entered, the security closed the area for a while. There was a sign that illustrated, closed for maintenance. Genelia did not notice Ryan as he waited in the corner. She chatted away and clicked pictures. When she turned around Ria was not to be seen. She realized she was talking to herself.

She saw Ryan as he peeped out from the curtains and was staggered. She could feel goose bumps all over. She thought she woke up from a strange dream but it was not. She saw Ria standing next to him.

Ria said contritely, "I am sorry. This was all for you. You guys need to talk and all the best." She hugged her and left.

Genelia went behind her, too. She wanted to escape. "Genelia don't leave. Coming to the zoo, all the way from London was no joke," said Ryan aggressively.

She turned around and asked, "Seriously, what are you doing here? I am dazed, Ryan. Can't believe this?" Genelia felt restless and knew she could not flee from the situation and took a few steps closer to him. She did want to talk to him and now when he was here she was in dilemma. She took a deep breath. This was still a shock to her. She sat on the carpet completely quiet.

Ryan sat beside her and held her hand. As he held her hand, he felt Genelia was very warm and nervous. She sensed the contentment and affection Ryan was conveying. She felt the same way when he had first asked her out at Ria's party. It was so hard for her to escape and pretend then. Her emotions were at the same slate she anticipated.

At that point, Genelia was happy that she met up with Ryan unexpectedly. She thanked the Lord for turning the tables and sent him as a surprise package. She was truly loved, she contemplated.

"How are you doing, Ryan?" asked Genelia. She managed to get her hand away from him.

"Good. I think of you of everyday and thought of visiting. I presumed, you might be engaged or maybe not. I did not want to regret it at all. There were days where I felt my heart was being hit by a metal bar. It was uneasy to breathe and I was so drawn deep into thoughts about you. I could only let go if I knew that you are really happy. Long distance relationships are not difficult. It is us who makes it difficult. Anyway, then I decided to call Ria, and planned the whole zoo thing. Sweety I am so happy to see you. Are you still dating that man?" expressed Ryan genially.

"NO! I broke it off a few weeks ago. I tried but could not do it," said Genelia sentimentally.

Ryan was so happy to hear that. He was elated and spoke with zeal, "This is awesome, awfully quixotic!"

Genelia could not say much because she was feeling reticent and still could not believe the fact that she was actually sitting beside Ryan at the underwater aquarium. He conveyed how much he had missed her, and told her, "A companion is the utmost grateful feeling and brings all sorts of emotions in our life like a vibrant cocktail. I want to hug you tightly, talk to you all the time. Say something."

"I missed you. I wanted to listen to everything you had to say which would have been surely comforting. Today, I believe that compassion exists and long distance relationships do work. I am glad you came. You are a surprise package for me. Sorry, I messed up," spoke Genelia passionately.

"You should be. If I never came here, you would have never told me anything. You would just put a stop to everything. It would have been devastating. How could you allow that to yourself?" Ryan said intensely.

"No! Don't take that for granted. I broke up for a reason. I would have called to check on you...soon. I never had a day when I didn't think of you," said Genelia optimistically.

"This time I am not hearing to any kind of downbeat story. By the way, would you want to visit London? I would love to show you around," asked Ryan.

"Sounds great! I need a holiday and have so much to tell you. Construction has started at the site. It should be ready by 2012. You know what you said about the cocktail, it is so true. Life is great when we have people like you around. Sorry and Thanks for coming to rescue me," articulated Genelia. She pinched him on his waist line playfully. She chuckled and gave him a flying kiss.

Ryan spoke with fondness, "Remember you spoke about maple leaves? Whenever I saw them, I remembered every word you said." Genelia was so happy and was going to share this with her mother. She knew this would keep her from finding new proposals, she considered.

Ryan told Genelia gently, "I love you alot." He texted Ria.

Genelia grinned and held his hand with adulation. They walked out of the aquarium and went to feed the elephants.

Ria was also intoxicated with zeal and happy for Ryan. Love was a crazy journey for anyone's life. It brought mischief, nuisance and blithe in volatile ways. It was all good to sip and experience, she considered.

She was proposed by Miguel compassionately, which felt amazing and jubilant. "I am leaving next week to Chicago and after four or five months, I shall visit back."

Ria was alright with it. Miguel loved every moment they were together and of course the bumpy ride was still on. All he did not need was a U-turn.

He commanded Ria with empathy, "Next time, you are coming with me to Chicago."

"Sure! We can go for another road trip and have loads of cocktails," said Ria flirtatiously and winked.

Acknowledgements

I would start by thanking my family for their support and push towards perfectionism. My younger sister Milan is no less than a spring of positivity. She made sure I put my new world into writing and sharing it with the whole world. Gratification and love is conveyed to my parents who have always desired the best for me. My brother, Ritesh always sent his encouragement with his quote, "You MBA, you can do it. You make me proud."

Special thanks to the Khemlanis', Sidhwa Family, Sadouzai Family, Aunty Tanaz, Balani Family, Rahul Sharma, Sahaj Marg and WHDC. I appreciate and express gratitude towards my editors Tinny and Rhonda. Leadstart publishing house has been encouraging and made sure at every step of this publication the best would be given.

Where family is part of an everlasting support so are friends. My friends have always been there and were so excited to see my labor of love. I would not be fair if I did not mention their names; however, there has been loads of support from many people who have been part of my journey of life. To do justice to some of my friends the list goes: Samreen,

Alisa, Bina, Rachna, Tina, Nimo, Rasee, Anjali, Pooja, Kiran, Sunantha, Gopi, Sharina, Priya, Loveleen, Radhika, Preeti, Naina, Natasha, Lavina, Sherry, Rach, Yogeeta, Ekta, Julie, Amnat, Samir, Meaz, Ausanee, Sheena, Tharsini, Deepali, Aashima, Uma, Nisha, Tina (ESTINNA), Aarti, Ritika, Bharti, Sangeeta, Dipa, Sonam, Rachana, Oindrella, Mamtha, Nicki, Debbie, Zia, and our Divas' Komal, Meina, Diya, Shareen, Tinny, Shalini, Rekha, Poonam, Falguni, Neha, Aleeisah, Shahen, Rushnaz, Amy and Sunisha. There are many more whom I shall remember and thank always.

My true inspiration and enthusiasm also came from the mind of the innocence, my students. They have always brought about a better day to my life. When I started teaching, I noticed that the emotional and joy ride the students contributed in my life was magnificent.

Last but not the least; I thank the Almighty God, My Master and the beautiful dream of the stars and moon smiling at me. Without the embrace of positivity and support this would have not happened. I shall write more and share more.

Thank you all.

Bhavna K.